THE BRIDGE

Books by Stuart Prebble

The Insect Farm
The Bridge

THE
BRIDGE

STUART PREBBLE

MULHOLLAND BOOKS

LITTLE, BROWN AND COMPANY

NEW YORK BOSTON LONDON

Mulholland Books / Little, Brown and Company
Hachette Book Group
1290 Avenue of the Americas, New York, NY 10104
mulhollandbooks.com

First Edition: March 2017

Mulholland Books is an imprint of Little, Brown and Company, a division of Hachette Book Group, Inc. The Mulholland Books name and logo are trademarks of Hachette Book Group, Inc.

The publisher is not responsible for websites (or their content) that are not owned by the publisher.

The Hachette Speakers Bureau provides a wide range of authors for speaking events. To find out more, go to hachettespeakersbureau.com or call (866) 376-6591.

ISBN 978-0-316-35538-4
LCCN 2016957617

10 9 8 7 6 5 4 3 2 1

LSC-C

Printed in the United States of America

THE BRIDGE

ONE

_____

IT WAS A sunny Saturday afternoon, and sightseers and tourists from all parts of the world crowded onto the South Bank, streaming in both directions across Waterloo Bridge. Some were walking to or from Covent Garden or the theaters; others stopped to admire the spectacular London skyline. At first glance the Madman seemed harmless enough, just a little the worse for wear from alcohol perhaps, or maybe celebrating a victory by his football team. Dressed in blue jeans and a gray hoodie, he muttered to himself and danced light-footed as he progressed, lifting his legs high like a week-old pony. Once or twice he paused and bent his knees to speak at eye level to a child, but later no one could identify the accent or decipher the words. Parents kept a watchful eye, but there seemed to be no reason for alarm. Then, with no warning, in a single sweeping movement and before anyone could intervene, the Madman scooped up the first tiny child, a four-year-old boy apparently selected at random, and swept him over the barrier.

There was a momentary snapshot of paralysis. The boy had made no sound. Was it some trick? Had the man switched the real boy for a dummy in some bizarre and ill-judged entertainment? Before anyone could take a breath the Madman had run half a dozen steps farther towards the next child, a three-year-old girl in a pink dress with birthday ribbons in her hair. Once again he gripped the child under the arms and swept her up and over the barrier, her legs suddenly pedaling through nothingness. Even now, shock and disbelief immobilized bystanders. He darted forward again and grabbed another, and yet another. Each child was seemingly as light as a wafer, flicked up to shoulder height and thrust out into emptiness. Four small people, infants and toddlers, lifted up in the space of twelve or fifteen seconds and thrown over the wall before the Madman took to his heels and vanished like a phantom into the holiday crowds.

A mother fell to her knees, cracking bones against pavement, and shuffled towards the wall as if drawn towards it like a magnet. It took more moments for the screams from the bridge to catch the attention of people below on the South Bank, and fuller realization of what had occurred spread through the crowds like waves of poison gas across a battlefield. Scores of people held their heads and covered their ears as if to prevent the news from penetrating. Eyes were turned upwards towards the sound of the cries and then followed the pointing arms into the water below. Desperate and still confused, one father jumped from the bridge and hit the surface with the slap of raw meat against concrete, but even as he submerged, already the bobbing heads which were still visible had traveled a hundred yards in the churning foam. Another brave man jumped into the water from the riverbank and struck out with an urgent stroke in the direction of the fast-moving shapes. Both were overwhelmed within moments by the strength of the swell.

The first police officers arrived on the bridge within two minutes and began trying to calm the hysteria sufficiently to understand what had happened, but it seemed that no two accounts from among the many were sufficiently similar to produce a consensus. He was variously described as eighteen years old at one extreme to about thirty-five at the other. He had brown hair or black hair or auburn hair. He was tall, medium, and short, and had an athletic build or was running to fat. The only clear agreement was about the jeans and the gray hoodie, which made him a match for about two hundred other young men in the vicinity that afternoon. CCTV recordings examined later lost track of him minutes before the incident and lost him again as a pinprick in the crowd within seconds after it.

The prime minister interrupted his holidays to visit the scene and consult on camera with the chief constable. On TV he pronounced himself to be "shocked and horrified by this appalling and inexplicable act" before commiserating with the bereaved families and promising that the culprit would be found and prosecuted to the full extent of the law.

Police appeals for drivers who had passed through the area to come forward produced immediate responses. Like a storm or an earthquake, it was the kind of incident which compelled complete strangers to seek solace in sharing the horror. Men swore out loud that *they* would have reacted more quickly after the mayhem had started. Women sucked on their teeth and silently thanked God it was not them or their families. Parents of small children kept them under more vigilant surveillance or held them just a little bit tighter.

"Good God, that's only a couple of miles from here," said Alison. "Didn't we pass near there ourselves earlier?"

"I guess we must have been a few hundred yards away." Michael's immediate instinct was to put whatever distance he could between the incident and themselves. "We drove by Waterloo Station, but that would put us among literally tens of thousands of people."

The couple was part of a group of families and friends waiting for visiting to start at the Greenacres care home in Battersea. This was not the first time that Michael Beaumont had introduced one of his girlfriends to his grandmother, but it was the first such occasion in the three months since she had moved from the apartment he shared with her and into the home. It was just eight weeks since he had met Alison, and he was still getting to know her, but Michael already knew enough to be sure that he wanted her to meet his grandmother. Not that he needed Rose's approval, but there was no doubt that she was the only person whose good opinion he cared about. Rose had brought him up as her own child, and he had her to thank for everything he was or had ever achieved. Michael knew that it was all a bit soon, but there was also a part of him — one that he did not want to acknowledge — which was anxious not to delay.

Alison had joined the other visitors gathered around the TV news and was absorbed by the continuing live coverage of the scene at Waterloo Bridge. By now the first photographs of some of the murdered children were available. Small hopeful faces looked out from beneath peaked school caps or smiled from sunlit beaches. Three of the dead children had been identified, while one remained unnamed until all next of kin had been informed.

What seemed to be an unending series of witnesses was queuing to give their accounts, and already the police were expressing concern at the apparent disparity in what had been seen; all they had in common was their expressions of disbelief and horror. Many wept as they described their perspectives, and Michael saw Alison wipe away a tear from the corner of her eye. He went towards her, taking her hand, and she half turned to acknowledge him, attempting a smile.

"Those children," she said. "Those poor families."

The clickety-click of heels on the hard floor alerted them to the approach of the nurse who would unlock the doors which kept the residents secure. Michael felt the need to shift attention back to the main purpose of their visit and wanted to reassure Alison one last time. "I always hope for the best, but mentally I prepare for the worst."

She smiled more freely and squeezed his hand in return. "It'll be fine, don't worry." Her accent was her souvenir from the eight years she had spent working as a tour guide on the other side of the world, and from where she had returned only a few months ago. "I promise not to bite her if she doesn't bite me."

The couple tagged along at the back of the group which proceeded through the main corridor, one or more of them peeling off in turn as they passed the open doors of the residents' private rooms. Michael glanced into them, and in almost every case saw that TV screens were tuned to the terrible news from central London.

"Does she always know who you are?" They had arrived outside of the door of Rose's room—number 23—and paused for a moment before entering.

"Not always, not recently, and it feels really weird when

she doesn't. It's like someone you know well has had their own personality transplanted and had it replaced by a complete stranger's. Honestly, it can be a bit freaky."

Before they turned to enter her room, Michael could see through the open door that the TV on the wall was also tuned to the news, which was now recapping for what must be the hundredth time the events of earlier in the day. The interviewer was speaking to witnesses who had seen what happened from below, on the South Bank, and only then did he realize that he and Alison had also eaten lunch not far away from the bridge and could so easily have been caught up in the incident. The thought made him shudder, and he inhaled deeply, trying to refocus on the needs of the moment. He mouthed a silent mantra of hope for what was to come, tightened his grip on Alison's hand, and stepped inside.

His grandma Rose had never been what people would describe as a beauty, but she had about her a poise and elegance which had not deserted her in older age. One of the nurses at Greenacres said when she first arrived that Rose reminded her of Jessica Tandy in *Driving Miss Daisy*. Michael had not seen the film but was happy that the comparison had pleased his grandmother. Now, though, she was sitting in an upright armchair next to her bed, seeming neither surprised nor pleased and betraying no hint of whether or not she recognized him. He noticed that her once-striking pale blue eyes seemed to be a shade paler, and perhaps her stare was a touch more vacant in the few days since he had last visited. He stood between his grandmother and the TV and then was not sure whether her gaze had moved at all from the direction of the screen.

"Hello, Grandma." Michael spoke in the most upbeat tone he could summon, and the sound of his voice drew her eyes a few millimeters towards him. Still he could not be sure whether she had registered, but in a few seconds a small light seemed to be dawning and a flicker of recognition dug a deeper crease into the crevices which fanned out at the edges of her lips. Hoping to build on a kick-start of reaction, Michael continued, "I've brought someone to see you." Alison had entered the room after Michael and was partially obscured behind him. She stepped forward and spoke.

"Hello, Mrs. Beaumont." Her tone was cheerful, and her accent sounded carefree. "I'm very pleased to meet you. I'm Alison." It was not the sound of her voice which drew Rose's eyes but her further movement forward with hand outstretched. Rose's gaze followed her visitor from the open hand, up her arm, and finally to register her face. When she got there, Grandma Rose looked at Alison for a few seconds, seeming to struggle to adjust her focus, and then, rather than looking up and into the outside world, it was as though she was looking in reverse into her own head, into a labyrinth of long-buried memories.

And then she started to scream.

TWO

I CAN'T SAY with any certainty what could have brought that on."

Ten minutes later, back in the waiting area, the young doctor from Greenacres was trying her best to offer consolation. Michael and Alison were both shocked by what had happened, and as she sipped from the cup of tea which had been hurriedly provided by one of the nurses, he could see that her hand was trembling. The scream had seemed to be an expression of anguish rather than of fear and was somehow far too big to emanate from so small and fragile a frame.

Rose had screamed until she ran out of breath, only to start over as soon as her lungs recovered. The nurses came running and flocked around her like birds until the wail subsided into a series of sobs that racked her body until it would rattle apart.

"Maybe she was upset earlier by the dreadful news from Waterloo Bridge this afternoon," said the doctor, whose name badge identified her as Bernice Williams. "Like everyone else she's been watching the TV, but it's not always easy to tell with Rose just how much of these things she is taking in. Possibly it was all percolating around her head and just chose that moment to come out. It's a terrible, awful business."

Michael and Alison both embraced the explanation willingly and assured Dr. Williams that there was no harm done. It was just that it had taken them by surprise.

"I've noticed that bit by bit she has been getting less like herself recently, but that's the first time I've seen her lose it quite like that," said Michael. He ran the fingers of both hands through his hair and clasped them together behind his head. "Has it happened any other time when I haven't been around?"

The doctor continued to look at her notes and turned the top pages on the clipboard. "There are a few references to her having been distressed from time to time, though there's nothing here to indicate what we saw today. But it's not all that unusual. Alzheimer's can manifest in different ways."

When he and his grandmother had first received the diagnosis nearly a year ago, Michael had gone to some trouble to educate himself about what it meant and what it might mean in the future. There were very few certainties, but one of them was that over an unspecified period, the person he knew would become a person he did not know, and likewise she would not know him. It was terribly distressing for all concerned, and the only consolation was that the patient herself might have little or no awareness of her lost faculties and failing capacity. Most of the upset would be felt by those closest to her. The thought had provided some comfort for Michael, which was part of the reason that the incident today was of such particular concern.

"Do you mind if I ask something?" Dr. Williams continued without waiting for the permission she seemed to be seeking. "Is there anything in her past that she would have been upset by, having to do with Australia?"

Michael was puzzled. "I don't think so. Why do you ask that?"

"No special reason. It's just that you said her outburst might have been triggered when your friend spoke to her." Her smile towards Alison was warm and polite. "I notice you seem to have a slight accent. I just wondered if hearing that set off something in her memory. Just an idea."

The discussion was interrupted by a nurse who came in to assure them that Mrs. Beaumont was calm and resting and asked if they would like to make another attempt to see her. Michael looked to Alison, whose expression indicated that she was willing to give it a go.

"You know what?" he said. "Let's leave it for today. It's great that she's calmed down, and we can always try again another time." Everyone seemed content with the decision, and Michael thanked the doctor once again.

"Try not to worry," said Dr. Williams. "Things like this can be very upsetting, but chances are she'll be right as rain next time you come — and she won't have the slightest idea that she has met you before." The doctor shook hands with them both, smiling warmly. "It gives the lie to the old saying that you only get one chance to make a first impression."

Their route from Battersea towards Michael's apartment in Kingston took them onto the South Circular, heading against the weight of traffic which was flowing back into London at the end of the day. Michael turned on the radio news, and their conversation on the journey home alternated between what had happened at the care home and the events on Waterloo Bridge.

"I can't imagine what the people who were on the bridge must be thinking now," said Alison. The BBC reporter had been interviewing witnesses, several of whom were saying how everything had happened so quickly that no one could have done anything to prevent it. "Isn't it amazing how you can just be minding your own business, having a nice day out, and then fate puts you in a situation which is going to affect you for the rest of your life?"

Michael thought about what she had said. "It is amazing, but it's also amazing how people like those witnesses react as though something has happened to them, when in fact it's happened to the children and their families. It seems to me that everyone is encouraged to consider how they feel about stuff themselves, when what they should be feeling is sympathy for the people who've been affected directly."

"The bystanders *have* been affected directly," said Alison. Her reaction seemed to Michael to be more vehement than the situation justified. "Everyone they ever meet from this day onwards will have in the back of their minds the question why they didn't act more quickly to stop what was happening. And despite what they're saying right now, they'll also be asking themselves every day of their lives whether they could have done more to prevent it. What happened today will affect them forever, and all because chance put them in the wrong place at the wrong time." She turned towards Michael, apparently anxious that he should take on board what she was saying. "Do you see what I'm getting at?"

"I do. I see that. In fact, as you pointed out, it could so easily have been us who found ourselves in precisely that situation." He paused. "I don't think I've seen a report of exactly what time all this happened, but we were not far from there this morning. Half an hour either way and we might have been witnesses ourselves." The couple drove in silence before Michael spoke again. "I wonder if what the doctor said might be true— that Rose had been watching the news reports before we got there and was traumatized. I've never seen her like that. It was shocking." He took his left hand from the wheel and covered hers. "I'm so sorry that you had that to deal with," he said, "it wasn't at all what I'd had in mind."

"What did you have in mind?"

"That she would instantly fall in love with you and would quietly take you to one side and tell you what a great bloke I am and how lucky you are to have found me."

Alison smiled. "OK, yes, I see now why you were disappointed. You'd hoped for a scene out of *All My Children,* and what you got instead was more like something out of *The Addams Family.*"

Alison squeezed his hand in return. The traffic was now even heavier and was at a standstill in both directions. Michael pointed out the bright-red faces of some of the people who had been all too keen to enjoy the first proper heat wave of the year. Alongside their Vauxhall, but traveling in the opposite direction, an open-topped bright-blue BMW contained a family of mum and dad in the front and two listless kids strapped into the rear seats. The driver was in his late thirties and clearly had been in the sun for too long. His thinning red hair was streaked across his pate and had done little to protect him, so that the skin covering his skull was pink and freckled. A heavily tattooed forearm decorated with elaborate patterns rested on the door and was so close that Michael could have touched it. Alison caught the other driver's eye for an instant and saw his expression change from irritation to something like a leer. She looked away quickly before Michael might notice, but just at that moment her boyfriend turned his head and also caught the attention of the stranger.

"They want to catch that lunatic and string him up from the fucking bridge," said the man. "That's what I'd do."

"Yeah, me too," said Michael, but when both cars had moved on he turned to Alison. "I hate it when that happens. It's like finding yourself having to agree with racist taxi drivers, because you don't want to get into an argument, but you hate yourself afterwards for not disagreeing with a skinhead."

Alison smiled and nodded. It was the kind of remark which had attracted her to Michael in the first place, and as they drove along slowly and in silence, she thought about how she had been drawn to him from their very first meeting just two months earlier in a wine bar in Brighton.

———————————

Alison had been on a rare evening out with colleagues from the local travel agency where she had worked since her return from Australia; Michael had come down from London for a stag weekend with a few friends from the TV postproduction house where he was a runner. Her attention had first been drawn in his direction by the irritating noise of their partying, and one of the women from her own group had suggested that they should make a complaint, but Alison and Michael exchanged glances and both felt the same tug on an invisible string.

He found a reason to break away from his friends, leaving them to continue their adventure into oblivion without him. There were similar knowing looks from Alison's workmates as she peeled off to speak to Michael. The couple remained in the wine bar for a while, and when the noise became too loud to bear, they left together to continue talking and drinking in the saloon of the dismal seafront hotel where he was staying overnight. They did not speak of anything serious or significant on that evening, but seemed to hit it off from the start. She was twenty-six with curly shoulder-length blonde hair, soft brown eyes, and skin which had been dipped in the Australian sunshine. He was twenty, sandy haired, good-looking, and athletic. The attraction was instant and mutual, but any idea of consummation was rapidly put to flight by the boisterous return of the stag party, several of whom stood on the stairs making obscene gestures through the reinforced glass. Alison took this as her cue to say good night and insisted on leaving him at the hotel entrance when she hailed a taxi. Nevertheless she borrowed a ballpoint pen from the sleepy receptionist and scribbled a telephone number on the back of Michael's hand. What might have been a kiss turned into a brush of cheeks as she turned her head at the last moment, but he went to bed that night thinking about her and awoke early the next day counting the minutes until he could persuade himself that it would be okay to call the number. He lasted until 8:30 and then irritated a couple of sleeping innocents before realizing that her 7s looked very much like 9s. She answered on the second ring, and they agreed to meet at the entrance to the pier.

Alison wore only light makeup, and her hair, which had been so full last night, was tied back in a ponytail. Her skinny jeans showed off the slenderness of her hips. Michael thought she looked even more attractive this morning than he remembered, but at the same time wondered whether her apparent lack of effort meant that she felt little inclination to make herself of interest to him. Still, she had taken the trouble to turn out early on a Sunday morning, so that must count for something.

Alison showed the way towards a fifties-style café close to the esplanade called the Pelican and ordered cappuccino, which came in brown smoked-glass cups with an almond-flavored biscuit going mushy in the saucer. Michael was amused to see Alison using her biscuit to scoop the froth from the sides of the cup before popping it into her mouth.

"Better not let my grandma see you do that," he said, prompting her to smile and press him for more information. He continued, and was surprised to find himself speaking about aspects of his life which he usually kept private. "My grandma Rose brought me up after my mother left home when I was a baby. She'd had a mental breakdown soon after I was born and was unable to look after me. She walked out of the house one day, and we never saw her again. Rose's husband, my grandfather, had also recently died of a heart attack, but despite all that she just stepped in and did what anyone else's mother would have done for them. When I was little I just assumed that she was my mum, but she never wanted me to call her anything but Grandma. So that's what she has always been to me—Grandma Rose."

"She sounds like a marvelous woman. Do you still live with her?"

Michael had been doodling with the back of his spoon in the froth on top of his coffee and had unconsciously rearranged the chocolate sprinkles into the shape of an unhappy face. "I did, until a month ago. Unfortunately, last year she was diagnosed with Alzheimer's, and she and I stayed at home together for as long as I could manage, but eventually the doctors told me that it was too dangerous to leave her alone."

The decision had been hard to take, but followed a series of incidents which gave cause for concern. Once again Alison encouraged him to say more, and Michael recounted how one day he had come home from work a little later than usual to find their apartment empty. He knocked next door, but Elsie, who was about the same age as Rose, had neither seen nor heard anything for several hours and assumed that his grandmother was out. He telephoned the number of the mobile phone he had pleaded with Rose to carry everywhere and heard it ringing on the table next to her bed. He hurried out into the street and across the ancient stone bridge over the Thames, scanning the heads of shoppers as he went. Eventually he was drawn towards a crowd of people surrounding a juggler performing in the main pedestrianized thoroughfare in front of the shopping mall. The man had picked someone out of the crowd to act as his assistant, and Michael was horrified to see his grandmother, dressed in her floral housecoat and slippers, carrying a dozen shiny silver rings over her left arm like a handbag, and a flaming torch in her outstretched hand. She seemed absorbed by the act and unaware of the intermittent gasps from the audience. Unsure of what to do, but anxious not to cause her any danger or embarrassment, Michael waited for a pause in the act before intervening to rescue her. Only when the crowd gave her a spontaneous round of applause did Rose seem to become aware of them, and she beamed a smile of untarnished pleasure. As he escorted her back over the bridge towards their apartment, Michael reflected on how horrified his usually discreet and shy grandma Rose would have been by such an incident had it occurred just a few weeks earlier.

"But that's enough about me and mine." Michael had promised to rejoin his friends at Brighton railway station at 11:00 AM for the journey back to town. Now it was 10:40, and he felt no inclination whatever to say goodbye to Alison. "It's your turn to tell me more about you. In the alcoholic blur of last night I can only remember you saying that you worked as a tour guide Down Under. How do you come to be on the other side of the world in sunny Brighton?"

Their conversation the previous evening had scarcely touched on anything personal, but now that he had told her so much about himself and his family, it felt appropriate that she should reciprocate. She seemed to pause to consider whether or not she would take that next step, but eventually the question appeared to be resolved.

"I'm not Australian, actually." The sentence was delivered with an interrogative at the end, as if she were seeking confirmation from him that what she was saying was true. "I went to Oz eight years ago and have lived and worked there since then. That's how I've picked up the accent. I know I have to try to get rid of it now that I'm back."

"Which part of Australia were you living in?"

"Sydney?" Again it was not clear from her inflection if she was asking whether he had heard of Sydney or if he could confirm that she had lived there. He smiled and nodded. "Why are you smiling?" At last an actual question.

"No reason. It's just that you sound every bit as Australian as Crocodile Dundee."

"I'm not sure if that's a compliment?"

They walked eastwards with the sea on their right, along the length of the front and all the way to the marina. It was mid-February, and only the most hardy were braving the biting wind which blew off the Channel. The waves were gray and powerful, their huge weight crashing noisily onto the beach and rearranging the shingle like the pieces of an impossible jig-saw. When they turned around to come back she slipped her arm through his and tilted her head onto his shoulder. At the railway station he moved to kiss her, and this time she did not turn away. When he asked if she would come to London to spend a day with him the following weekend, she said that she thought she might.

On the train journey back to Victoria, thoughts and feelings about his meeting with Alison filled Michael's mind. He watched the Sussex countryside through the window, her face imposing itself on the reflection in the glass, and already his brain was committing to memory the various images which would preoccupy him more or less continuously in the days ahead. They spoke on the telephone every evening for the next week, and when her train arrived at Victoria Station at 9:52 on the following Saturday morning, Michael was there on the platform to greet her. He pulled her to one side, away from the quickening crowd, and they kissed the kiss that he had imag-ined for the past six nights. It was every bit as exciting as he had hoped.

They felt the need to do something together, and it tran-spired that Alison had never been on the London Eye, so they queued among the tourists for the 11:00 AM flight. He was far better informed about the history and geography of Lon-don than she was, and so Michael enjoyed pointing out the main landmarks, and he loved it when once again she took his arm and seemed to be genuinely impressed by his knowledge. They ate sushi in a Japanese restaurant next to the Royal Festival Hall, and she folded the corner of her napkin to remove the trickle of soy sauce from the side of his mouth. She could not stay overnight, she said, but later they took the suburban train for the half-hour ride to the apartment in Kingston which until recently he had shared with his grandmother. Though it seemed inconceivable that Rose would ever be able to return to her home, Michael would not take Alison to the double bed in her room, and they held each other tight between the cold sheets on his single, which he had had the foresight to put on fresh that morning.

After they made love for the first time, and then for a second, Alison lay beneath the sheets and looked around the room which had been his since he was a small boy. His interest in Chelsea Football Club had evaporated some years ago, he explained, but the posters remained in place because to remove them risked leaving a mark on the wallpaper. The paperbacks which were stacked along a set of self-assembly shelving were a mix of the classics, studied for GCSEs and A levels at the local grammar school, and novels by authors such as Ian McEwan, Lee Child, and Iain Banks. By the side of his bed Alison found a copy of *The Great Gatsby,* a bookmark positioned two-thirds of the way through, and asked if it was any good. She was not, she explained, a great reader of novels.

"I've always loved to read travel books," she said, "especially by people who can take you on a journey to places you probably won't ever get to yourself. There's a great big world out there."

"Is that why you went to Australia? To see for yourself how much world there is?"

At their first meeting in Brighton, Alison had spoken about her time in Australia and how she had loved her life there but eventually missed her home and decided after eight years to return to the UK. Now Michael was surprised to realize that while she had told him a little about her work and her friends, he had no idea whether his new lover had parents still living, or brothers, sisters, or cousins. She was six years older than him, and for all he knew she might even have been married and had children of her own.

Suddenly the stuff that had seemed so irrelevant before felt important, and he wanted to know everything she was willing to tell him. Once again, however, as in Brighton a week ago, she seemed reluctant to speak about herself. When she did, she chose her words carefully, individually, as if she needed to test them to check that they expressed what she wanted to say.

"I don't have any parents," she said, pausing just long enough for the thought to settle. "They died in a car accident when I was very young, eight years old, and I had no other close relatives, so I was brought up in a children's home. It's not like it's a big secret, or anything I'm ashamed of, but you can probably see why I don't necessarily bring up the subject unless I have to." Michael experienced several emotions all at once. First among them was empathy from having grown up without parents himself, but hard on its heels was a realization that his situation had been nothing like hers. He did not know what to say, and he told her so. "That's OK," she said. "People seldom do. That's another reason why I prefer to avoid the subject if I can. People get embarrassed, but it's not as though it's anyone's fault. It's just stuff that happens."

"But what about adoption, or fostering? Couldn't the authorities find you a family to live with?"

"I did stay with a few families for short periods when I was very young," said Alison, "but for one reason or another, none of them worked out. And if no one has adopted you by the time you get to nine or ten, it's sort of assumed that you must be a problem of some kind, and so people steer clear. Most couples who want to adopt are looking for cute babies. Anyway, by that time I was so used to living in an institution that I probably wasn't sufficiently domesticated to fit into an ordinary family."

Michael was aware that perhaps he was asking too many questions all at once, but for the moment his curiosity was taking priority over his discretion. "So did you go to an ordinary school? How did that work out?"

"Yes, I went to the local comprehensive, but I was never going to do all that well because every other kid in the school went home to their mums and dads and their food cooked and ready on the table. I had no parents to help me or encourage me with homework, and nowhere suitable to do it even if I'd been that way inclined. And to tell you the truth, I probably wasn't going to be a brainbox anyway." Alison's tone had become sad, and her eyes turned down towards the floor.

Michael knew that she had said as much as she wanted to about her personal history, but still there was one aspect he needed to know more about.

"And what about boyfriends? I guess there must have been quite a few."

She smiled. "One or two."

"But no one special?" His raised eyebrows indicated the hope of confirmation.

"No," she said. "No one special."

"And no one now?"

"No," she replied, and for an instant he thought she was going to continue, but she did not.

"Unless you count me?" he said.

"Well, I suppose I'm hoping that as we've spent the last few hours making love, I can count you as a boyfriend, but maybe it's a bit too soon to say whether you're going to be someone special?" A flicker of concern crossed his mind before he recognized her teasing for what it was and shut her up with a kiss.

It was half an hour before they spoke again, and by then it was dark outside and the only light was the yellow hue from streetlamps edging through a gap between the curtains. Both were happy to remain silent as they lay side by side, hand in hand, contemplating the ceiling and the delicious glow of a new relationship. She propped herself on her elbow to drink some water. "And so now you live here on your own, do you?" He was about to point out that she had not finished telling her own story, but she continued, "That's very cool—hardly out of your teens and you have your own place."

Michael explained that the apartment belonged to his grandmother, but that when they had first been given her diagnosis, he and she had agreed that she would grant him power of attorney over her affairs. They had done nothing about that as yet, but he felt that the time to do so was approaching. Anyway, he was her only relative and beneficiary, so while he had to find money for council tax and utilities, he was at least spared the expense of paying a mortgage.

"I used to drive her around, to doctor's appointments and stuff, before she went into the care home. I reckon I'll have to sell the car sometime soon, but now I come to think about it, I don't even know where she keeps the documents."

For a little while, the only sound was of early evening traffic on the busy streets outside. Eventually Alison said she needed to be on the 10:30 train back to Brighton, and so Michael rummaged in the kitchen drawer for a menu from the nearby takeaway.

It was nearly midnight by the time Michael got back to the apartment in Kingston after having seen Alison off on the train at Victoria Station. His thoughts turned within themselves on the journey back through the suburbs, and he luxuriated in the new sensation in his stomach as he relived the previous hours. He had spent much time in the past week imagining undressing and making love to her. He had known that she would be beautiful, and her body was every bit as thrilling as he had anticipated, her skin brown and soft, and kissing her had been like a narcotic. Though she was by no means his first girlfriend, these feelings were all very new to him, and he felt a twinge of regret that he had no one, no sibling or close family member, with whom to share the novelty of his emotions.

Michael looked forward to the prospect of returning to bed so that he could further indulge his reverie, but that night, a dream he had dreamed many times as a young boy and adolescent returned to discomfort him. In the past the dream had begun in different ways, but always he was with a group of boys around his own age when he found himself somehow having become separated. Sometimes he was alone in a dark alleyway, or occasionally on an anonymous wasteland, when suddenly he was grabbed by strong hands. Instantly his body would go limp, any power to resist draining away, and he felt himself being held tightly by his arms and legs. The force of the violence lifted him bodily off the ground, and the pressure became more and more intense, until he felt the strain at the joints where his limbs were attached to his body, and suddenly there was a danger that he would be torn apart. The pain increased still more, so that at the moment when his limbs and flesh must tear, a single scream from deep within his throat pierced the night and woke him, cold yet sweating, and he would be found clawing frantically at the sheets as though it was they which held him down.

When he was a child, his distress was quickly comforted by his grandmother, who would rush into his bedroom, alarmed herself by the noise of his sudden awakening, but urgently reassuring him that he was safe. She would hold him tightly to her, her cool hands stroking his brow, and whisper soothing words in a singsong voice that he came to love. Eventually he would return to sleep, and she to her bed, and seldom was the matter referred to again in the morning. At last she became so concerned by the frequency of his nightmares, however, that she consulted the doctor. Michael was aware of whispered conversations in which he played no part, but over the years the bad dreams disturbed his sleep less frequently, and gradually the problem faded to the back of his mind.

This night, though, for the first time in several years, the dream returned. It was as before, except that on this occasion he could make out the shadowy outline of his assailants. They were not people he recognized, but he could see the shapes of their faces. As so often before, it was at the point when he felt the flesh on his shoulder begin to rip apart that he woke with a jolt and realized that he was totally alone in the aftermath of his ordeal. There was no one to soothe him or whisper that he was safe, and Michael wept quietly for his loss.

THREE

IN THE DAYS after the incident on Waterloo Bridge, newspapers and news programs on TV and radio carried wall-to-wall coverage. "Madman Throws 4 Kids off Bridge" screamed the *Daily Express* headline the following morning and, as if by agreement, the other tabloids adopted the same description. "Madman on the Loose" was the *Mirror*'s version, while the *Sun* went for "Police Hunt Mad Child Killer." The label was repeated in the wider print media and on radio phone-ins. Like unseasonal rain, the crimes became an add-on to conversations about anything else. "Have they found that Madman yet?" was heard as commonly as the hope of a decent summer.

Grieving relatives, neighbors, sympathizers, and tourists came from far and wide to leave flowers and tributes at the scene, and soon the carpet of bouquets and wreaths began to obstruct traffic on the bridge. With care and respect the police moved them onto the South Bank, where the walkway was wider. Frequent updates on television revisited CCTV footage from the bridge and the nearby streets, and a single frozen frame of a blurred white face in the shadow of a pulled-down hood became a national familiar. It seemed that every person in Britain was looking for this man, despite the fact that the shot gave no realistic chance that he could be recognized. Anyone wearing blue jeans and a hoodie was likely to be viewed with suspicion, and there were several reported cases of unjustified beatings by vigilantes.

Continuing interest in the story obliged journalists to resort to ever-more-ingenious means to keep it on the front pages. After the backgrounds of all the dead children and their families had been investigated and reported, there were the funerals and the grieving relatives. There were extended profiles of the "brave hero"—a twenty-three-year-old man who had dived into the water from the South Bank in a futile attempt to rescue the children. His body, along with that of the father who jumped from the bridge after his five-year-old daughter, was eventually washed up in the mud at Greenwich.

There were reports from inside the police operation and analysis of the capabilities and limitations of CCTV monitoring. TV and radio staged debates about the merits of Big Brother–type surveillance, and criminal psychologists were brought into newsrooms and studios to opine on the kind of mind which was capable of dreaming up such an outrage. Child murder by drowning, it turned out, was by no means as rare an incident as might be expected, but usually it was committed by deranged parents who sought revenge on former partners by killing their children. There seemed to have been few previous examples of random acts of this kind of violence. Speculation was rife that the culprit would turn out to be a father who had been denied access to his own children.

There were discussions in pubs and social clubs about whether the wearing of hoodies should be banned in public places, and everyone seemed to have their own opinion about the civil liberties issues arising therefrom. But gradually, despite the very best efforts of editors and reporters, the specter caused by "fear on our streets" began to fade, and after more time the subject was relegated to inside pages and then was absent altogether.

Michael's job in the postproduction house involved very long hours during the working week but almost always allowed for freedom at the weekends, and so every Friday night since that first time, Michael would travel to Brighton, or Alison would travel to Kingston. One Sunday when he was in Brighton and making plans to return to Kingston for the week ahead, he received a call on his mobile to say that there had been a break-in at the production house. No one was sure if anything had been taken, but most of the staff would not be required until Tuesday. Michael was glad of the opportunity for an extended weekend with Alison, but her job in the travel agency was more difficult to juggle, especially at this time of year when people were booking their summer holidays. He remained in bed that morning but arranged to pick her up at lunchtime for a bite to eat.

As he waited in the foyer, he enjoyed watching her through a glass panel and witnessing her best efforts to remain patient with customers who were trying to organize every last detail of their trip of a lifetime. She looked smart and efficient in blue uniform and tied-back hair, and he smiled to himself as she struggled to be polite in the face of a series of entirely unrealistic requests, when all she wanted to do was to get out of the office and spend time with him.

He was also aware that he was an object of curiosity among some of the other staff who worked with Alison, and guessed that he had been the subject of office gossip. He found that he rather liked the idea that she had talked about him, and when he saw two women who seemed close to Alison's age obviously pointing him out, he tried not to appear self-conscious when he smiled back at them.

"That was Angela and Pauline," said Alison as they walked arm in arm back to Alison's apartment. "Angela is a great mate of mine. She's thirty and has been through the mill in her love life."

In the space of seven or eight weeks, the couple had fallen into something resembling a routine, and increasingly Michael began to feel the need to reintroduce Alison to Grandma Rose. The visit had fallen on that terrible day and had not gone well, so there were no immediate plans for a repeat. He had been to see his grandma many evenings since that first time, but Rose had not referred to it, and he, hoping for the opportunity of a fresh start sometime in the future, had decided not to raise the subject.

Alison's apartment consisted of two rooms and a tiny bathroom on the second floor of a large Victorian terrace, three or four streets back from the seafront in Brighton and surrounded by the bustle of everyday and every-night life in the popular tourist town. There was seldom a quiet moment. One Sunday, a few weeks after their visit to see Grandma Rose, they spent the afternoon making love and had fallen asleep in front of a black-and-white movie playing on the TV, which she propped up on a recycled hospital trolley at the end of her bed. The kitchen was arranged along one wall of the living room down the corridor from the bedroom, and the two did a "dip, dip, dip" to decide which of them would go to make the tea. Michael won and stayed in bed watching the news while Alison slipped on a yellow terry-cloth robe, using both hands to flip her tousled hair from inside the collar, and padded barefoot down the hallway. He loved to see the shape of her as she pulled the dressing-gown cord tight around her waist. The report was about a recent hike in house prices, featuring interviews with first-time buyers who were describing their struggle to get on what the newsreader kept referring to as "the housing ladder." The story was illustrated by animated graphics of people on ladders, which made Michael wonder if he was watching *Play School* rather than the news.

A picture of Waterloo Bridge appeared in the frame behind the newsreader, and he reached for the remote to turn up the volume. The words BREAKING NEWS suddenly appeared in the rolling text at the bottom of the screen, and an immediate change in the newsreader's demeanor indicated that this was a big story.

"And we are just getting word of an incident which has taken place just a few minutes ago in the south coast seaside resort of Brighton. Reports are coming in that an unidentified man walking on the pier has taken hold of a number of children and thrown them into the sea. Let me repeat that, a man appears to have grabbed and thrown three children from the pier at Brighton into the water, and first accounts suggest that he has fled the scene and escaped. We are hearing that several passersby gave chase, but the man is believed to have vanished into the holiday crowds." All the while the newsreader was looking off camera towards a computer screen beside his desk, and now he put a finger to his ear to indicate that he was receiving more information.

Michael yelled to Alison to come through from the kitchen, and only at that moment did he realize that she was unable to hear him because she was speaking to someone on the telephone. He could not make out her words, but when the tone of her voice suggested that the call was coming to an end, he shouted to her once again.

"There's been another incident involving that lunatic, and it's just down the road from here, at the pier. Three kids thrown into the sea." Alison appeared at the door, drying her hands on the corner of her dressing gown, and sat on the bed beside him.

The newsreader continued, "We have no certain word about the condition of the children who are reported to have been thrown over the barrier into the water. We will bring that to you as soon as we hear more. So, to repeat for those who have just joined us, we are receiving news . . . " The story was told again, but as yet there were no new facts.

"Fuck fuck fuck fuck fuck," said Michael. "That's unbelievable. More or less the same thing, in broad daylight, and they say that he got away again." Alison did not speak, but gently shook her head while she remained transfixed by the TV screen.

"Who was that on the phone?" he asked distractedly. Alison seemed momentarily confused. "I called you when the news came on, but you didn't hear me. I think you were on the phone."

"Oh, just Angela," she said. "Some problem at work. Nothing to bother about."

Over the following minutes the news channel began to fill out the story with hurriedly sourced maps showing the location and archive shots of the pier, viewing it from a variety of angles. At last, and with some relief in his voice, the announcer said that they had an eyewitness on the telephone. The screen graphic read "MADMAN" STRIKES AGAIN: EYEWITNESS IN-TERVIEW.

"We were just enjoying a day out with the kids, nothing un-usual, and then we hear this ruckus coming from the pier."

"You were on the beach at this point?"

"Yeah, playing with the kids, and we hear this scream from above our heads and then a splash, and we look up and at first we can't see anything, and then there's another scream and we see this kid just, like, flying through the air. A second later she lands in the water, and then we see that she's landed beside an-other kid who is lying facedown. It was shocking."

The TV screen cut back to a shot of the presenter in the stu-dio.

"That was an eyewitness who was on the beach at Brighton when this incident occurred just a short time ago. And I'm be-ing told that we can now go over live to our reporter James Connelly, who has recently arrived on the scene. What can you tell us, James?"

The presenter was looking off camera, and nothing hap-pened for a few seconds until he started to look uncomfortable and began shuffling the papers on his desk.

"He's gone to the outside broadcast before they're ready," said Michael. "There'll be panic in the control room right now. They're all over the place."

Just then the screen changed to an unstable camera shot, which jerked around for a few seconds before coming into fo-cus on a young reporter who seemed harassed and ill prepared.

"Yes, Bill. I've just arrived at the scene, and while our cam-eraman was setting up, I've been talking to eyewitnesses. They've been telling me that this incident you've just heard about took place just fifty yards or so along the length of the pier, and by the time anyone realized what was happening, the man had turned and sprinted away at what's been described to me as lightning speed. He leapt the turnstiles at the exit to the pier, apparently, and then ran through the traffic, into the Lanes and alleyways beyond. I have with me Brendan Carlton, who's holidaying here with his family and who tried to apprehend the person responsible." The shot widened to include a large man aged about thirty, wearing an undershirt and with sunglasses perched on top of his head. "I've been told that you're the hero of the hour. Can you say what happened?"

"Well, I just seen this bloke running off the pier," said the man, "and someone shouted something like 'There he is,' so I ran after him, and I managed to grab him by the arm, but he struggled and kept on running, so I wasn't able to keep my grip."

"So he ran into the Lanes? Can you say what he looked like? What was he wearing?"

"Yes, he had on blue jeans and a white T-shirt and sneakers. He had what looked like a red bandanna covering the bottom half of his face. He seemed to be young, but honestly I couldn't say more than that. He was strong, though, and very, very fast."

Two of the three children thrown into the sea had been rescued and taken to hospital, where they were said to be expected to survive; one had been caught up by a wave and slammed against the props holding up the pier and had sustained serious head injuries. Within ten minutes of the first report the news was carrying video footage taken on mobile phones showing the limp body of a small boy being carried ashore, and what seemed to be frantic efforts to breathe life into him.

"Jesus H. Christ," said Michael, "that's absolutely unbelievable. This crazy bloke has done more or less the same thing again. Just weeks after the last time."

Their original plan had been that Michael would catch the return train to London at around 6:00 PM, which would get him back to Kingston in time to sort himself out for the working week ahead. When he began to pack up his belongings, however, Michael was aware that Alison had not spoken for some while, and when he looked over at her, he saw that her eyes were turned down towards the floor and she was unwilling to raise her face to look at him.

"Are you going to be OK?" he asked her. "Is it this stuff that's going on . . . ?" She shrugged and shook her head, but he knew that she was evading the question. "I know it's upsetting. Especially happening just up the road like this," said Michael. "It's upsetting for everyone, but is there something in particular?"

He had been trying his best to express sympathy, but when she turned to look at him, the look of sadness on her face had been replaced by something closer to indignation, and her voice sounded brittle. "Why would you ask that? I'm just upset like any normal person would be."

Her response took him by surprise, and he wondered how to row back. "I know. Of course. As you say, any normal person would be. It's just that——"

"Just nothing. I'm upset. Don't worry. You need to get off home." She said "home" with an emphasis that underlined that her home was not his. He waited for a few moments to try to absorb what had happened and to allow the spat to die down. He was confused and anxious not to part on bad terms.

"Tell you what," he said finally, "why don't I stay tonight and get off early in the morning."

At first Alison was reluctant to acquiesce, her body remaining stiff and unyielding, but then gradually she seemed to soften. "Sorry," she said finally, her shoulders visibly relaxing as she spoke, "that's a nice thought, but we've got no food in the apartment. We'd have to go out."

The bars and restaurants in the center of Brighton were always busy at weekends, but as they went out into the streets it seemed to Michael that there were even more people about than usual, and there was something resembling a buzz of excitement in the air. Barroom TVs, which were usually switched to sports or music channels, were tuned to twenty-four-hour news instead, and every few seconds the wail of police sirens drew customers close to doors and windows to see what was happening outside.

The couple was close to giving up and buying takeout when Alison remembered a bistro in a nearby lane which was run by a French couple and had no TV. She noticed that the streets appeared to be populated by a greater-than-usual number of groups of young men, and maybe it was just her imagination, but it seemed as though many of them were wearing blue jeans and T-shirts. Occasionally one member of a group would dart across a road, as though fleeing, and the others in the crowd would cheer and shout, "There goes the Madman! After him!"

"Fucking morons," Michael said, shaking his head.

They felt a sense of relief and refuge when they entered the relative calm of the restaurant. Alison had eaten there before and was on friendly terms with the couple who ran it. She greeted the owner, Claude, by his first name, and they were shown to a small table in a quiet spot farthest from the windows. Straightaway Claude's wife, Renee, came over to take their order.

"Something happening outside it seems?" said Renee. She wore a black leather skirt and a T-shirt with red and white hoops for the sake of the tourists, but there was nothing staged about the accent. "There seems to be lots of noise. What is it all about?"

"There's been an incident on the pier. Haven't you seen the news?" asked Michael. "Just like what happened on Waterloo Bridge a few weeks ago. Some mad bloke started grabbing kids and throwing them over the side into the water."

A length of white string attached to her belt saved her writing pad from hitting the floor as Renee gasped and used both hands to cover her mouth. "Oh, but that is terrible. Here? In this town?"

"Yes, just at the pier, a few hundred yards away," said Michael. "Bloke wearing a red scarf, jeans, and a white T-shirt apparently."

Just as last time, in Greenacres, the incident drew people into conversation, and two women sitting at the next table seemed to want to join in. Both were in their midtwenties and were dressed and made up, ready for a big night out.

"Has there been any news of the kiddies?" asked a woman with dyed-blonde hair and heavy mascara. "When we came out they were saying that a couple of them were going to be okay, but one was in a bad way."

Alison had her back to their table and made no effort to turn around. Michael felt a twinge of anxiety that her reluctance to respond might give offense and so sought to fill the gap. "We haven't heard anything more recent than that," he said. "That was what they were saying when we left home about half an hour ago."

Michael and Alison both ordered galettes and drank white wine, which they consumed to the accompaniment of the more or less continuous sound of emergency vehicles screaming back and forth in the streets outside. The events of the last hours had cast a long shadow over what had been a lovely weekend for both of them, and Alison in particular seemed to have withdrawn into her own thoughts. Michael made several further attempts to lighten the conversation before eventually giving up, accepting that they would eat their food in silence.

Three or four more couples came and went in the course of the next hour, and Michael noticed that the blonde woman at the next table was glancing in their direction and speaking to her friend. He caught the same gestures two or three times and said nothing, but then he saw that they were preparing to leave and the woman was approaching their table. Michael had no time to alert Alison before she was alongside.

"Sorry to bother you"—the accent was more south London than south coast, and she was directing her words to Alison—"but I know you, don't I? It's Lizzie, isn't it?"

Alison had been looking at Michael, and for a moment she did not turn her head or acknowledge the interruption. The situation was just at the point of becoming embarrassing, and Michael was about to speak when Alison turned to face the woman.

"Sorry," she said. Michael thought that her tone was awkward, and her smile seemed forced. "I think you've got the wrong person. My name's Alison." The woman did not respond straightaway but continued to look directly back at her, as if trying to decide whether or not she was right. "That happens to me quite a bit," Alison was continuing, and Michael wondered whether the Australian lilt in her accent sounded if anything a little more pronounced than usual. "I must have one of those faces that people think they know."

The woman continued to stare back at Alison without speaking and seemed about to persist when suddenly she changed her mind. She stood upright and spoke again.

"OK, sorry, love. My mistake. Yeah, you've probably just got one of those faces. Sorry to have bothered you." The woman turned to look at Michael with an expression he found difficult to decipher and returned to join her friend. He watched them leave the bistro and head into the street.

FOUR

RATHER THAN RISK another surprise which might have the same outcome as before, Michael thought it best to warn his grandmother that he was bringing someone new to see her. On the evening following the incident at Brighton Pier he went to Greenacres with the intention of telling her about his new girlfriend and preparing Rose for the idea of a meeting.

In the first two or three weeks after she first moved into the care home, Michael had visited his grandma every day after work and twice each weekend. Initially he had in his mind that he would continue with this pattern, but it quickly became clear that work commitments would make that impossible. When he began to feel that she was settling into her new home, he allowed the number of his visits to reduce, usually to twice during the working week—dropping in quickly in the late evening—and once at the weekend. More recently his regular trips to the coast, or otherwise the visits from Alison to Kingston, meant that he missed seeing his grandma on either Saturday or Sunday. He didn't feel too good about it, but if Rose had noticed his decreasing attentions, she had not mentioned it.

She was not in her room when he arrived at Greenacres, and he went straightaway to the dayroom which was shared by all the residents. The space was light and airy and looked out over a small but well-kept garden. In a far corner a television was playing *On Golden Pond* at a volume Michael would have found equivalent to torture had he been forced to endure it. Immediately he saw his grandmother sitting at a small table with three other people, playing cards. It seemed to be a game of bridge, and Michael watched for a few minutes and was happy to see the smile which spread across her face as she put down what was obviously the winning card of the hand. It was clear that she was on good terms with the other players and it gave Michael a boost to see Rose enjoying herself. How weird it was, he thought, that her condition seemed to vary from entirely lucid and apparently carefree on one day to a state of evident torment on the next. One of the group looked across and spotted Michael standing in the doorway, and he was further gratified to see her beaming smile turned in his direction. She excused herself from the table and walked slowly towards him, arms outstretched in welcome. They embraced as usual, but when he hugged her he noticed that she felt just a little more frail. They returned to her room where she made tea for two, taking her own good time over every element of the process. After ascertaining that she was well and in good spirits, Michael introduced the subject which had been on his mind.

"If it's OK with you, Grandma, I'm going to bring someone to see you on Saturday. She's a new friend of mine, a girlfriend."

This was the first mention he had made of Alison in the weeks since he had originally brought her to Greenacres, and

Michael was relieved that she showed no indication of recognition or recall. A second chance to make a first impression, as Dr. Williams had said. This was one of Rose's good days, and the prospect of the visit seemed to please her.

"Oh, well, that will be lovely, dear. Perhaps we can see if we can get some cake, if it's a special occasion."

Michael smiled broadly at the idea of taking tea and cake with his grandma and Alison together. He still felt an echo of the trauma from his first attempt to introduce Alison to Rose, and he was surprised to find a small tear forming in the corner of his eye. He wiped it away before Rose noticed.

One of the ancillary staff who cleaned and tidied the rooms knocked on the door to bring in the flowers Michael had left at reception, following the house rule. Esme was among the people who had been most welcoming to his grandma when she first arrived at Greenacres. At first it had seemed a strange and slightly forbidding place, and Michael had made sure to express his gratitude to her. Esme was in her fifties, large and black, with a big warm smile, and when Michael first greeted her by the name on the brooch pinned to her uniform, she pointed out that it was "Ez-may," not "Ez-mee," but that if it was all the same to Michael, she'd just be calling him "sweetheart." Michael confirmed that he was happy to be called sweetheart. He discovered that Esme had a particular fondness for Quality Street chocolates, and so Michael always made sure that his grandma had a bowl of them on her bedside table and that he refilled it regularly.

Esme had arranged the flowers in a plain glass vase, six white lilies with a hint of pink—his grandmother's favorites—and their fragrance instantly went into battle for ascendancy over the more familiar smell of antiseptic.

"Would you be kind enough to put them over there please, Esme?" said Rose. "Next to the daffs."

"You're a very popular girl today," said Esme, moving the daffodils to one side to make room. "We're going to run out of vases if you get any more admirers."

"They're lovely, Grandma. Where did they come from?"

Michael glanced at Rose's face and saw immediately that the question seemed to have made her uncomfortable. He wondered whether perhaps his grandma had an admirer among the older gentlemen in the care home and was momentarily unsure whether to repeat the question, when Esme spoke next.

"She's a very popular lady, your grandma is."

"Michael has a new girlfriend apparently, Esme, so it looks like you've lost your chance." Esme had told Rose early on what a handsome grandson she had, and it was now a running joke among the three of them that romance was in the cards. Michael noticed the deft change of subject by his grandma, but chose not to pursue the matter.

"Oh, I'm just biding my time," said Esme. She had produced a yellow cloth from a pocket and was flicking dust from the top of the sideboard. "He'll come to his senses and see what he's missing in the end."

Fifteen minutes later Michael said goodbye to his grandma and promised to come in again later in the week. He was on his way to the car park when he saw Esme at the far end of a corridor. She was walking slowly away from him, and for a moment he was undecided, but then turned and increased his pace to catch her. He was still a few steps behind when he spoke up.

"Thanks for taking such great care of Rose, Esme. She seems to be having a better day today, and I know she loves having a good laugh with you."

"Your grandma is a lovely woman." Esme's face broke into a smile. "It's no trouble whatever to sit and chat with her. I'd do it all day if it wouldn't get me into trouble."

"I was pleased to see those other flowers in her room. Where did they come from, if you don't mind me asking?"

Esme seemed unaware of any mystery. "Oh, they're from that woman who comes to see her now and again. I've only seen her in the distance, but I haven't met her. I assume she's an old friend or neighbor of your grandma's. Why do you ask?"

"No reason," said Michael. "It's just that I can't get here as often as I'd like, and I thought I was her only visitor, so it's great if she gets to see someone else."

"Your grandma isn't lonely, Michael. That's the best thing about a place like this. On her good days she is a great mixer with other people. She's very popular. On her bad days, she's . . ." The words trailed away, but Michael nodded. He did not need her to complete the thought.

Michael's cell phone pinged as he reached the car park, and he hoped it was a message from Alison. He was disappointed to see that it was from Stephen, his boss at the postproduction house, asking him to report for work early in the morning. URGENT. NEED YOU IN. NEW FAST-TURN-ROUND SHOW FOR CHANNEL 4 was as close as it came to an explanation.

His main responsibility as a runner at the Hand-Cutz post-production house in Soho was to fetch and carry for the producers and directors who used the place for editing programs for television. Everyone in the media seemed to need a lot of maintenance, and the demands of running back and forth, carrying skinny lattes or sushi, kept him busy. His deal with the management was that he could spend any spare time at the back of one of the two sound-mixing studios, watching the engineers at work. Michael had studied media at A level, and his ambition was to be a sound mixer for TV and maybe eventually on feature films, with a long-term dream of Hollywood. He was only too well aware, however, that there was a lot of competition for his current job, in what was anyway a highly competitive industry. Lots of people wanted the opportunity to progress in the business, so it was important to stay on top of his game. UNDERSTOOD, he texted back, SEE YOU AT 7:30.

The fast-turnaround commission turned out to be an hour-long news special about the hunt for the Madman. It would be produced by Matterhorn, which specialized in quick-response current-affairs programming. The production team had been gearing up over the weekend anyway and so had been able to move quickly when the latest incident occurred on Sunday. First rushes were already in and being ingested into the editing system, and the director wanted to view the new material shot to date as well as some footage from the archive. When Michael went into the off-line suite at 7:45 to ask if anyone wanted breakfast, the director was watching footage shot in the streets around Brighton Pier shortly after the incident. It showed a lot of the groups of young men who had caused such irritation to Alison and himself, and once again he noted the high proportion of them who were dressed in jeans and T-shirts.

"I was in Brighton on Sunday evening," Michael said. "Everyone seemed to be behaving like total idiots."

The director appeared to be completely absorbed. "Huh? Did you say something?"

"I was just saying that I was down in Brighton when all this happened. On Sunday." The director still gave no indication that he had heard or absorbed Michael's words. "As a matter of fact I got a good up-close look at the bloke who did it, and I think I recognized him. He looked a bit like you, actually." Michael waited for a reaction, but there was none. "So I assume you don't want breakfast then?" he said, and went to the next suite.

The demands of the last-minute production meant that Michael was required to work overtime every day that week, which meant in turn that he would be unable to keep his promise to get back to Greenacres before the weekend. He telephoned and spoke to the receptionist, who said she would pass his message on to Rose, but that she seemed perfectly content and was at that moment playing cards with her usual group of friends.

The Channel 4 show was on schedule for delivery for broadcast on Friday evening, and Michael was able to free up some time to observe in the dubbing suite while the commentary was recorded. This was the moment when the whole production came together and one of the things he most enjoyed about working in television. The team had been allowed access inside the police operation hunting the killer, and the producers had brought in a criminal profiler from America called Professor Aaron Miles to give his view about the psychology of what he persisted in calling "the perp."

"The murder of children by drowning is the eighth-most-likely method of killing," said Miles. "The most common motive is where you have a father who has become estranged from his partner and is angry that he is being denied access to the children. It's as though the perp is saying, 'If you can't have them, no one is going to have them.'" The professor put on his specs and glanced at his notes before continuing. "The most recent similar case in America involved twenty-seven-year old Arthur Morgan, who picked up his five-year-old daughter, Tierra, from her mom, telling her they were going to the movies. He stopped the car off the Schoolhouse Road bridge over Shark River in Wall Township, tied his daughter to a car jack to weigh her down, and threw her off the bridge into the water. He told the court he could still hear her crying as he drove away, and after the verdict, he was caught on camera winking at the prosecution. He got life."

"And is it always men who do this?" asked the interviewer.

"Usually but not always," said Miles. "In 2005 in the San Francisco area, a twenty-three-year-old woman named Lashaun Harris stopped her car next to Pier 7 and threw her three sons, all between one and six years old, into the bay. She said that God had told her to send them to heaven. Only one of the bodies was ever recovered. And it's been less than ten years since Andrea Yates in Houston, Texas, was convicted of drowning all five of her children in the bathtub. In both cases the juries brought in verdicts of insanity."

There followed an extended interview with the senior officer leading the investigation. Chief Superintendent Norman Bailey was the Met's most successful detective, apparently, and his neatly trimmed mustache might have been contrived to emphasize the military precision of his approach to his work. The central theme of his interview was that the killer was likely to be someone with a grudge against society in general and children in particular, but who was capable of blending in with ordinary life. In the middle of the recording the dubbing mixer turned to Michael and whispered, "Is that what's called a blinding glimpse of the totally fucking obvious?" and the two had to suppress their laughter. The unavoidable conclusion of the program was that after an investigation lasting five weeks, the police were no closer to catching the culprit than they had been on the afternoon of the first crime.

Alison caught the train from Brighton after she finished work that Friday, and Michael was able to get away by 7:00 PM so that he could meet her at the station. He arrived with a few minutes to spare before her train was due and spent the time watching passengers coming and going on the busy concourse. Most were commuters, many of their faces showing all the lines and shadows associated with the end of a long and exhausting week. But Michael noticed that every time he saw a family getting on or off the train, the children were being kept unusually close by the adults. In cases where the children were of an age when they might be expected to run free, they were held tightly by the hand. In other cases, parents with toddlers were using nylon harnesses to keep their children safe. The Madman's crimes had had their effect on just about every parent and child in the land, and there was no sign that the police had the first clue about his identity.

Michael felt the same rush of pleasure that he always experienced when he saw Alison after an absence of a few days. It had been raining earlier in the day, and she wore a flimsy white raincoat, tied at the waist. Her blonde hair hung in loose curls onto her shoulders and seemed to bounce in slow motion as she walked towards him. The corners of her eyes crinkled into a fan when she spotted him.

"Wow," his reaction was involuntary, "you look like a TV advertisement for something irresistible." He loved it that she always seemed so pleased to see him, and the couple embraced, fully indulging their moment of total disregard for the teeming humanity all around.

"You're looking pretty good yourself," she said, "and if you play your cards right you might not find it necessary to resist."

They had planned to have an early dinner in town before getting the train back to Kingston, but their sudden urgent need for some privacy changed their minds for them. One hour later they were making love in his single bed, and an hour after that both pronounced themselves overcome by the need for food. She put on his dressing gown and tidied the apartment while he slipped on his clothes and walked across the bridge to buy pizza.

"So are you sure you're happy to go to see Grandma Rose again tomorrow?" He had forgotten to say "no anchovies" and had been delicately extracting them with his fork as he made his way through the deep-dish. "She seems to be going through a really good spell, but there's no way to be certain. The last thing we want is another scene from a horror movie."

She smiled but did not reply, pointing to her bulging cheek by way of explanation. When she had emptied her mouth, she spoke. "No worries. It's all fine. I reckon she'll be OK, and if she isn't, it's not the end of the world. I've seen a lot worse than that in the children's home."

It was the first time that Alison had referred to her upbringing since she had originally given Michael her potted life story, and he was keen to know more.

"You haven't said much about all that. Is that just a coincidence, or that you don't want to talk about it?"

"I don't really like talking about it," she said, and suddenly her tone was becoming just a little more strident with every word, "for what I hope are obvious reasons. I was unhappy there." Her inflection implied that Michael had raised the topic a number of times before and that she was getting impatient with him. "As far as I'm concerned I got out of all that at the first moment I could and have put it behind me and am moving on with my life." She stopped suddenly, as though realizing that she had been overreacting. Michael was reminded of her response some weeks earlier when she had spoken about how fate had dealt an unfair blow to the witnesses on Waterloo Bridge. He wanted to say something like *whoa* but then had an instinct that she already knew that her response had been inappropriate, and that pointing it out probably would not help.

"That's completely cool," he said instead. "I can totally understand why you prefer not to talk about it. Sorry I raised it." His instant retreat seemed to confirm for Alison that her reaction had been unfair, and it was her turn to conciliate.

"There's no need to be sorry. It was a perfectly innocent question. I guess it's just been a long week." They put the unfinished pizza to one side and she curled up alongside him on the sofa. They slept in each other's arms that night and woke to a light drizzle which put a soft-focus filter over the view from their window.

The lingering smell of deep-fried food and overcooked vegetables permeated the security doors to the waiting area, reminding Michael of school lunches. He recalled that his grandma had always been fastidious about healthy eating, even before it was fashionable, and he wondered out loud what she made of the mass catering at Greenacres.

"Presumably it's not compulsory to eat it," said Alison. "Personally the smell would be enough to put me off."

"I noticed the other day that she's getting thinner. There was nothing of her to start with, so she can scarcely stand losing more weight." He was keen not to be making complaints at Greenacres, but made a mental note to mention his concern to Esme when he got the chance. By the time the moment came for the introductions, Michael was so wound up with anxiety that he could scarcely get his words out.

"Grandma, I said I was going to bring someone to meet you." They had arrived in her room, and he was immensely relieved to see his grandmother rise from her chair and put out her hand. "This is Alison. She and I have been seeing a lot of each other."

"Hello, Mrs. Beaumont." Alison's smile was broad and engaging. "It's lovely to meet you."

The two women shook hands, and Michael wasn't sure whether Alison didn't do a little curtsey. He noted again how tiny his grandmother looked, and how fragile. After the formalities they all sat around a table which Grandma used for taking meals when she chose to eat her food in the privacy of the room. It was very obvious that Rose was having a good day, and now Michael reproached himself for not having been more careful in preparing for the visit the first time he tried it. They talked casually about the weather for a few minutes, until there was a knock on the door and Esme came in pushing a trolley with tea. Michael leapt to his feet to hold the door back against its spring.

"Michael has brought his new friend to meet me, Esme," said Rose. "Looks like you've missed your chance." Esme greeted Alison warmly. She put the teapot and cups onto the table and removed a layer of tinfoil to reveal a homemade Victoria sponge cake. "Esme made this cake herself especially for the two of you." Rose had a little bit of mischief in her voice. "I told her that Michael was bringing a special friend, and for some reason she thinks the cake they usually serve here isn't good enough."

"I knew it was an occasion, is all," said Esme. "Nothing wrong with the cake at Greenacres." She turned to Rose and wagged a finger. "Don't you go getting me into trouble with that careless talk." The two women were obviously great friends.

Alison was quick to respond. "That was really kind of you, Esme. The cake looks completely delicious. I'm always in awe of anyone who can bake."

Esme was clearly pleased. "It may take face powder to get 'em, honey, but it takes baking powder to keep 'em." Everyone laughed, and she finished laying out the crockery and headed for the door, but turned to Michael before she left. "She seems far too good for you, mind. Make sure you look after her."

"That's the plan," said Michael, and everyone smiled again.

After Esme had gone and Michael poured tea, Alison complimented Grandma on the comfort of her room, and Rose explained how the care home was organized. All the residents had their private space in which they could put their own furniture, ornaments, and pictures, but they were welcome to take meals and mix with the others in the communal areas. It all worked rather well.

"Is that Australia I detect in your accent?" Rose asked. "Whereabouts does your family come from?"

"I've been working in Australia for quite a few years," said Alison, "but originally my family came from the south coast of England."

"Oh, that's nice," said Rose. "I know that part of the world well. My husband and I used to spend a lot of time in Hove. Whereabouts did you grow up?"

Michael was aware that his grandmother was straying into territory he knew Alison to be sensitive about. He was about to interrupt to change the subject, but Alison seemed ready with her answer. "I went to school in Brighton," she said, but Michael thought he detected just a slight change of tone in her voice. He decided to try to intervene.

"I'm sorry I haven't been around much, Rose," said Michael. "It's been a busy time at work and I've been putting in a lot of extra hours."

Rose did not respond to Michael's interjection, and when he glanced up at her, he saw that his grandma was continuing to stare in silence in the direction of Alison. It was not easy to read her thoughts, and after a few more seconds had passed he wondered if she had lapsed into a daydream. "Grandma? Did you catch what I said? I was saying sorry that I wasn't around last week." Still he had not managed to get her attention, and now Alison began to show the first indications that she was feeling embarrassed. Rose was continuing to stare at her, with a look that suggested she was trying to work out a puzzle which was eluding her.

"Rose? Are you OK?" The change of tone in Michael's voice finally got his grandmother's attention, and suddenly she regained animation, as though coming out of a trance.

"Sorry, I was miles away," she said. "I was just thinking about something else." She turned back to Alison and smiled. "Please do forgive me. My mind does wander about these days. I can't always remember . . ." and now her words trailed away.

Michael got to his feet and started to collect the cups and

plates. "Listen, Rose," he said, "we're tiring you out. And anyway you've got to keep your wits about you to cope with those cardsharps I saw you playing with the other day."

The spell was broken, and Alison also got to her feet, taking care not to let the crumbs from the cake fall onto the carpet. "Thank you for the tea and cake, Mrs. Beaumont," she said, "they were delicious."

"Thank you. Actually I have the wonderful Esme to thank. When I told her that Michael was bringing a special visitor, she told me not to order the cake they serve you here and that she would bake one. I gather that it's her specialty." Rose's smile suggested no awareness of the repetition of their earlier conversation.

"Well, maybe we'll see her on the way out, but please give her our thanks and compliments if we don't." Michael had taken his jacket from the hook behind the door and was slipping it on. "I don't know when I'll get here next, but I'll be sure to pop by sometime in the week."

Rose reassured him that she always loved to see him, but that he mustn't exhaust himself on her account. "And anyway, you've got Alison, who'll need your attention now." She spoke with no apparent trace of regret. "You can't be spending your spare time with a daft old woman like me." Michael told her that she was talking nonsense and gave her a careful hug. He glanced back as Rose prepared to close her door behind him and was disappointed to see that once again his grandmother's expression had returned to the stony stare which suggested that she was retreating into another world.

FIVE

IT WAS A less busy week at work, and Michael was given some opportunities to sit in with the sound engineer as he mixed the music and effects for an ITV drama which was in postproduction at Hand-Cutz. He never ceased to be amazed at the skill involved in blending a dozen or more unrelated tracks together in a balance which sounded as though it was all meant to be. He watched as the engineer, his friend Stephen, placed each of his fingers on a different fader like a concert pianist and edged down the volume of the music tracks as the sound of a passing car came through the frame, and nudged down the blasts from a series of gunshots just at the right moment so that the screams from the victim would cause appropriate alarm.

"Now you try."

The great thing about the digital suite was that everything could proceed by trial and error until the perfect mix was achieved, and so no mistakes were final. Michael spent a happy hour trying different balances between the sound sources and eventually produced a sequence which Stephen declared to be "not at all bad." He then suggested that Michael should try mixing in some dialogue, but they had nothing suitable readily available, and so Michael went into the sound booth. They both had trouble keeping a straight face as he read aloud from the lunch menu which they offered to outside clients. The eventual mix of a dramatic shoot-out accompanied by the voice-over describing a range of pizza toppings caused hilarity and eventually was declared by Stephen to be a good morning's work, which had made him need some food. That was about as high a compliment as Michael had ever heard from Stephen, so he was pleased with himself. They had a client coming in for a voice recording at 2:00 PM but agreed that they could spare an hour to go to the local pub for a sandwich. Security at the production house had been tightened since the break-in some weeks earlier, and they set the lock on the door of the dubbing suite before they went to lunch.

The Ploughman's Arms was an unlikely watering hole for the middle of Soho, but it was only a few hundred yards away, and Michael and Stephen arrived to find a collection of colleagues already ensconced at a corner table, where they had saved two seats.

"Looks like I've arrived just in time to buy the drinks," said Michael. "Funny how that happens."

"Put it on the company account," said Stephen. "I reckon that what we've done this morning counts as working through lunch, so Hand-Cutz can pay."

"Nice one," said Michael. He wrote down an order from everyone at the table and queued at the bar while his friend sat down. The room was decorated more in keeping with a village in the Cotswolds than an inner-city district where the clientele was a mix of workers from the media and the sex trade. The walls of the Ploughman's were covered with sepia photographs of men driving cart horses through fields of wheat. Leather straps decorated with horse brasses adorned the bar area, and as he waited, Michael perched himself on a stool which seemed designed along the lines of a saddle. He glanced ahead and caught the eye of a young woman who was in conversation with a friend.

The woman immediately looked away, but something in that moment told him that they had recognized each other. She had blonde hair and was heavily made up, and Michael wondered whether the woman was employed in the other industry for which Soho was famous. He always enjoyed exchanging banter with the girls who stood outside of the clubs and bars describing the temptations within, and wondered whether that was where he knew her from. She did not look back at him after that first glance, and it seemed that her conversation was coming to an end. Something told Michael that the woman already knew the answer to the question he was trying to solve, and it was only when he had paid for the drinks and delivered Stephen's pint to the table that he remembered. He looked up again and saw that the friend was just leaving the bar, and the woman he recognized was also preparing to depart. He excused himself from the group of workmates and walked towards her.

She turned to face him with a look which suggested that she had guessed what he was about to say: "Didn't I see you in Brighton, at that French restaurant, on the day when those kids were thrown off the pier?"

"That's right," she said without hesitation. She was collecting her things and showing no signs of stopping. "Work around here, do you?" She picked up her cell phone from the bar and put it into her handbag.

"Yes, just down the road. But have you got a minute for me to ask you something?"

The woman's face was a picture of disinterest, as though she knew she was not about to help him but was resigned to going through the motions. "Go ahead. I'm not in any great rush."

"Well, you thought my girlfriend was someone called Lizzie, which she isn't, but I had the feeling that you didn't believe her?"

The woman looked into Michael's eyes, her own darting from side to side, and eloquently conveying a sense that she doubted his intelligence.

"I don't want to go about calling anybody a liar. I just know what I know, is all."

"So you don't think it's possible that Alison just looks a lot like the person you know? How long is it since you last met Lizzie?"

"Look, like I say, I don't want to get into anyone else's business. Everyone has their own reasons. All I'm saying is that I know what I know. I'm not saying anything more."

Michael stared hard at her, as if a study of her face might give him a clue as to the explanation. Her blonde hair was overdue for having the roots done, and the thick and clumsily applied makeup did nothing to enhance what might otherwise have been an attractive face. He did not think she was telling lies on purpose, and there had been something in Alison's response when they met in Brighton which suggested there was more.

"And are you willing to tell me where you think you know her from?"

The woman said she had to go and slung her bag over her shoulder. "If you want to know that, I suggest you ask your girlfriend. If she hasn't told you, it's probably because she doesn't want you to know. Know what I mean?"

Michael did know what she meant, but could see that he was unlikely to make any further progress.

"OK, sure. Sorry to have disturbed you." She seemed surprised when he put out his hand. "My name is Michael. Can I ask yours?"

She appeared to be in some doubt and hesitated. Then she shook his hand and replied, "Joanna. Joanna Potts, but if you want my advice you won't go telling her you've met me," and she turned and walked out into the street.

SIX

MICHAEL'S USUAL ROUTINE on a day when he didn't need the car to visit Rose was to take the overground train from Waterloo to Kingston, drop into the local shops to buy food and whatever provisions he needed, and then walk across the bridge towards the apartment. On his way home that evening the sun was still shining, and the Thames was a buzz of activity. Diesel-driven passenger ferries masquerading as Mississippi steamers transported tourists backwards and forwards from Richmond to Hampton Court, stopping to load and unload on the Kingston side of the water. One- and two-man canoes dodged between fast sculling boats, which darted at what seemed to be alarming speed up one side of the river and down the other.

Michael stopped in the center of the bridge, put down his carrier bag of shopping on the side of the pavement, and leaned against the parapet. On the right-hand-side bank he could see one of the ferries loading up with passengers, and beneath him a boat rowed by four strong-looking men about his own age sped like an arrow through the water. He looked again at the passengers embarking on the ferry and noticed, as he had before, that parents or grandparents were holding on tightly to the hands of small children. He watched as one child, aged about six or seven, pulled himself free from his mother's grasp and set off at a run along the river's edge. She called after him in a pitch of hysteria, which in normal circumstances would have seemed far out of proportion. There was a collective sigh of relief among the people surrounding them when she regained hold of the little boy's hand, but Michael was less happy to witness her administering a sharp slap on his leg, which seemed to echo around the concrete arches. His scream temporarily drowned out all other sounds.

When Michael reached the apartment ten minutes later, he was about to put the key in the lock when his next-door neighbor came out into the shared hallway.

"Hello, Michael. I was hoping to see you." Unlike his grandmother, Elsie had chosen to fight the ravages of time through the use of hair color and heavy makeup. He knew from Rose that she had been what his grandmother described as a "girl about town" in her youth, and Michael felt just a hint of discomfort to see the twinkle in her eye when she spoke to him. Nonetheless, she had been a good friend to Rose, and he was always glad to pass the time of day with her.

"I do hope your grandma is keeping well, Michael," she said. "Will you be sure to tell her I was asking after her?" Michael assured her that he would and that her good wishes would be returned. "I just wondered if you or Rose have such a thing as a large white envelope I could borrow? I've just found an old photograph I want to send to my son, and ideally I want one of those stiff ones. If not, maybe I could use an ordinary one and put a bit of cardboard inside?"

Michael said that he didn't think he had anything like that

himself but that there might be a large envelope among Rose's papers. He offered to go in to have a look, and he would knock on Elsie's door in a few minutes if he could find anything.

He let himself inside and went immediately to the dark wooden bureau in the corner of Rose's bedroom where she kept her papers and stationery. It still felt a bit odd to come into Rose's room when she wasn't there, and he reminded himself that he should open the windows from time to time to keep the room aired. Writing paper and envelopes were usually stored in the drawers below the pull-down flap, and he rummaged through several pads of pale-blue Basildon Bond. In among the papers was a selection of greetings cards which had obviously caught Rose's eye and been kept for when appropriate occasions came along. There were several books of postage stamps, and he also found a number of brown envelopes which contained formal documents and certificates. Most were duplicates, because the originals had been destroyed in a fire caused by a faulty electric heater in the house where they had lived when Michael was a baby. He had no memory of the event, but the story had been used throughout his childhood as a vivid warning about the danger of carelessness.

Continuing to rummage among the papers, Michael came across a blue cardboard file on which was written the word "Michael" in his grandma's hand. He opened it and began sorting through a batch of his own GCSE and A-level certificates, which were tucked in alongside a pile of his end-of-term reports from junior school. The discovery replayed for him a memory of bringing them home in a sealed brown envelope and of being required to sit next to his grandmother on the sofa while she read them from beginning to end. He pictured Rose remaining very still with her specs perched on the end of her nose and tilting the angle so that the neatly typed pages caught the best light. She would give away little other than a mumble of disapproval or otherwise, until she got to the last comment, and then she folded the paper, returned it to the envelope, and cooked his favorite meal of fish cakes, chips, and peas.

"It's marvelous to see you learning so many different and wonderful things," she said to him as they ate together one evening after his report had been read and stored safely away. "The only worthwhile thing I ever learned at school was from one particular teacher who told me something which has always stayed with me."

"And what was that, Grandma?" said Michael.

"That when someone else is behaving badly, to try your very best to see the world from their point of view. If you can do that, you'll usually find that what they're saying or doing makes sense to them, even if it doesn't to you. It's a piece of advice I've always tried to live by, and you would do very well to do the same." His grandma's smile was full of warmth and love, and he knew that he would always do his best to make her happy and proud if he could. That was then, and that was now, too.

Michael was just about to give up the search for something which would meet Elsie's needs when he came across a small bundle of white stiffened envelopes. He was glad to be able to help her after all, and his neighbor seemed delighted when he delivered one of them next door. He returned to settle in for the evening and opened a bottle of beer.

Michael still felt a nagging disquiet about the encounter earlier in the day with the blonde woman in the Ploughman's Arms. The incident had added to a level of concern which was already bubbling away in his mind about Alison, and in particular about the account she had given of her early life. Of course it was understandable that she would be reluctant to talk about what had obviously been a very difficult time in her childhood, and perhaps it was not surprising that the circumstances which led to her being brought up in local authority care were sketchy. No one would enjoy saying much about a car crash in which her parents had been killed. However, he had now seen on several occasions that Alison tended to overreact when anything to do with her past came up, and the incidents caused him a growing sense of discomfort. He wondered what, if anything, he might do to rid himself of his anxiety, but something made him feel reluctant to embark on anything resembling an investigation. Though he had his doubts about what Alison had told him, the last thing he wanted was for his relationship with her to be undermined by suspicion or distrust.

Michael reached across to his shoulder bag and took out his laptop. He switched it on and checked his emails, and then hesitated for a few moments more before turning to Google. He put the cursor in the search box and carefully typed in the words "couple die in car crash" and pressed the space bar. Alison had said that she had been eight years old at the time, which would put the date at around 1995 and so he entered another space and typed in "1990–2000." He put in another space and then typed "Brighton." Now Michael hesitated for yet a few seconds more before making up his mind and clicking on search. The system produced 450,000 results in 0.67 second, and he began to scroll through the first few screens. Immediate headlines included a broad assortment of tragedy and mayhem, but none of the first five pages he looked at suggested anything remotely similar to what he was looking for, and already the relevance of entries seemed to be getting more remote. He narrowed the search to the Brighton *Argus* web-site and once again could find a series of road accidents, but nothing which might have been the incident involving Alison's parents.

Michael sat back in his chair and breathed deeply, still trying to get a perspective on his feelings. At one moment he felt worried that he did not know as much as he wanted to know about a woman he was becoming more and more involved with. At the next he was impatient with himself for wasting his time on a stupid search which was never likely to yield any-thing helpful. "If you care enough about it," he said aloud to himself, "just ask her, for God's sake."

The thought reminded Michael that the time was approach-ing 6:00 PM, and he had gotten into the habit of phoning Alison as she left the office in Brighton so he could speak to her during the walk back to her apartment. He was still sorting through papers, but keeping an eye on the clock, and he waited for a few minutes after the top of the hour and dialed her number. Alison had expected his call and seemed happy to hear from him.

"How was your day?" she asked, and he could hear the buzz of traffic in the background.

"It was good," he said. "I spent some time with Stephen do-ing a trial sound mix on a drama we are working on. He was pleased with me and said they might soon give me a formal at-tachment to his department so I can do some proper training. What about you?"

"I had to spend more than an hour with this couple who wanted to book a round-the-world cruise," said Alison, "but I didn't seem to be able to make them understand that seaports have to be visited in the order they appear around the globe, rather than in any order you select." By now she could see the funny side and both of them laughed.

"And you'll never guess who I saw in the pub at lunchtime?" said Michael. Of course she could not guess and did not want to try. "Remember that crazy woman who came up to you in the restaurant in Brighton? On the day the Madman was throwing kids off the pier? Thought she knew you . . ."

"Of course I do. Horrible piece of work, I thought. Did she see you?"

"Yes, she did. As it happens we had a little chat."

"You did what? Why on earth would you do that?" Once again Michael was taken aback by the sudden stridency of Alison's response. For a moment he struggled for an explanation, before realizing that he didn't really need one.

"No reason. Why shouldn't I? The poor woman is convinced she knows you. Obviously she's off her head, or you have some strange doppelgänger walking round. If so I'd love to meet her . . ."

Still Alison did not seem inclined to see any lighter side of the conversation. "Why do you say she still thinks she knows me? What did she say?"

Michael repeated the conversation as far as he could remember it but was careful not to give any hint that he might suspect there was any truth in what the woman was saying. "Maybe she has changed her appearance so much that you don't recognize her? She told me her name. Something like Joanna Potter or something?"

"Look, Michael," said Alison. "Let's be clear. I don't know her. I've never met her, and I've never heard that name."

"Okay, okay," said Michael. "I get it. You don't know her. Of course you don't. I just think it's interesting that she is so convinced that she knows you, and I'm surprised you aren't curious. If there was someone walking around who was a spitting image of me, I'd want to know more about it. Anyway she's obviously off her trolley, but for whatever reason she's mistaken you for this Lizzie woman."

It seemed clear enough that this was not going to be the best moment for Michael to pursue the questions which had been accumulating in his head, and so he turned the conversation to their plans for the weekend. It took a few more minutes before the tone of Alison's responses began to thaw, and soon she declared that she had arrived home and would call to speak to him again at bedtime. They had just rung off when there was a knock on Michael's door, and when he answered, he was surprised to find that it was Elsie. She was holding the envelope he had given her in one hand, and in the other she held a photograph. He assumed that she wanted to show him the picture she was planning to send to her son.

"Hello, Michael. Good job I checked. I'd put my photo in the envelope and was about to seal it when I thought it was a bit bulky. I looked inside and found this. It looks like an old holiday snapshot. Your grandma must have put it in here to stop it from getting creased."

Michael took the photograph from Elsie's outstretched hand and glanced down at it. It was a faded color picture of a group of people he did not recognize, apparently at the seaside. He thanked Elsie, told her she should keep and use the envelope anyway, and closed the door.

Suddenly he felt famished and returned to the kitchen to search the cupboards and fridge for inspiration about what to make for his supper. He had cooked eggs in every different way he knew over the last few days and decided to ring the changes and open a can. Ten minutes later he was sprinkling Worcestershire sauce on a plate of baked beans on toast and looking round for something to read while he ate. He noticed that he had placed the old photograph on the far edge of the table and leaned across to retrieve it, popping a corner of toast and beans in his mouth. As he put the photo on the table beside his plate, a blob of hot sauce dripped from his fork and onto the picture. Cursing under his breath, he reached for a tissue from a box on the counter behind him and wiped the surface. He was irritated to see that the heat from the sauce had blurred a small area of the picture, and even now he experienced a twinge of concern about what his grandmother would say.

He looked more closely at the photograph and felt quite sure that he had never seen it before. It had been taken on a promenade at a seaside resort, which looked as though it might be Brighton. It was of a group of four children, caught midaction, as though instructed to stop whatever they were doing to pose for the camera. He looked more closely to see if he could recognize the faces, but if they had ever been clear, they certainly were not recognizable now.

SEVEN

ON THE FOLLOWING weekend Alison was due to come to Kingston, but she had been troubled for some time by a leaking tap in her apartment and told Michael that she would have to wait at home on Saturday morning for the plumber. She planned to set off on the train as soon as the problem had been sorted but would be unlikely to arrive before midday. Michael had anyway been feeling uncomfortable that he had not visited Rose much at weekends recently and so said he would take the opportunity to see her in the morning. Maybe then he and Alison could meet for some lunch? He had been thinking on and off about the photograph, and before he left the apartment on Saturday morning he slipped it into an inside pocket.

Saturday morning was the busiest time for visitors to Greenacres, and he was not able to find a place in the car park and so drove around the local streets for ten minutes trying to find a space. He was listening to the news on the radio, and once again it occurred to him that the hunt for the Madman had disappeared from the bulletins. Two of the three children thrown into the water in Brighton had survived and were back with their families; the third had not recovered from the head injuries caused when he was battered against the metal props beneath the pier. This meant that the Madman was responsible for the murder of five children, as well as the two adults who had drowned in the Thames trying to rescue them, and Michael wondered whether these terrible crimes would ever be solved.

Eventually he found a space in a residential street and tried to ignore the hostile glare of the woman standing in the bay window of her house as he parked directly outside. The care home was a few hundred yards away, and he felt anxious about how his grandma would be today. Since that awful occasion when he first tried to bring Alison to meet her, she seemed to have had some better days. However, he had never since that time been able to anticipate a visit without a gnawing feeling of concern that a similar scene might occur.

Michael checked his wristwatch. Visitors were admitted to Greenacres at 10:00 AM on Saturdays, and it was just coming up to 10:15. He enjoyed the thought that Rose would not be expecting him and hoped that his visit would give her a nice surprise. He went into the main entrance and through to the foyer, glancing across to check that the waiting room was empty and that the visitors had been admitted. There seemed to be no one about, and so he pushed open the door leading to the main residential corridor and walked through. Doors of individual residents' rooms were open as usual, and Michael glanced in at the children, grandchildren, nephews, and nieces who would no doubt have preferred to be off at the skate park rather than giving up Saturday mornings to visit ancient relatives.

He was about halfway along the corridor, just outside number 12, when he heard the scream. Instantly Michael knew where it was coming from and felt the effect of a cold hand gripping his heart. It had exactly the same piercing resonance that he experienced up close from his grandmother those few weeks ago—the kind of scream you might hear in a horror film when the heroine is being attacked by an axman, as though life itself was in imminent danger. It was a primordial alarm call, and the human instinct was to run towards it, ready to fend off whatever was causing the terror. Today, though, a more powerful force seemed to stiffen Michael's legs and bring him to a standstill. He was aware that members of the nursing staff were running past him in the direction of Rose's room and saw Bernice Williams, the young doctor who had been on duty on that first day, striding from the other direction towards her door. She and two nurses had entered the room, and more seconds passed before the screams stuttered to a halt, only to be replaced by a sound of wailing and sobbing reminiscent of a mother grieving for her children.

Michael had a sudden impulse to turn on his heels and head out of the building, return to his car, and drive away as fast as he could. A moment later he felt ashamed of his reaction and forced one foot to step in front of the other. He was just a few yards away from the doorway to number 23 when a woman he had not seen before strode out of Rose's room and was past him before he was able to see who it was or get an impression of her appearance. He turned around to watch her walking quickly away and saw that she broke into a run as she reached the double doors which led outside. His first thought was that she was a doctor or member of the care-home staff, perhaps hurrying to get some emergency equipment for Rose, but then he saw the main doors swing open and realized that she had left the building.

He paused outside the door to Rose's room and waited for his grandmother's distress to subside. It was as if he had been traumatized by the earlier incident, and this echo of it brought back the shock. He waited for perhaps thirty seconds more before taking a deep breath and turning the corner through her doorway, only to find that his grandmother was lying on her bed but was concealed by the two nurses and the doctor who had rushed to her. He was surprised and pleased to see Esme standing in the corner. Straightaway he caught her eye across the room, and they exchanged a watery smile of greeting.

When finally Rose had calmed down sufficiently for the nursing staff to withdraw, Dr. Williams took Michael aside. "It's good that you're here, but I don't think she's going to know it today," she said. Michael asked if this kind of thing had happened in recent weeks since that first time, and the doctor thought that it had not. "She's probably having more and longer periods when she's not quite herself, and there's no doubt that her short-term memory is beginning to suffer more. But this is certainly only the second time this has happened while I've been on duty." She said that this type of event was not unusual in patients with Rose's condition, but that they had no idea at present what would cause an individual incident. When they had finished speaking, the doctor said she would leave Michael alone with Rose and that he could stay as long as he liked.

He sat by his grandmother's bed and watched as she dozed, halfway between consciousness and sleep. Even now she seemed to be troubled and was mumbling under her breath as though arguing with someone in a dream. Michael tried to make out what she was saying but could not decipher anything clearly. Then he noticed that Esme was still on the other side of the room and was putting extra energy into her dusting and polishing.

"Esme." He spoke just loud enough to attract her attention. "Were you in here when all this kicked off?"

"Yes, Michael." Esme tiptoed back towards the opposite side of Rose's bed. "But I was over by the sink washing up a few cups and plates. I have no idea what brought it on."

"But I saw a woman coming out of her room just after she started screaming," said Michael. "She hurried past me and I didn't get a chance to speak to her. I assumed she was a doctor, but then I thought she might not be. Do you know who it was?"

Esme nodded. "I don't know her name, but that's the woman we talked about a few weeks ago. Remember? She brought those daffodils? I guess she's a friend or neighbor of your grandma's. She pops in to see her from time to time."

"OK, but that feels so weird," said Michael. "It's great that Grandma has friends and visitors, but I don't feel happy that I don't know who this woman is. Could you hear what they were talking about? I'm just wondering if it was something she said that set Rose off?"

Esme replied that she had been washing dishes and not listening to the conversation. She doubted, though, that the outburst was caused by it. "I really don't think there was anything unusual. Just like last time when you brought Alison to visit, it seemed to come out of the blue."

"I guess so, and I'm sure it's just a coincidence, but it does seem odd that the reaction should come on just as this mystery visitor was in the room. I think I'd better ask at reception. Presumably she would have had to sign in when she first came to Greenacres?"

"She would, I'm sure she would," said Esme. "But I'm as certain as I can be that you'll be wasting your time. If there had been anything out of line, I would have noticed it. Best thing is just to put this down to your grandma's condition. Chances are that she'll be as right as rain and have forgotten all about it by teatime."

Michael was about to ask more questions but caught sight of the clock on the wall of the reception area and realized that the unexpected turn of events meant he was likely to be late to meet Alison from the train. He thanked Esme again for taking such good care of his grandma. Suddenly he felt a powerful wave of gratitude towards her and gave her a kiss on the cheek as he said goodbye.

On the way back to the car Michael tried to telephone Alison's mobile, but his call went to voice mail. He described briefly what had happened and that he would probably be another half an hour or so. He suggested that they could meet at the sushi restaurant near to the Festival Hall where they had eaten when she first came to London to see him. He was aware that sometimes messages left on her phone did not get through immediately, so he finished by asking her to send a text to confirm that she had heard and understood.

The traffic going into town was heavier than usual, and it was closer to forty-five minutes before Michael arrived on the South Bank. He parked the car on a patch of waste ground near to the London Eye and hurried towards the restaurant. As he weaved his way through the tourist crowds he could feel his stress levels rising and hear his own heart beating hard and fast. He had not heard from Alison since leaving the message and feared that she might still be waiting at the station. Michael had the unwelcome thought that his grandfather, Rose's husband, had died of a heart attack and that coronary disease is usually hereditary. He had no idea whether his own father was alive or dead, but none of this felt very encouraging, and he wondered if Rose would ever again be well enough for him to be able to ask some of his many unanswered questions.

A few minutes later Michael was jogging alongside the Festival Hall next to the giant sculpture of the head of Nelson Mandela. The Japanese restaurant was on his left, and he peered through the glass to see if he could make out Alison at one of the tables. There was no obvious sign of her, and so he stood in the doorway and looked around. A waiter asked if he wanted a table, and he said that he was just looking for someone. Still he could not locate her. He had been carrying his cell phone in his hand, and he looked again for any messages. There were none.

Michael was about to call her again when he decided to head towards the river just to check if by any chance she was waiting there. He half walked, half ran, the hundred yards to the promenade area alongside the river and looked left towards the railway bridge heading into Charing Cross and then right towards Waterloo. There was the usual crowd of tourists, and he turned east with the river on his left and walked a hundred yards or so but could see no sign of Alison. He was about to retrace his steps back towards the restaurant when he saw the silhouette of a person he thought could be her. The young woman had her back to him, and it was hard to be sure because she was obscured by a crowd of tourists, most of whom were following a large and noisy tour guide. Michael caught a further glimpse of the woman he thought looked familiar, but now he saw that she was talking to someone else and that it wasn't Alison after all. He decided to walk just a bit farther, continuing to look around among the crowds, and realized that he was heading towards the carpet of flowers and tributes which were still being renewed each day in the shadow of Waterloo Bridge. It dawned on him that he must have come too far and turned back on himself. After retracing his steps for fifty yards, he glanced again at the woman he had spotted a few minutes earlier and was surprised to see that in fact it was Alison. He was about to call to her when he saw that she was still speaking with someone else and that their conversation seemed animated and even possibly hostile. Michael was astonished to realize that the other person was the blonde-haired woman he had met in the pub in Soho.

For a moment Michael felt slightly winded, as though someone had punched him in the stomach. The women were entirely absorbed in their conversation, and neither had noticed him. He was undecided about what to do and was about to make himself known, but then he had a feeling that he should back off. He remained where he was for a few seconds, regaining his breath and his equilibrium, and then turned again and walked briskly away until he reached the flowers and messages which had been laid on the ground and propped next to a parapet beneath the bridge. Many were scrawled in crayon in the writing of young children, and Michael felt a weight inside as he read the tributes. "Always in our hearts." "The sunshine of our lives." And "Forever young." The ink from some of the writing had run in the raindrops and spread like multicolored tears over the paper. Tiny dolls and teddy bears had been propped up but had fallen over in the wind and weather. He decided that he should take a detour round the Festival Hall back towards the restaurant.

Michael asked for a table for two and sat alone for a few minutes. He ordered green tea and tried to sort out the tangle of thoughts fighting for ascendancy in his head. The first was an immediate feeling of indignation that Alison had lied to him so blatantly, but then quickly he remembered the important lesson his grandmother had taught him: always to try to see any situation from the other person's point of view. So he considered the various possible reasons that Alison might have misled him. Just then he heard a plink on his phone, a text. JUST GOT YOUR MESSAGE. BAD SIGNAL. DON'T WORRY— TRAIN WAS LATE ANYWAY. WILL BE THERE IN 10. A. X

Michael was glad that he would have a few more minutes to sort things out in his mind before Alison arrived. Clearly she had deceived him more than once about knowing the blonde girl. The most likely explanation was that they knew each other in the children's home where Alison grew up, and perhaps it was understandable that she wanted to put all that behind her. On the other hand, there seemed to be no obvious reason that she should not have been able to admit that she knew her, even if she insisted on saying nothing more than that. When he put this together with his suspicions about what Alison had told him about her parents' car accident, Michael felt increasingly uncomfortable about what else she may not be telling him, and whatever might be the reasons for her evasions.

He still had not decided how to handle the situation, but now he saw her through the window approaching the restaurant. When she arrived at the door he stood up and waved his hand to catch her attention. She looked flushed and troubled, but even as she came towards the table he could see that she was regaining her composure. He hoped for a moment that she was about to volunteer an explanation which would clear things up without his having to ask.

"So sorry," she said, and leaned across and kissed him on the mouth. He liked the kiss but tasted the salty perspiration from her top lip. She tasted it, too, and reached for a napkin. "Oh God, I'm sorry. I'm all hot and bothered," and she smiled warmly. "Hope you don't mind."

"I don't think I'm ever going to mind a hot kiss off my girl-friend." She sat and already a waiter was hovering, so she also ordered green tea.

"The train was delayed and the mobile signal wasn't work-ing, so I was going nuts not being able to tell you I would be late. I didn't get your message until we were just coming into the station."

"Oh, that's OK," said Michael, "and so did you come straight here from the train?"

"Yes"—she did not hesitate—"straight here," and she turned her attention to studying the menu.

They ordered sushi, and while they were waiting, Michael was still struggling to arrange his thoughts into some sort of or-der. He knew that he could not ignore what he had seen, but equally he feared the consequences of a confrontation. He de-cided to give himself more thinking time, and so he related what had happened earlier at Greenacres.

"I know these outbursts are just part of Rose's condition, but still it was terribly traumatic to see," he said. Alison leaned across the table to squeeze his arm.

"I know it's not very endearing to look at it this way," she said, "like 'It's all about me,' but in a way I'm relieved that it happened without me being there. I know they said it wasn't so, but there was a little part of me which feared that it was something about me which had caused her reaction the first time we saw it."

Michael smiled and tried to reassure her. "They say these things often happen to people who suffer from Alzheimer's, and they have no idea why. It could be something or nothing. There was something a bit weird, though. Just after the screaming started I saw someone I don't think I've seen before leaving her room. I thought that was a bit odd." Michael told Alison what he could recall about the woman and what Esme had said about her. "It would be nice to know who she is sometime. Esme thought she might have been a former neighbor, but if so I've no idea who it could be. It certainly wasn't Elsie from next door."

They ate without speaking for a few minutes, and Michael was beginning to regain some perspective on the events of the morning. He took the opportunity to look carefully at Alison, wondering again what might be about to unfold, but all he could think about was how lovely she was. Alison glanced up and caught him smiling.

"Is something funny?" she asked.

"Nothing's funny," he said. "Just you. I'm just enjoying the look of you. But Alison," he paused to check himself that he really wanted to go ahead with the course of action he had decided upon.

"Yes?" she prompted. She seemed to have no clue about what was coming next.

"You've been telling me all this time that you don't know this girl Joanna who says she knows you. The thing is . . ." Once again he hesitated but managed to renew his determination to plow on. "I know that you do know her, because I just saw you speaking to her by the river. Just now." He waited a few seconds to allow his words to sink in, then he had to continue. "And while we're on the subject, I can easily understand why you wouldn't want to talk much about the children's home and your early life there—and you're going to have to forgive me if I'm wrong about this—but I'm afraid that I also don't think that what you've told me about what happened to your mum and dad is the total truth either." Michael looked steadily at her, waiting for a reaction, but her demeanor revealed nothing of what was going through her mind. He reached across the table and covered her hands with his own. "You know I care about you, and that I want to know all there is to know about you. And I hope you also know that nothing that has happened in the past will matter to me, but I do need you to tell me the truth."

Alison remained silent, still giving no indication of whether she was about to explode or explain. At one moment she opened her mouth as if to speak, and then seemed to change her mind. "Let's take a walk," she said finally.

Michael paid the bill, and five minutes later they were back among the crowds on the embankment, meandering to avoid the parties of schoolchildren and tourists. At first Alison walked apart from him, and then she moved alongside him and took his arm.

"I'm sorry that I lied to you about my parents." She seemed to find it easier to speak as they walked, rather than looking directly at him. "I've told that version of events for so long that I almost believe that it's true myself. And I've told it because it's easier for me to face up to than the actual truth."

Michael stopped and turned to her, easing around so they were face to face. "Look, Alison, you need to understand that it doesn't matter what the truth is. Whatever it is, do you get that? I just need you to feel able to be honest with me."

She paused and searched his eyes with hers, and then nodded, turning again to continue walking. "Well, since you insist on knowing it, the horrible fact is that my parents put me into care because they couldn't cope with me. Not because of anything I did, or so I was assured by about a hundred social workers over the following ten years. They couldn't cope because they were alcoholics and junkies, both of them, and they preferred to give me up rather than to go on the wagon." She paused again. "So that's the top and bottom of it. They didn't want me, and neither, as it turned out, did anyone else. I think you can probably see why it's easier to tell people that they died in a car crash, rather than that I was such an appalling kid that they just didn't want to have anything to do with me."

They continued walking, and Michael made sure that she had no more to say before he spoke again. "So I think I can see why you aren't keen to talk about all that, but obviously none of that was your fault. Where are your parents now? Are they still alive?"

"I neither know nor care," she said. "They never came to visit me and never asked after me, so far as I know, and I never asked about them. They may be alive or they may be dead, and I hope you might understand when I say that I don't really care either way. Just as they obviously didn't care about me."

Michael thought for a further moment about what Alison was saying, and then continued, "And Joanna? What's the story about her?"

"I knew Joanna in the children's home. She was a dreadful bitch then, and she's an even more dreadful bitch now. I'm sorry that I lied to you, but you and I hadn't been together for very long at that time, and the last thing I wanted was her coming along and complicating things. She knows what really happened with my mum and dad, and if she'd blabbed something about was I back in touch with them or something like that, you'd have known that what I'd told you was untrue, and that would probably have been the end of us."

"It wouldn't have," said Michael, "but I can easily see why you might think it would."

The couple continued to walk until they were alongside the piles of wreaths and bouquets and children's toys marking the Madman murders. "When I see anything like this," said Alison, "it just reminds me of families and all the bloody tragedies that come with them. No family has ever done anything for me, so I find it hard to deal with stuff like this. I know everybody does, but I have a lot of my own particular demons."

"And that's the sum of it?" said Michael. "The whole story? Nothing else you need to tell me? I won't mind, whatever it is."

Alison turned and held the cloth of his jacket, pushing him gently a few steps so that his back was against the wall. She put her arms around his waist and looked upwards to bring her face close to his.

"No, that's it. There's nothing else. That's the entire sorry story." Then once again she linked her arm through his as they headed back alongside the edge of the deep water.

EIGHT

MICHAEL FELT MOMENTARILY disoriented when he woke the following morning. His sleep had been one of those which could have lasted for ten minutes or ten hours; the curtains were drawn closed and the room was dark, and it might have been the small hours of the morning or late in the afternoon. He stretched out his hand to confirm that the space beside him was empty, and only then did he sense the movement of someone in the kitchen. He could hear the soft clatter of cups and the sound of the radio. Gradually it came to him that it was mid-morning and that he had slept for nearly nine hours.

Still struggling to place himself firmly in his space, Michael now recalled that, for the first time, he had decided that they should sleep in his grandmother's room. Until then they had made do with his single bed, but at last it seemed crazy to disturb each other throughout their sleep when there was a larger one in the next room.

"Are you sure you are happy about this?" Alison had asked. For a moment they'd felt like two teenagers sneaking into a parents' bed while Mum and Dad were away. Except that neither of them had grown up with any experience of a mum or a dad, and there was no one who might come back unexpectedly and catch them. Alison's revelations on the riverside had brought Michael a huge surge of relief, and he felt entirely comfortable when he assured her that it was fine; he had thought about it for a long time and reckoned that he was overdue to get on with making the adjustments he would need for living alone. He had made up the bed with fresh sheets several days before, so that he could move in when the time was right.

Michael looked around the room at some of the objects which made it such a familiar backdrop. There was a pair of candlesticks on the dressing table, and he could picture Rose placing them carefully on a sheet of newspaper on the kitchen table for polishing, methodically turning them this way and that to ensure that she got into all the tiny corners. It was a job she had carried out on the first weekend of every month for as long as he could remember. Next to the candlesticks was a small decorative china bowl containing multicolored potpourri, which had never to Michael's knowledge been refreshed since the day he had bought it for her as a birthday gift, perhaps ten years earlier. Alongside that was the framed photograph of himself at school, which, he noticed for the first time, had been turned to face the wall. He was amused that Alison must have looked at it, but wondered why she had repositioned it in the wrong place. He saw the door handle turning and was about to leap out of bed to help, when it was nudged open and Alison edged inside carrying a tray. He was surprised that she was fully dressed.

"Wake up, sleepyhead," she said, and placed the tray on the space beside him. As well as making tea and toast, she had been out to get the Sunday papers.

"Wow. Breakfast in bed. What a treat. How long have you been awake?"

"Only an hour or so," she said. "You were sleeping for England." She plumped up the pillows beside him and sat down, lifting her legs onto the bed but remaining outside of the blankets. She opened the newspaper. "It was the funeral of that child from Brighton yesterday. His name was James Mitchell apparently. They called him Jamie. He was one that was thrown off the pier."

"That's been a while," said Michael. "Those poor parents. I guess that in a case like that they can't release the body until after the postmortem or whatever, and the coroner has done his thing." Neither spoke further as they scanned the headlines and photographs of the child's family standing at the graveside. The main header was "Goodbye to Our Darling Boy," and the picture showed the mother and father, clinging to each other in their shared grief. Inset was a smaller picture—a close-up of the same words in handwriting on a tag attached to flowers.

"Did the family have any other children?" asked Michael.

Alison continued reading. "It doesn't say so. No brothers or sisters are mentioned. The parents must feel as though they've lost everything."

Michael sat up in bed and reached for his tea, drinking in silence while Alison read on. He watched her profile as she scanned each line of the news story.

"What's going through your mind?" He knew it was an odd question, and it seemed as though she was not going to reply.

"Just the idea of drowning," she said finally. "I've often thought what a terrible way that is to die. Some people are terrified of fires or falling off a cliff or whatever. My personal terror has always been to die in water. Trying to hold your breath until you can't any longer and then eventually having to inhale, and at that moment your lungs fill up and you just black out there and then." She visibly shuddered at the thought. "These poor kids. These poor bloody parents."

Michael put down his tea on the bedside table and placed a hand on her arm, giving it a gentle squeeze. "I don't really have a special fear of death. My nightmare is this odd thing I sometimes dream, of being manhandled and then pulled apart by a group of men. Just at the moment that I think my limbs are going to be torn off, I wake up."

"I wonder what that's all about," said Alison, but she had not turned to him, and he could see that she had scarcely been distracted from her reading.

"I don't suppose we ever know where these things come from," he said. "Unless we go to see a shrink or something, and I'm hardly likely to do that."

"Maybe you should." She turned to him, at last appearing to focus on what he was saying. "They can sometimes be very helpful." He did not know how to answer and merely looked back at her for several moments, trying to read the expression on her face. "Your toast is getting cold," she said.

His grandmother's most recent meltdown at Greenacres made Michael realize once again that the time had finally come for him to establish a power of attorney over Rose's affairs. The sight of her in a near-catatonic state was a vivid indication of what might soon become a more or less permanent situation, and he dreaded the notion of having to deal with things on her behalf without her permission. On the other hand, despite her clearly expressed view that this would be a necessary step at some point in their future, Michael worried that anyone should think he was trying to take control of his grandmother's life or property before the time was right. Something about it seemed to smack of grasping relatives, and he was not that.

Michael had never before needed the services of a solicitor, and he could not remember Rose ever needing to use one, so had no clear idea where to start. Then he remembered being told on his first visit to Greenacres that among the staff was a welfare officer who was available to give advice. So one day the following week Michael stopped at the care home on his way to work and knocked on her door. She seemed happy to see him, introducing herself as Edwina Morrison, and declaring that she would be glad to help in any way she could. Mrs. Morrison was in her late fifties and looked highly professional in a smart gray suit and starched blouse. If the outfit had been put together to give a sense of reassurance and wisdom gained by experience, it worked.

"When my grandmother and I first got her diagnosis more than a year ago, we agreed that at some point she would want to hand over control of her decision-making. I'm her only living relative, and there's no one else who's very close. She was fine for a long time, but she's been becoming more forgetful recently, and there've been a couple of incidents that have made me worry that she's deteriorating. So I wondered if this would be a good moment, and if it is, what do I have to do?"

Mrs. Morrison was happy to reassure him that this was something they had to deal with very frequently at the care home and confirmed that this was a good time for him to proceed. "It's best to do it while your grandmother is still completely compos mentis for at least some of the time, so that we can all comfortably put hand on heart and say that she knows what she is doing. 'Sooner rather than later' is always my motto."

Michael said that the last thing he wanted was for anyone to think he was trying to take charge of his grandmother before it was necessary and in her best interests.

"I don't think anyone would think that. And if they did, no doubt anyone here could put them right."

Mrs. Morrison told Michael that the forms were very clear and simple to complete. "You can download them and fill them in online, or I can provide you with some hard copies which you can post. You'll also need a few key documents, like the relevant birth, marriage, or death certificates. Do you know where your grandmother keeps all that kind of thing?"

Michael had an idea where they were. "Let me try to sort them out within the next few days," he said.

Michael still had a few minutes before he needed to set off for work, so he walked around the corner into the corridor which led to the residents' rooms. This was outside of normal visiting times, but in the past he had found Greenacres to have a reasonably relaxed attitude in such circumstances. He was still carrying around in his pocket the photograph which Elsie had retrieved from the envelope and had in mind to ask Rose who the children were—but he doubted that there would be an opportunity to do so this morning. Michael found these days that he had a little less of a spring in his step as he considered the prospect of seeing Rose. Despite his great love for her, the two recent incidents had left him traumatized, and since that first time he always felt a trace of apprehension about how she would be.

He knocked on the door of number 23 and waited for a few

seconds. There was no response from inside and he thought he would try the handle before seeking her elsewhere. He hoped that perhaps she was already up and dressed, and playing cards in the dayroom. Instead he found her still in bed, lying in semidarkness with the curtains all but closed. He could not immediately tell if she was awake or asleep but thought that through the gloom he could see a small movement from her eyelids.

"Grandma?" he whispered as softly as he could, so as not to wake her if she was dozing. "Are you asleep?" He closed the door softly behind him and tiptoed closer to her bed. "Grandma? It's me, Michael." Now almost alongside her, he could see that Rose's eyes were open and that she seemed to be staring at the ceiling. Her head was on the pillow, her pure-white hair merging with the crisp white linen, but she did not turn to acknowledge him. "I'm on my way to work, but I was a bit early, so I thought I'd drop by. I came on Saturday, but you were not feeling so good."

Still Grandma Rose looked at the ceiling, and only the fact that her eyes were blinking reassured him that she was conscious. After a second she lifted her left arm to take Michael's hand in hers. She held it and gave it a gentle squeeze, but still said nothing nor did she look towards him.

"You must still be tired, Grandma," he said. "Maybe you had a bad night. Have you been getting enough sleep?" She turned her head ever so slightly, and as he caught her gaze he wondered whether the water in her eyes was from tiredness or sadness. Her expression was impassive and gave no clue to her emotions. "I won't stay and disturb you. You should sleep. I just wanted to say hello." Michael continued to look at her face for any trace of a reaction but found none. He determined to retreat slowly back towards the door and whispered softly, "You go back to sleep and have lovely dreams." He was about to turn to go when he saw just a flicker of movement from Rose's lips. Was she trying to speak? "Did you want to say something, Grandma? Is there anything you need? Shall I see if I can find a nurse for you?"

Still there was no sign of expression on Rose's face, but she seemed to be trying to form some words. He came back to be closer to her and turned his head to one side to place his ear next to to her mouth. "What are you saying, Grandma? Do you need anything?" He heard her breathe again, as though wishing to put some voice behind her whisper. She was trying to speak, and he could make out some individual sounds but nothing that he could form into a word. After two or three more tries, she appeared to give up, and when he looked again at Rose's face her eyes were closed, and she was breathing deeply. Michael turned back and walked lightly towards the door, opening and closing it as carefully as he could. Now he was running short of time, and so he put on a pace as he left the main building and walked towards his car. What had she been saying? Nothing that made sense. He played what he could remember of the syllables over and over in his head, trying to turn them into something recognizable. "Dancey Lisa"? "Dant Sea Lisson"? And then it hit him like a cricket bat across the top of his skull. He believed that he knew what she had been trying to say.

"Don't see Alison."

NINE

WITH THE ANNUAL Dragon Boat Festival due to take place on Saturday, activity on the river at Kingston was more than usually frenetic. Some thirty-five boats, crewed by men and women of all ages and abilities, were making their final preparations to take part in a series of colorful races throughout the day. Each of the boats was crewed by sixteen people, eight rows of two, with every person wielding a single paddle. Momentum and coordination would be maintained by keeping time with the beating of kettledrums at the rear of the boat, which traditionally represent the heartbeat of the dragon. Every summer thousands of sightseers looked forward to a special family day out, and the riverbanks were crowded with people enjoying the spectacle.

Having its historic playing fields adjacent to the river meant that Teddington Junior had a long tradition of excellence in all water-based activities, and over the years the school had attracted onto its staff a number of teachers with distinguished careers as oarsmen or sailors. The deputy head Adrian Dunlop had rowed in the Cambridge eight which won the 2004 boat race by a record margin after a controversial clash of boats at Fulham Reach. Mr. Dunlop was known to be highly competitive, and with so many teams using the river during the daytime, few of the students and parents were surprised when he suggested some extra training after dark. Not only would the river be less congested, but it would give him a chance to put into practice some of his secret training techniques without being so easily spied upon by the opposition. The idea of paddling their multicolored boat like crazy, in time with a frenetic drumbeat, was already exciting enough for the eight-year-olds in the crew, and the sense of subterfuge further added to the anticipation. The additional thrill of training by the light of Oriental lamps and spotlights placed it somewhere close to fever pitch. Mr. Dunlop was alongside in the motor-powered safety boat as the thirty-foot-long canoe went into the water.

"Alexandra!" She was head girl of the school as well as captain of the canoe team. "Get a grip on things there, will you?" Parents who were sharing steaming coffee from a vacuum flask were amused to hear their eight-year-olds spoken to as if they were Olympic athletes.

Minutes later the children settled into their seats, and the canoe was shoved towards midstream. With a gentle tide running against them, Alexandra picked up the padded drumsticks and followed Mr. Dunlop's instructions to begin very slowly. At the outset there were two or more seconds between each beat. Then, as the boat began to steady and to move through the water, the rhythm of the drumming gained pace. Gradually the vessel picked up speed, cutting its path through the pitch-black river. Mr. Dunlop steered his motorboat just a little distance ahead to check for floating logs or other debris, motoring into the shadow of the railway bridge which carried suburban trains between Hampton Wick and Kingston. Once he was through and clear, the water reflected vivid streaks of yellow light from the streetlamps on the road bridge which crossed up ahead. Now the paddles were synchronized perfectly with the primordial rhythm of the drumbeat, and the full power of the gathering momentum helped to thrust the canoe through the water like the mythical dragon advancing on its prey. Mr. Dunlop yelled encouragement as he watched the children straining every muscle, but the smiles on their young faces told their own story as the boat forged forwards. The oncoming tide caused the teacher's boat to slow and put him alongside.

The object came out of the deep black sky with the dull thud of a meteor landing in a desert. The first that Mr. Dunlop knew of it was the shattering sound as it smashed into the canoe, more or less dead center, miraculously landing between the four children clustered around the fulcrum of the vessel but hardly pausing in its descent. The boat jackknifed in the middle, launching the children sitting at each end into the air like stones from a catapult. Their limbs momentarily flayed out of control before they splashed down hard on the water and disappeared into the inky blackness. The wake splashed against Mr. Dunlop's boat, which now careered out of control and smashed into the concrete plinth of the bridge, tossing him, unconscious, into the water.

———————————

Ten children managed to swim or cling to the splinters of wood for long enough to get to the bank, but six of the sixteen, all ages either eight or nine, were drowned on that night. The incident had taken place well out of sight or sound of the school at Teddington, and so parents were still chatting and drinking coffee under the stars when the police arrived twenty minutes later with the terrible news that would change all their lives forever. Mr. Dunlop was taken to hospital suffering from shock and exhaustion and would never teach or be seen on the water again.

"So, are you telling me that there is no CCTV coverage of Kingston Bridge, day or night?" Detective Chief Superintendent Norman Bailey had been working late at the incident room in Charing Cross and had reached the scene in less than thirty minutes. He knew that it was not fair to make the local sergeant feel personally responsible for the omission, but right at this moment he did not care. "A main thoroughfare crossing the busiest and most important river in the country, and we don't have a bloody thing?"

"And so we don't even know if the bastard arrived in a car, on a bike, or even on foot?" Detective Constable Georgia Collins was Bailey's deputy.

The sergeant confirmed that both assumptions seemed to be true. The two senior officers walked to one side of the pavement.

"What do you think, sir? Is it him?" asked Collins.

"It's him, all right," said Bailey. "He is going to keep on keeping on until no one feels safe having their children anywhere near anything deeper than a puddle. I just wonder what the fuck is going through this sick bastard's head."

TEN

MICHAEL WOKE EARLY but tried to remain quite still to avoid disturbing Alison, who was lying curled up in the bed beside him. After half an hour spent staring at her bedroom ceiling, he was badly in need of coffee and was wondering whether he could make some without waking her, when suddenly the problem was solved by the radio switching itself on. Only a few words of the news bulletin were audible before her bare arm appeared from beneath the sheets and she fumbled to find the off switch.

"Oh God," she said, "I always intend to reset the timer at the weekends and always forget."

"Could we listen to that?" said Michael. "I thought they were saying something about Kingston."

"What?" She was still only half awake. "What about Kingston?"

"On the news," said Michael, and something was making him increasingly anxious. "Would you mind switching it back on?"

Both instinctively sat upright in bed, unable to say anything sensible while the newsreader related the story of the events of the previous evening. The reporters seemed to have very little information beyond the basic facts, but such was the enormity of the crime that once again they were stretching every resource to find new things to say. Michael felt immediate horror that such an appalling crime could occur, and somehow it felt even worse that it had happened so close to his home.

"God, I know it's terrible to look at something like this from your own point of view," he said, "but I'm just so glad we weren't there last night." Alison did not respond, and the two of them remained silent as the newsreader introduced interviews with reporters who had been to the scene and with the police. News coverage was open-ended on TV and radio, and Michael and Alison moved to the sitting room to watch the live reporting from the area they knew so well. At one point the camera panned across the riverbank, and Michael could just make out a corner of his own apartment building peeping between two more-prestigious blocks. "There goes the neighborhood," he said, and immediately realized that his weak attempt at levity was entirely inappropriate. "Sorry," he added quickly, but still Alison had not responded. He turned and saw that her face was transfixed in a stony stare and that there were tears streaming down both of her cheeks. She made no attempt to wipe them away, and Michael continued to look at her as the dark droplets fell onto her T-shirt.

"Oh, baby," he said, "I'm so sorry. There's you reacting like a normal and sensitive human being, and there's me trying to be funny." He reached forward and grabbed a handful of tissues from a cardboard box on the table in front of them. He handed them to her, but instead of taking them from him, Alison took the cue to cover her face with the open palms of both hands, and he heard a muffled sob as she seemed to try to regain herself. Michael put his arm around her shoulder and reached for the remote control. "Let's not watch any more. There's nothing we can do about anything, and it's only depressing me and distressing you." Alison agreed, and after a while Michael suggested that they should take a walk along the seafront to try to blow away some of the horror.

The weather was warm but windy, and they retraced the path they had walked that first Sunday, along the promenade towards the marina. Their route gave them a chance to see every level of life in Brighton, from the rows of grand and elegant Victorian homes to the tackiest and most popular forms of seaside entertainment. It was the mix which gave Brighton its particular charm. The bracing smell of ozone in the air was overlaid from time to time by the sweet wafts of cotton candy, the aroma of cooking onions, and that familiar whiff of burning oil, remembered from childhood, as the miniature railway trundled past on its track at the top of the shingle.

Hardly a moment had passed in the last few days when Michael had not been thinking about his last visit to Grandma Rose, and his view of what had happened alternated between extremes. Most of the time, he thought that he must have misheard what she said, and over and over again he replayed the words she seemed to be trying to whisper. Could it have been "Don't see Alison"? How could it have been? It was ridiculous, the sort of thing that might happen in a nightmare, an odd narrative made of unrelated thoughts joined together. At other moments, though, Michael felt sure that he had correctly interpreted what she was trying to say, and if that were so, then somehow or for some reason his grandma must have recognized Alison. He recalled that first time he had brought her to meet Rose and the violence of his grandma's reaction.

They had all convinced themselves that it was coincidence, but maybe there was something more?

A confusion of thoughts and feelings went around his head until in the end Michael worried that he was losing his grasp of reality. Surely he was making a mountain out of something absolutely trivial.

"It's unbelievable that that should take place just a few hundred yards from your place." Alison's words brought Michael back sharply to the present. He was glad that she appeared to have gotten past the apparently overwhelming distress which had affected her earlier. "What kind of a mind dreams up something like that?" she was saying. "To drop a heavy weight on a boatload of children? You just don't know how to start believing it, do you?"

"According to all the news I've read, killing children by drowning isn't as unusual as you'd want it to be. They said on that program they made at work that usually the killer knows the kids . . . most often they are from the same family. There've been a few examples of random acts of this kind, but not many . . ."

Michael was set to continue when the cell phone in Alison's handbag started to ring. It was the third time it had happened since they left her apartment, but she had ignored it before and she was ignoring it now.

"Don't you think you should answer that?" he said. "It might be important. Whoever it is certainly seems to be persistent."

"I know who it is," said Alison. "It's an idiot girl from work who wants me to go to some silly bridal shower next week. Angela's friend Pauline. I've said I don't want to go, but she won't take no for an answer."

They walked and talked some more, and gradually the sea

air began to do its work, and Michael felt himself beginning to relax. The notion of "blowing away the horror" had some merit after all. On one side of the road, the cliff rose sharply up to a hilltop path, and Michael saw that just ahead one carriage of the funicular railway was coming down to meet them. He suggested that they might take a ride to the top of the cliff and enjoy the views on the way back from the different perspective. The attendant took their fare and opened the doors, and Michael and Alison were the only ones in the carriage as the wheels creaked and the mechanism groaned, gradually lifting them two hundred feet up the side of the cliff face. They stepped out at the top and stood for a while to enjoy the seascape.

"Last time I stood on these cliffs was about ten years ago on a school trip, a project about our history as an island," said Michael. "It's so strange to think that this tiny stretch of water has protected us from invasion for a thousand years. The French have tried it, the Spanish have tried it, the Germans have tried it more than once. Just a few miles of water between us and being overrun by enemies."

Alison turned to look at Michael, her face suddenly breaking into a smile which he found difficult to read. "What a curious man you are," she said finally. "Here I was, wondering where you're going to take me for a plate of fish-and-chips, and here you are thinking about the Battle of Britain."

"Well, that's probably why you love me then . . . because I'm fascinating and unpredictable." There was a moment of silence. She had not ever said that she loved him, but now she turned back to look out to sea and slipped her arm through his. She pressed the side of her body against him and leaned her head on his shoulder.

"Yes," she said at last, "must be."

They stood for a while without speaking, and occasionally he tightened the grip of his arm around her shoulder, and she responded by pulling him closer at his waist.

"Set off back now?" he said.

Alison said that she needed to use the ladies' room before they started walking again and asked Michael to look after her handbag while she was away. No sooner was she out of sight than he could hear her cell phone ringing once again from within the bag. He saw the phone lying on top of her other belongings, and the light on the front panel said UNKNOWN NUMBER. He pulled it out and tried without success to locate the button which would shut off the noise. He thought he had found it when suddenly the ringing stopped and the flashing screen was replaced by a notice reading TEXT RECEIVED. He kept pressing buttons more or less at random, and before he knew it the incoming text was revealed.

THERE'S NO POINT IN TRYING TO PROTECT HIM.

Michael felt as though a cold hand had grabbed at his insides. He did not want Alison to think he was prying into her business, and for a moment he was undecided about what to do. Glancing quickly towards the entrance to the ladies' room, and with fumbling thumbs, he tried to locate RETURN on the panel. He pressed several buttons before the message disappeared off the screen altogether, and was unsure whether he had deleted it. He replaced the phone in Alison's bag just as she emerged and rejoined him. He handed it over.

"Your phone was ringing again. I tried to find the button to stop it but don't know what I've pressed. I hope I haven't screwed anything up."

"You didn't see who was calling?"

"No, I think it said 'unknown number,' but by the time I got to it, whoever it was had rung off. It was probably that same woman from work—Pauline, did you say?"

"Probably."

They continued their walk without speaking, and once again a whole new round of questions filled Michael's head and began to multiply and overlap with one another. He had only just managed to find a perspective on the words he thought he heard from his grandma, and now there was this. THERE'S NO POINT IN TRYING TO PROTECT HIM? What on earth could that mean? Protect who? And from what? And who could such a message be from? Whoever the sender, Michael felt pretty sure that it was neither Angela nor Pauline. It all felt deeply troubling, but then again, all those doubts and questions were set against his increasing happiness about what seemed to be the deepening intimacy between them. She had recently owned up about her lie involving the deaths of her parents and about Joanna, and the admission had caused Michael to feel a weight lifting from his shoulders. He could completely understand why she might want to erase any memories of having been abandoned by her mother and father. Having dealt with those earlier uncertainties, the last thing he wanted now was a further series of doubts to get in their way. She had not said that she loved him, but neither had she denied it when the idea came up. He did not wish to break the spell by introducing another subject which would push her away. Several times he was on the brink of blurting out one of the questions which seemed to be accumulating, but already there was something in her demeanor which brought down a barrier that he felt unable to penetrate. He would bide his time, he decided. Clearly she still had secrets, but surely she would choose her own moment to share them.

ELEVEN

AT THE FRONT of the dayroom, a magician was producing a white rabbit out of a hat. Michael smiled broadly at the thought that it was still possible to make a living by doing old-fashioned conjuring tricks, but then reflected that the man entertaining forty or fifty old folks at the Greenacres care home was unlikely to be doing it for the money. Magic had been his hobby since he was a small boy, most probably, and a chance to entertain an audience of real people was as much a treat for him as it was for those who were currently pretending to be amazed.

Michael looked around at the men and women—mostly women—who were laughing and joking together in the dayroom. He thought, as so often he had before, how at first sight this seemed to be a group of old people, when in fact it was just a group of people who had been around for a long time. Yesterday they were sending their children to school and college, running a medium-sized engineering business, employing forty people, and paying their taxes. They were teachers, lawyers, musicians, shop assistants, and businesspeople. Now they were eighty years old and were watching a not-very-good magician performing tricks that might have impressed them when they were eight.

When he found himself with time to spare at Greenacres, Michael had gotten into the habit of studying some of the individual faces of the residents. He discovered that if he looked carefully and for long enough, he could still see the eight-year-old boy or girl for whom this kind of entertainment had been designed. There they were, a bright young optimistic face, buried beneath many layers of experience and passing years, but deep down they were still very much present. Some had taken the opportunity of growing older to rediscover that eight-year-old's carefree approach and humor. Many more had not.

This was Saturday morning, and Michael's grandma Rose was among the audience, and now when he looked at her he thought how she had grown old under the weight of the responsibility of raising him. He had watched as she transformed from the busy and bustling older woman she was when he was a child to the slower and slightly stooping elderly lady that she had gradually become. It had been like watching the post-script stages of the ascent of man—from upright to bowed over in the course of twenty years. The odd thing was that, if anything, it had been the onset of her progressive condition which had helped Rose to shed some of the burdens which reduced her and to rediscover the eight-year-old within. The developing Alzheimer's had freed her of responsibilities and complications and released her to sit and be amazed each time the tiny ball vanished under one of three small red plastic cups and seemed to reappear under a different one. But what had been her progressive escape from the cares dictated by reality was now being reversed, and Michael fretted to know more about whatever it was that seemed to be blighting what might be her last weeks and months.

He joined in the vigorous applause at the end of the entertainment, and only then did Rose look around and realize he was there and waiting to see her. Since he met Alison, there had been fewer opportunities for him to visit on weekends, and he hoped that she would be pleased. As it was, though, he thought her movements seemed significantly more labored than of late and that if anything it took her a moment to acknowledge him. She got up from her seat slowly, and they linked arms and walked carefully along the corridor to her private room, where he made her sit while he brewed a pot of tea.

"That was fun, Grandma," said Michael. "Was this his first time at Greenacres, or have you seen him before?"

Rose turned to look at him when he spoke, seeming to notice him for the first time. When she replied, her words were an effort, as if she was struggling to stay alert. "Oh, Geoffrey's been here loads of times. When I first knew him, he was the local butcher's boy at a stall in the market. He went on to be a manager at the Co-op Bank in the high street. Now he's reduced to patronizing old folks with nothing better to do and nowhere to escape to." She paused, and Michael thought she had finished speaking when she added, "Like me." Michael turned and saw that Rose seemed close to tears.

Michael was sad to see his grandmother apparently so depressed, and he adopted as light a tone as he could while they had tea together and he told her all his news. When he asked how she was feeling, she said only that she had not been sleeping well, and after half an hour Michael sensed that she was tired and that he should leave. He was of two minds on whether to ask about the photograph that he had found in her bureau. He had been waiting for the right moment, but Rose's apparently fast-diminishing faculties made him worry that if he did not ask soon, the chance to do so might be lost forever.

"Oh, just one thing, Grandma." He reached into his inside pocket, feeling for the picture, which he had been carrying around with him. "I was looking for some stationery the other day, and I came across an old photo in a drawer. It's a bit blurred, but I don't think I've seen it before, and I didn't recognize any of the people in it." Michael handed the picture to Rose, who hesitated as she took it from him, and then held it up, moving it back and forth as she tried to bring it into focus.

While she appeared to be looking and thinking, Michael took the opportunity to stand up and collect their teacups and saucers, and he carried them to the sink ready to be washed. He turned his back to her, and a few seconds passed before he realized that it had been a while since he asked the question. When he turned again towards her, he saw that Rose's face was fixed in an expression he had never seen before — a mix of surprise and dismay. Gradually it seemed as though she knew what she wanted to say but could not find the words to say it.

"Are you OK, Grandma?" said Michael, suddenly concerned that he had inadvertently upset her. Perhaps the photograph had triggered an unhappy memory. "Is it something about the picture?"

Rose looked directly at her grandson, still unable to find the right words, and still apparently in growing distress. He saw that her head was gently shaking from side to side and that her hands were trembling. When she spoke, her voice was soft and suffocated.

"It was a family who used to live next door to us before you were born. They broke up, and it was all very difficult for the children. I'd forgotten I had the picture, and it's brought back some sad memories."

"Oh, I'm sorry, Grandma," said Michael, and walked forward to put his arm around her shoulder. "I had no idea. I wouldn't have mentioned it."

That night Michael's sleep was once again visited by the dream which so often had haunted his childhood. In it, he was playing with other children and somehow become separated. He found himself alone on an area of waste ground, lying flat on his back, and had the feeling of being grabbed by strong hands and lifted up bodily into the air. The pressure tugging on his legs and arms increased until he was spread-eagled, and he felt pain in his shoulders and hips as if in danger of being torn apart. It was just at the moment when the hurt became excruciating that the scream formed in the bottom of his throat and built and built until it was actual and audible, and moments later he found himself grappling with the bedclothes. As a child he had frequently woken in this way to hear the words of his grandmother Rose soothing him and to feel her soft cool hands on his brow. This time the hands touching and holding him were different hands, and her words were spoken by another voice—"It's all right, Michael. It's all right. I've got you. You're all right. It was just a bad dream." These were the hands, and this was the voice, of Alison.

As soon as Michael knew where he was and realized what had happened, his first concern was for her. He knew that it had been his own scream which had woken him, and that therefore she must have been woken in the same way.

"Oh God, I am so, so sorry." He sat up in bed, leaning forward and pressing his forehead into his cupped hands. "What a terrible thing to do to you. You must have been scared out of your wits."

She was at his shoulder, her arm around his back, and running a hand through his hair. "Not at all. You had an awful dream and woke yourself up. Poor baby."

Neither of them spoke again for a little while, and finally Michael felt his equilibrium returning. He was keen to try, if he could, to lighten the mood. "By the way," he said at last, "I've been meaning to ask you. I know I may not have been the best-looking boy in the class, but was there some reason why you turned the photo of me as a schoolkid to face the wall?"

Alison glanced up to look towards the dressing table. "I don't think I did, did I?" She paused. "Sorry. I think I did look at it but thought I'd put it back as I found it." Now she smiled. "Did you think I thought you were so ugly that I didn't want to look at you?" She grabbed a pillow from beside him and cuffed him gently across the head.

The team from Matterhorn Productions had been commissioned to make a further program about the police hunt for the Madman, and once again the off-line editing and postproduction was being done at Hand-Cutz. For several days the following week, Michael was in and out of the editing suite and, like everyone else, he was curious to know whether the police were any closer to finding the killer. Coverage in the newspapers and on the radio and TV had reached new levels of hysteria, and wherever two or three people were gathered together it seemed as though the crimes had replaced most other topics of conversation.

This latest program was due to be broadcast on Sunday, and so Michael was required to work long hours during the week. He had tried to get to Greenacres after he finished work on Thursday, but by the time he arrived at the care home it was 9:00 PM and too late to visit. He ran into Esme at the end of what had been a long shift for her and offered to give her a lift to the train station. Once in the car, he asked how she thought Rose was doing and, unusually for Esme, when she spoke she was not smiling.

"To be honest with you, Michael, I am a bit worried about her. She is off her food and has been sleeping a lot during the day. When she's awake, she seems to be agitated, as if something's upsetting her."

Michael told Esme about what had happened when he visited a few weeks earlier after seeing the welfare officer, but he stopped short of repeating the words he thought she had said.

"Yes, she's been a bit like that," said Esme. "Like I say, sleeping a lot during the day—says she can't sleep at night—but when I'm cleaning her room sometimes she seems troubled. She lies there, just staring at the ceiling, muttering and mumbling."

Michael did not reply, but drove in silence. "By the way," he said eventually, "did you ever find out anything about the woman who visits Rose from time to time? The one who brought the daffodils."

"Ah yes," said Esme. "I was meaning to mention it to you. I think she must be a neighbor. I asked reception to look her up in the visitors' book. She's been coming in now and again for more than three months—I thought I was right about that. She put her name down as Rawlinson. Eileen Rawlinson, I think it was. Mrs."

"That doesn't ring any bells," said Michael. "But why do you say 'put her name down as'? Is there any reason to think that's not her real name?"

"No, not really. It's just—I was a bit surprised. I didn't recognize Eileen as the name your grandma has been calling her. I can't remember what name she uses—maybe it was just a nickname. I've been racking my brains, but I can't re-member it."

Michael said he would try to check with an administrator next time he came to Greenacres. "But you haven't seen any reason to think she is upsetting Rose in any way? That her visits could be unwelcome?"

Esme shook her head. "No, quite the opposite. Rose always seems pleased to see her—but you know that she's sometimes been getting upset for no apparent reason." By now the car was drawing to a halt outside Queenstown Road Station, and Esme was about to get out. "It's not my place to say it, Michael, but I'm afraid that what's happening to your grandma is prob-ably no better and no worse than you should expect. I've seen this before. Sometimes people fade away happy, and sometimes they fade away sad, but all of us fade away in the end. It's just upsetting for everyone who loves them, is all."

Once again Michael thanked Esme for looking out for his grandma and watched her as she walked across the pavement and into the station. There was hardly any traffic at this time of night, and so forty minutes later he was opening the door of the apartment in Kingston. For some reason he could not name, he felt an instinct to go into his grandmother's bed-room.

The photograph of himself on his first day at grammar school was back in its place, and Michael picked it up and peered closely into the scrubbed clean and shiny young face. He remembered the terror he had felt at the prospect of going to the big school where almost all of the other kids seemed to be so much more worldly than he was. He remembered the other kids in the class talking about their brothers and sisters, or their mums and dads, and of remaining silent himself because he had nothing to contribute. Sometimes a bully would make fun of him, but always the teachers intervened quickly to save him from his embarrassment. Nonetheless, he had felt the isolation of being an only child and had found most of his friends among others in the same situation.

Michael put down the school photo and picked up the only other framed picture on display. It was a black-and-white shot, in a gilt frame, of Rose's wedding day. He looked closely at the bride and struggled to match this lovely young woman whose face was full of hope and happiness with that of the troubled and much older person he knew. Next to her was his grandfather, sporting an impressive and handsome mustache and looking every bit as overjoyed as his new bride. It occurred to Michael that he knew next to nothing about the people standing on either side of the happy couple and made a mental note to ask Rose more about his great-grandparents—if only he ever got the chance to do so.

The thought reminded him of the photograph which Elsie had retrieved from the envelope found in Rose's bureau, and which Rose had said was of a family of neighbors. He tried to remember which jacket he had been wearing when he had shown it to her, and now he went into his own bedroom and fumbled through his clothes, eventually finding it. Once again he returned to his grandmother's room and sat on the edge of the bed. He turned on the bedside light and examined the picture carefully.

He could see the outline of four children; there seemed to be two young boys, an older girl, and a baby. The face of the older girl looked as though it had been unclear in the first place and had been further damaged by the hot sauce he had accidentally spilled on it. Michael held the photo under the light and examined it closely. The child was about seven or eight years old and was holding the handles of a stroller and standing in an attitude which suggested that she was proud to be in charge. Her face was neither smiling nor frowning, but there was something about the arrangement of her features which seemed familiar to him. Michael felt frustrated. He had spent his entire life with Rose and had never before known or heard any reference to this family who apparently had at one time lived next door. He wondered what their story could have been that would be so bad that Rose was still upset to be reminded of it. He stood up and went to the door but turned to have a last look around before he switched off the light.

The next day was Friday and was likely to be another long day looking after the needs of the team from Matterhorn. By midmorning the program was in postproduction, and Michael became aware of an unusual flurry of activity. He joined a group of people gathered around the TV in the foyer, which was always tuned to twenty-four-hour news.

"What's happening?" Michael's question was to no one in particular.

"There's been another incident involving the Madman." It was one of the receptionists who answered. "But no one seems to know what."

Michael's first instinct was to wonder how that might affect the schedule of the program they were making, and therefore how long he would need to stay at work. It took him only a few seconds more to feel a sting of shame about his reaction. Somewhere out there a desperate human tragedy was probably going on, and all he was worried about was how it might affect the end of his working day.

The television was showing live pictures of a news conference being set up by the police searching for the Madman. Someone next to Michael wondered out loud if they were going to announce that they had made an arrest, in which case the program in production would probably have to be shelved. The officers were settling down into their seats, and in the studio the newsreader announced that the channel would be showing the statement live.

"Ladies and gentlemen, thank you for gathering at such short notice." The face of Detective Chief Superintendent Norman Bailey had become familiar to anyone following the news in recent weeks, and Michael thought that he looked exhausted. "We always appreciate the help of the public and members of the press, and there has been a development which we hope may represent a significant breakthrough."

"Has there been an arrest?" It was one of the journalists shouting out from the back of the pack of assembled reporters, but the cameras did not follow the disembodied voice.

"I'm sorry to say that I'm not in a position today to announce an arrest. However, we have received what we believe to be a significant piece of evidence which we wish to share with you."

It seemed that everyone held their breath as they waited to know what the new development was. In the foyer of Hand-Cutz, you could have heard a pin drop as the detective leaned forward to the keyboard of a computer on the desk in front of him.

"Most of you are aware that the inquiry into what have become known as the Madman crimes is one of the biggest investigations ever carried out by the Metropolitan Police. So far we have been deploying sixty-five detectives and have followed up more than fifteen thousand leads." Bailey looked down at his notes, but then placed them on the table in front of him and directed his words straight into the camera. "Recently we received a package from an anonymous source, containing a recording of the voice of a man. We believe that this voice may be that of the person we are looking for in connection with the incidents at Waterloo Bridge, on Brighton Pier, and in Kingston. We have not ruled out the possibility that this may be a hoax, but in view of the chance that it's genuine, we feel the need to share it with the public so that anyone who recognizes the voice can let us know. So, ladies and gentlemen, in a moment I'm going to play this recording to you, and then we need to hear quickly from anyone who thinks they recognize the voice on the tape."

Once again the silence in the room was absolute. The detective looked around to check that everyone was ready and then leaned forward to start the playback. There was another long pause before anything happened, and Michael felt an apprehension quite unlike anything he had experienced before. He sensed the same among the people around him. The hunt for the Madman was unique in his lifetime, and the fear he had witnessed among parents and families was also unprecedented.

The voice, when it came, echoed around the room, and around the world, like the voice of evil.

"I am the person everyone is calling the Madman." The effect was stunning. The pause was only two or three seconds, and then the recording continued, "I may be mad, or it may be the rest of you who are mad. Who is to say? Some of us have known for a long time that the world has gone mad, but it takes someone like me to make all the rest of you realize it." There was a further pause, and then an intake of breath. After a few more seconds the words went on, "And by the way, if I'm the mad one, how is it that you're no nearer to catching me than you were when I first started?"

Michael looked around the room and saw that everyone else was every bit as transfixed as he was. Did anyone recognize the voice? Michael tried to scan through a mental Rolodex of possibilities—maybe from school, from work, or from childhood. For a moment he imagined that there was something about it that seemed familiar, but then he checked himself, sure that he was allowing his imagination to run away with him. Still, there was a timbre in the voice which managed to get into his head and reverberate around it. It seemed to be that of a young man, without a noticeable regional accent. There was total silence as it was unclear whether or not the recording had finished.

"That's all for now. If you don't get any closer after the next time, maybe I will send you another message to get you on the right track." Now Detective Bailey leaned forward and switched off the machine. He sat back in his chair, as if unburdened from a huge weight, and began to speak again.

"That was it, ladies and gentlemen. That, we believe, may be the voice of the person known to the press as the Madman." Instantly, there was a bedlam of questions, none of which could be made out distinctly in the broadcast. Everyone who had gathered around the television in the Hand-Cutz foyer started talking to one another all at once, each offering instant opinions about who or what the voice sounded like.

"Well, that's me done for," said one of the women from the reception desk. "I won't be getting a wink of sleep until they catch the bastard."

"He sounded like the devil himself if you ask me," said another. "Enough to give anyone the creeps."

Everything was a hum of indistinct conversations, and then Michael's friend Stephen, who was standing just a few feet in front of him and closer than he was to the television, turned and spoke at a volume just loud enough to be heard by everyone in the room.

"You know what, Michael," he said. "That bloke sounds a hell of a lot like you."

TWELVE

MICHAEL HAD CONTINUED to postpone the business of obtaining a power of attorney over his grandmother's affairs, and the long hours at work had made it more difficult. However, with Rose's condition now apparently deteriorating more quickly, he made a new resolution to get on with sorting out the various papers he needed. On the way home that evening he stopped in the Blue Anchor fish-and-chip shop, which was just around the corner from the end of his street, bought his dinner, and ate his food out of the paper. Once again he reflected that he never would have done this while his grandma was living here. He felt sad and lonely as he sat at the kitchen table, but nonetheless made no effort to use a plate or cutlery.

Michael picked up the remote control and flicked through the options. It seemed as if every channel which was not showing cartoons or films had cleared its schedule and was carrying the latest news following the police press conference. Speculation about what it all amounted to was becoming frenzied.

An assortment of criminologists and retired detectives had been called into the TV studios to opine on what the words used on the tape might reveal about any motives for the murders. The consensus among the experts still seemed to be that police should be looking for a father who had been denied access to his children and had been driven crazy by the system. A representative of the Fathers for Justice campaign group was being given the opportunity, for what seemed the hundredth time, to explain the inequities of a system that he said was loaded against dads. Hence, he said, some of the more extreme stunts staged by protesting fathers. "Not, of course, that anything could possibly justify the kind of actions we are seeing here."

Experts in linguistics had also been brought in to give instant analysis of the geographical and social roots of the person speaking, while criminologists were called upon to pronounce on whether or not the tape was likely to be genuine. Veteran journalists and academics recalled the case of the Yorkshire Ripper, who had murdered thirteen women in West Yorkshire and across the north more than thirty years ago. Police hunting him received letters and a tape purporting to be from the killer, only to discover later that they had been someone's idea of a joke. Michael remembered that the way the original case had been covered by the newspapers had been a part of his media course at A level. Detectives had been convinced that the man on the tape and the killer were one and the same, which had thrown the investigation completely onto the wrong track. Lessons needed to be learned.

For the moment at least, it seemed that police were working on the assumption that the recording was genuine, and so the hunt was on to identify the voice on the tape. At the time he had tried his best to shrug it off, but now he began to think about Stephen's suggestion that the voice sounded a bit like his own. He thought it had been intended as a joke, but Michael was not feeling inclined to see a funny side. It was, of course, a difficult thing for him to judge, but if he considered it as objectively as he could, he supposed that the voice did sound similar to his. Certainly the person on the tape sounded relatively young, was probably from the southeast of England and from a reasonably good educational background. He ticked those boxes, but then again so did millions of others.

Michael did his best to banish thoughts about the hunt for the Madman, but the price he paid for doing so was that even-less-welcome thoughts occupied his mind. Try as he might, he felt unable to make any headway in his efforts to work out whether he was creating an issue from nothing or whether there was actually something odd going on relating to Alison. He wondered what the tension between her and Joanna could have been about and whether any of that was related to the strange text message received when they were walking together in Brighton. THERE'S NO POINT IN TRYING TO PROTECT HIM. What the hell could that mean? Michael had no way to know whether the text was from Joanna or what it could mean. Half the time he felt certain that there was something worrying going on, and the rest of the time he was impatient with himself for obsessing over what was likely to be a completely innocent set of misunderstandings. However, he knew that having these questions gnawing away at him in the background was not good for him or for the future of their relationship, and that soon he would have to confront this further mystery head-on. Always keen to avoid confrontation when he could, Michael did not look forward to the prospect.

He cleared away his food wrapping and rinsed his hands under the tap, then dried them on the tea towel and reminded himself that it should go in the laundry. He grabbed it and threw it into the washing machine and then had to press his knees against the glass door to force it to close. He moved into Rose's bedroom and went to the bureau where important family documents were kept. He knew that the papers he was looking for were stored in the second drawer, just beneath the section where he had found the envelope he had given to Elsie.

He folded and tidied away the school reports he had rummaged through recently, and next he came across a diploma he had been awarded when, at age eight, he had managed to swim one hundred meters unaided. He remembered his grandmother taking a special pride in that particular achievement— she had always given a very high priority to ensuring that her grandson could swim.

After a while he found his grandmother's birth certificate, which was in her maiden name of Williams. He knew that he would be unlikely to find a copy of her marriage certificate because that was one of the papers which had been destroyed in the fire. However, Michael knew that he would need a copy of his grandfather's death certificate as evidence that he was no longer Rose's next of kin. He reflected that he did not know, and had probably never been told, the actual date or even the place of his grandfather's death, so he hoped he would be able to find the original and not need to apply for a duplicate. Michael continued to sort through a whole pile of letters about pensions and family allowance. Finally there was just one aging brown envelope remaining, which he hoped would contain what he needed. The paper felt almost like old cloth in his hand as he carefully unfolded it, and he saw straightaway that it was what he was looking for. The document was headed "Certified Copy of an Entry of Death," and to one side was the imprint in red ink of a rubber stamp which said AMENDED COPY. Michael had no idea what that could mean but assumed it was a result of the house fire which he had been told about. Beneath these words was a row of boxes, each of which had been completed in scarcely legible handwriting. Under WHEN AND WHERE DIED the registrar had written "Hove, April 15, 1997." Under NAME OF DECEASED was written "George Frederick Beaumont." In the box headed AGE was written the number "64," and beneath the box asking for the cause of death was written a single word. Michael looked at it, and immediately something made him turn his head away for an instant, and then he turned back to look at it again. The word written in the box was "Suicide." Michael felt his legs give way under him, and he sat down on his grandmother's bed, his hands suddenly trembling uncontrollably.

An hour later Michael was still sitting in the same spot on the end of Rose's bed, the same bed he used to climb up into as a small boy when he felt in need of comfort. He had tucked his heels into the gap beneath the mattress, elbows resting on knees and the palms of his hands supporting his head. Now he realized that his back had stiffened painfully from remaining for so long in one position, and he rolled over onto his side and brought his knees up to his chest. Several times he arched his spine this way and that, trying to ease the cramp which gripped him. He felt himself shivering and pulled back the duvet to slip his legs under.

For all the aspects of Michael's young life which had been missing—parents, siblings, cousins, all the usual ties—there had always been one person he could rely on, one constant factor in the otherwise fragile framework of his world. Now even she, his beloved grandmother, had embarked on a journey which would eventually take her out of his life altogether, as though he could see her steps in the snow, and she was retreating into a deepening mist which would soon engulf her. Of course he had had time and opportunity over many recent months to absorb some of this, and had done his best to do so, but sometimes the reality hit him hard, and this was one of those moments. It occurred to him that the less form and structure he had in his life, the more precious were any constants that he did have. One of the few fixed points of Michael's life was that his grandfather, Rose's husband, had died of a heart attack when Michael was a small boy. Like all tiny children, Michael had always taken this at face value as something that happens when people get very old. He had no recall of being told that his grandfather was sixty-four when he died, but even if he had heard it at the time, this would have seemed to a small boy to be a ripe old age. Now that he was twenty, Michael knew enough to understand that sixty-four was young to die in any circumstances, and the idea that his grandfather had committed suicide seemed to yank away another part of his already flimsy foundations.

The shock of all this was exacerbated because it had come on top of all the other uncertainties that had been troubling him earlier in the evening. Such was the deterioration of Rose's condition that it might already be too late for him to ask her about the circumstances of her husband's death. Then he thought again about the photograph which Elsie had discovered in the envelope and wondered whether it was his destiny to have his entire history forever concealed by mystery.

Eventually Michael pulled himself together as best he could

and tried once again to apply the important lesson his grandmother had taught him: always to do his best to see any situation from the other person's point of view. Eighteen years or so ago, his grandma Rose would have had what must be one of the worst experiences it is possible to have — the suicide of her husband. God only knew what the circumstances had been, but suddenly she was facing a situation in which she had lost her spouse, and her daughter had walked out the door, leaving her to take care of a tiny boy. Certainly it was entirely understandable that anyone dealing with all that might choose to try to bring up the child in ignorance of the tragedy which surrounded his early life. How could suicide be explained to a small boy anyway, and what would have been the point of trying to do so? Michael thought he could understand why the story would have been kept secret from him, but nonetheless it was a shock to discover it in this way. The revelation had knocked him sideways.

His thoughts were interrupted by the sound of his telephone, and he was relieved to hear Alison's voice. After their usual greetings she wanted to talk about the same subject that everyone was talking about.

"I couldn't believe my ears when I first heard it. Everyone in the travel agency stopped work. My friend Angela said it would give her nightmares. Do you think it's actually him?"

Michael related what he could remember of the news reports about the similar situation with the Yorkshire Ripper, which had happened before they both were born. He thought it was dangerous for the police to assume that the person on the tape and the killer were the same. "Bloody Stephen at work said he thought the voice sounded like me. Shouted it out among a big group of us."

Alison hesitated while she tried to absorb what Michael had just said. Her first reaction was indignation, as though having a similar voice in some way associated her boyfriend with the crimes. "What's he talking about? It sounded nothing like you. And even if it had, that's not a very nice thing to say among a whole load of people you work with."

"I don't think he thought about it in that way. Remember he's a sound engineer—he's trained to listen to different voices. I think he just said the first thing that came into his head."

"Well, I think he's got some bloody cheek," said Alison. She was quiet again, and perhaps she was wondering whether there was indeed some similarity or not. Michael changed the subject.

"Did you ever sort out that woman from work who was on at you to go to the bridal shower or whatever it was? The one that kept on ringing you? Pauline, was it?"

Alison said that she had, and that it had all been a lot of fuss about nothing. Then she in turn seemed to change the subject quickly.

"How is your gran? Any change there?"

Michael told her that he had been trying to make progress with the power of attorney and that he had successfully located the key papers he needed. "But the weirdest thing has happened which has completely freaked me out. I don't know whether I told you, but my grandfather died when I was a baby, and I've always been led to believe that the cause was a heart attack." Alison said that he had not told her that, but urged him to go on anyway. "Well, guess what? The last document I needed, to prove that Rose has no other living family, was my granddad's death certificate. And I just found it at the bottom of a pile of other stuff, except that it doesn't say that his cause of death was a coronary, as I've been told. It says that his cause of death was suicide." Michael expected a reaction from Alison, but for a moment there was silence and he wondered whether the line had been cut. "Alison? Are you still there?" He heard a noise at the other end of the line, as though perhaps she was swallowing or breathing deeply. "Alison?"

"Yes, I'm here," she said finally. "I just don't know what to say." There was another long pause, and then when she spoke, there was a long hesitation between her next words. "That's . . . absolutely . . . awful."

THIRTEEN

MICHAEL HAD BEEN told to report for work at 10:00 AM for what seemed likely to be a long and hard day, so he decided to drop in at Greenacres early on his way into town. Strictly speaking, relatives were supposed to confine their visits to the prescribed hours, but he had found that if things were quiet and the medical teams were not on their rounds, no one seemed to mind him popping in.

It was just after 9:00 AM when Michael arrived at the care home. He was able to find a space in the car park, and he entered by the main door and made his way along the corridor in the direction of the residents' rooms. At the far end, beyond number 23, he could see Esme washing the floor using a bucket of soapy water and an old-fashioned mop. She caught his eye as he approached, and Michael walked past Rose's room to greet her. Last time they had met he had kissed her on the cheek, but now he did not know whether it was appropriate to repeat the gesture. There was a moment of awkwardness, and then he did and was glad.

"Hello, sweetheart," said Esme. "Your grandma will be

pleased to see you, but you'll get into trouble if you keep turning up here whenever you like."

"Yes, sorry about that," said Michael. "I'm having to work late a lot these days, and it's difficult to get here in the evenings. Anyway, I'm here now. How does she seem?"

Esme said that Rose had been sleeping a lot, but when she was awake she was alert and her old self for some of the time. "But you can see that she is gradually withdrawing, Michael. Part of the time she seems not to know where she is, and she gets very distressed. Once or twice she has woken up from a bad dream and has been shouting out."

Michael would have liked to ask more questions but was aware of having little time to spare this morning. He said that he would put his head round the door to see if Rose was awake but would have to get on to work shortly.

Rose was sound asleep when he entered her room. Michael looked at his watch and reckoned that he could spend a few minutes at her bedside. As he did so, he remembered that the watch on his wrist had belonged originally to his grandfather but had been given to Michael by his grandma on his eighteenth birthday. It was not especially valuable but had been Rose's gift to her husband on their silver wedding anniversary. Michael had been very moved to receive it and had promised to take special care, which he had. He looked at it now and wondered again what could have happened that was so terrible that it led his grandfather to take his own life.

As he sat at her bedside and looked at his grandmother's face, Michael tried once again to wash away the passage of time and imagine her as a much younger person. Despite the toll taken by the years, his grandmother was still, in her way, a beautiful woman. She had reached a point of her life when beauty was not about physical appearance but about the person behind it. Clearly Rose had been through more than her share of tragedy and disappointment, but she had been true to herself and had given him every opportunity and an enormous amount of love.

His time had passed, and Michael got up to leave. He was moving towards the door when he heard a soft knocking from outside and saw the handle turn. He took a step back to ensure that he was not in the way when the door opened, and as he did so a woman entered, clearly surprised to find a visitor in the room. She was shorter than Michael and did not look up at him as she spoke.

"Oh, sorry. I had no idea."

The woman was about fifty years old, with shoulder-length brown hair parted in the center and just a few streaks of gray. She had a pretty face and wore no makeup. She also seemed to be more flustered than might be expected by the surprise, and only then did she turn up her face to look for the first time at Michael. It took her a second or two to register him and then with no further words, she turned around and walked briskly out of the door.

The woman had come and gone so abruptly that Michael needed a moment or two to collect himself. He allowed the door to close, but then stepped forward to open it once again. He walked into the corridor, looked left and right, and saw that she had already reached the far end of the corridor and was hurrying out of the main door towards the car park. Seeing her running away made him realize that this was the same woman he had seen leaving Rose's room after he heard his grandmother screaming. The thought propelled him to quicken his pace, and a few seconds later, he burst through the door and cast his eyes around. He hoped that he would catch a glimpse of her getting into one of the cars and driving off, but there was no sign.

Michael was now at risk of being very late for work and so had no further time to consider or to follow up on what had happened. He remembered his intention to make more inquiries about the woman Esme had said was called Mrs. Rawlinson and regretted that he had not done so before. The earlier incident had faded from his mind, and now he determined again that he needed to find out more about Rose's mystery visitor. Certainly he had no objection to Rose receiving anyone so long as they were welcomed by her, but he was more curious than ever to know who this woman was.

The commuter traffic was just a little lighter since the main part of the rush hour was over, and Michael turned on the radio as he weaved in between the lines of cars. The news was still dominated by the police hunt for the Madman, with speculation about the significance of the recording still overshadowing every other story. It seemed that everyone had a view about it, and it was being reported that the police had received hundreds of calls from people who thought they knew the man on the tape. The police had released more details of the form in which the recording had reached them. It had been on one of those USB digital storage devices, of a type which had been adapted for use as a key ring. "That's a fat lot of use," Michael said aloud, and looked down at his own car keys, which were attached to a USB stick he had bought in a service station for less than a pound.

Michael parked the car in the underground car park, which was one of the few perks of his otherwise rather junior job. He and colleagues sometimes joked that the car parking in the center of London was worth more than the salary. He waved hello to the two young women on the reception desk, but both seemed to be immersed in conversation and neither acknowledged him. Michael thought it slightly strange that he passed no one else in the corridors on his way to the sound recording suite, which he used as his base. The doors into the recording area were unusually heavy in order to dampen the noise and were fixed with strong springs so that they closed quickly and completely behind whoever was passing through them. The last door into the sound suite had a glass porthole at head height to enable people entering to check that they would not be interrupting a critical moment of recording. As it was first thing in the morning and no red lights were on, Michael glanced quickly through the window at the same time as he pushed the door, and it was just a second before he realized that there were perhaps half-a-dozen people inside the suite, and that two of them were uniformed police officers. He stopped dead, taken aback by the unexpected sight, and then his amazement went into overdrive when he realized that he had interrupted them listening to a voice which was coming from the speakers, and that the voice was his own. Five men he did not recognize, plus his friend Stephen the sound engineer, were listening to the recording he had made a few weeks ago listing the items on the lunch menu.

"You must be Michael." It was one of the men wearing plain clothes whom he now assumed was a detective. "Please, would you sit down?" It did not sound like a request, and he gestured to the three-seat sofa which was positioned in front of the control desk and facing the screen. Michael made no movement, unable to take on board what he was seeing. Eventually his brain engaged sufficiently to enable him to speak.

"What the fuck? What the hell is going on . . . ?" He was still struggling to process the scene which confronted him.

"There's nothing to worry about, Michael." Stephen was sitting at the central seat in front of the sound console and was operating the equipment. "Apparently a few people have told the police that they think the voice of the man they are looking for sounds a bit like yours. They have to check everyone who's reported to them, they said, just for the purposes of elimination. So we haven't asked them for a warrant or anything. I hope that's all right with you?"

He could hear the words and he was beginning to be able to sort out what they meant, but the true import of what was going on still eluded him. Could it possibly be the case that someone somewhere thought he was the Madman who had killed eleven children? Even as the idea floated across his consciousness, Michael felt himself having to work hard to temper his reaction.

"I'm sorry to seem dense. I'm not usually quite so slow." Despite his best efforts, he felt that he was beginning to lose control of himself. He took off his jacket and threw it down on the chair. "Are you people listening to a recording of my voice to see if it matches the voice of a mass murderer?"

"As your colleague here says, Michael," said the detective, "we are obliged to check everyone who's been reported as having a voice similar to the one on the tape, and that includes you."

"But the radio said there have been hundreds of calls. Loads of people have rung in to suggest people with similar voices. How come you've got to me as what must be one of your first checks?"

"We're prioritizing people who've been named by the greatest number of callers. That's the only way we can do it."

Michael thought that his otherwise unjustifiable indignation was at last getting some traction. There was a hint of sarcasm in his tone as he asked his next question. "And how many people have called in to say it sounds like me?" The detective reached into his pocket and flicked open the pages of a notebook, which seemed to arrive instantly at the relevant place.

"Twelve."

Michael sat down hard on the sofa, clutching his head as if trying to force the information inside. "What? I don't understand. What are you saying? That twelve people have phoned you to say that they think that the man on the Madman tape is me?"

"I don't think that's what anybody is saying, Michael," said Stephen. "Certainly that's not what anyone here is saying, but the police have asked the public to let them know of anyone they think sounds like the man on the tape, so that they can be eliminated from their inquiries. And that must include you if only for the reason that twelve people who know you seem to think so. I for one don't think for a moment that you are the bloke the police are looking for, and nor do any of the others here, obviously. We're just doing what the police have asked us to do."

"So you phoned the police and told them that you work with someone who sounds like the Madman?" Michael did not know whether to be hurt or furious.

"No, I didn't," said Stephen. "It wasn't me, or at least it wasn't just me. It was eight of us from here. You do sound like the Madman. Your voice sounds like his. That fact might help the police, even though the Madman obviously isn't you. Or you are not him." Stephen waved his arms around helplessly. "Whatever."

"Obviously," said Michael, still completely nonplussed.

"We were just about to make a spectrogram comparison with your voice and his," said the detective, "so that we can rule you out and get on with checking the hundreds of other people whose friends and colleagues are as public spirited as yours are."

Michael felt that he had no choice but to sit quietly as the process continued, if only so that the misunderstanding could be cleared up quickly and be over. He now understood why the people on the reception desk had seemed preoccupied when he entered the building, and there had been no one in the corridors as he walked through. He watched the screen as Stephen set up the equipment so that it would project one graph on top of the other. The spectrogram was usually used in the suite to measure sound patterns on a digital recording, which helped when cueing background effects or commentary on a TV program. At the same time it was also measuring all aspects of the quality of a voice and in theory ought to be able to confirm that two recordings were made by the same person.

He felt a shudder go through him as Stephen played a few words from the tape which had become so familiar overnight. "I may be mad, or it may be the rest of you who are mad. Who is to say?" The recording suite was designed to absorb sound, but the words seemed to echo around the room and bounce into and out of the corners. Once again, Michael knew that he was unable to be objective, but as he listened to it now he thought he would have known in an instant that the voice was not his own. Or perhaps it was simply that he did not want it to be so. It was, of course, irrational to feel such hostility to the idea that his voice sounded similar to that of the Madman; how could that matter? In a way he should hope that the two were indeed similar, because the comparison might help the police to track down the geographical background of the real killer. But such was the evil associated with the Madman and his dreadful crimes that Michael thought that no one would wish to be compared to him in any way, even the most tangential.

At last the kit was set up and ready to make the comparison, and on the screen Michael could see two graphs, one colored red and one colored blue, superimposed over each other.

"So just to explain how this works," said Stephen. "The machine takes about twenty different aspects of the timbre of someone's voice and attributes a high and low to them on the graph. An individual speaker usually keeps within the same measurements whatever they are saying."

"Even if they are speaking at a different volume, or speaking into a different recording device?" asked the detective.

"That's right," said Stephen. "These aspects of a person's voice are fixed in any circumstances. They would be difficult to disguise." He turned to Michael. "With any luck, Michael, this'll take about three minutes, and we can let these good people get on with what they should be doing." If it was an attempt at an apology, it was too little and too late.

"Let's get it over with," Michael said, and sat back on the sofa, folding his arms tight across his chest. "Let's see if the Madman wants to order from the lunch menu." But there was no trace of levity from either the speaker or from anyone listening.

On the control desk behind him, Stephen pressed two buttons at once and opened two faders in parallel. Immediately there came the sound of two voices, speaking across each other. One was the voice of the Madman, continuing with the words he had used in the recording received by the police, the other was Michael reading out items from the menu. Had it not been so serious, it might have been comic. On the screen in front of the gathered audience, a wavy blue line began to run from left to right, and over it a separate wavy red line did the same thing.

"The blue line is the recording the police brought us this morning," said Stephen. "The red line is the recording of Michael we made a week or so ago."

No one spoke as the two recorded voices were played alongside each other, and the two lines progressed across the screen. Each voice was reflected in its own highs and lows at different times as their own individual syllables were spoken, but neither line went higher than the other at the top parameter of the graph or lower than the other at the bottom.

Michael felt a knot forming in his stomach as the significance of what he was witnessing slowly began to dawn and then to become inescapable. He found himself willing the top scale of the blue line to go markedly higher than its equivalent on the red, or the graph of the red line to do the same along the bottom register—but neither of them did. After a further ten seconds it was clear what the machine was indicating; nonetheless, the policeman asked the question.

"Is this machine telling us what it seems to be telling us?"

There was silence. Everyone turned to look at Stephen, but he did not speak. He could not speak. After a further five seconds the detective walked across the room and stood in front of Michael.

"Michael Beaumont. I am arresting you on suspicion of the murder of James Mitchell. You do not have to say anything, but it will harm your defense if you fail to mention, when questioned, anything that you later rely on in court. Anything you do say may be used in evidence against you. Do you understand what I am saying to you?"

Michael tried to stand up, but his legs would not obey him. When finally he opened his mouth, he found he had no voice and had to clear his throat before any words would come out. "You've got the wrong person."

Alison was eating lunch at her desk at the travel agency when one of her colleagues returned to work with the stunning news that police hunting the Madman had made an arrest. The whole office erupted in a spontaneous cheer, as though an invisible weight had been lifted from their shoulders. Just as the individual incidents had united everyone in their revulsion, so the prospect of an end to the national nightmare felt like a cause for collective relief. Of course, they wanted to feel sure that the police had gotten the right man.

"Did they catch him trying to do another one? Does anyone know the circumstances?"

"It'll have been that tape. Someone will have recognized it as their son or brother and grassed him up."

"Would you turn in your own son or your lover? Even if you thought he was the Madman?"

In the fast-flowing discussion which followed, Alison recalled what Michael had told her the previous night about the supposed similarity between his voice and that on the tape, but said nothing. The call to her mobile phone came in at exactly the same moment as she saw the TV news crew appear on the pavement on the other side of the street opposite the agency.

Personal calls at work were not encouraged, and so usually she kept her phone switched off. Now she was rummaging in her handbag to stop the ringing as quickly as possible. She saw that the call was from an unknown number and was deciding whether to answer it when she looked up again and noticed that the news crew on the opposite pavement had now been joined by four or five other people, some with cameras and some without. She was aware of growing interest among her colleagues, several of whom were collecting at the window to try to see what was happening. Alison answered.

"Is that Alison Parsons?" said a voice she did not recognize.

"Yes, it is. Who is this?"

"My name is Frank Miller, senior crime reporter from the *Daily Mail*. I wonder if we could just get your reaction to the news that your boyfriend, Michael Beaumont, has been arrested by the police investigating the Madman murders?"

Alison sat still and silent. She could not move, but remained transfixed, staring straight ahead, until she looked again through the window and saw that a dozen people had now gathered and were crossing the road as a group and heading in her direction. She could feel her mind struggling to take in the sudden onset of events, and a moment later the individual images in front of her began to swim and blur. The telephone hit the floor a split second before Alison keeled over.

_____

It was five or six minutes before Alison began to return to consciousness and found herself lying on a couch while three of the women she worked with attended to her. She recognized that she was in the back office, which was primarily for storage but which was sometimes used as a staff room. Her friend Angela was wafting a tea towel up and down to create a draft of cool air, while Pauline was standing to one side and fiddling with an electric fan which had not worked since the previous summer. Another woman from the office called Denise was perched on the edge of the seat next to her and holding a wet washcloth on her forehead. Alison was taking all this in and wondering what on earth had happened when the cause of her demise flooded back into her mind. She raised the palms of her hands to cover her face.

She could hear what sounded like an argument going on outside the door, between her other colleagues from the agency and the journalists trying to get access to her. It was a free-for-all, in which she could decipher phrases like "The public has a right to know" and "She must have known what her boyfriend was doing." Her mind was swimming in a chaos of thoughts, and she felt profoundly grateful to have these few moments to try to impose some kind of organization on them. As the noise from outside grew in volume, she tried to listen to more of what was being said, but then became aware of police sirens approaching from a distance. It was not the sound of a single car but of several merging from all directions into one, a level of cacophony usually associated with a major response by emergency services to a serious crime or accident. Moments later she heard the slamming of car doors and then more raised voices from outside.

FOURTEEN

SO BEFORE WE start, Mr. Beaumont, can we just make sure we've got a few of the basics sorted out?" The face of Detective Chief Superintendent Norman Bailey had become well known to Michael, as it had to virtually everyone else in Britain, and now the familiar look of determination from the police press conferences had acquired a renewed graft of steel. "Can you confirm your home address as number sixty-five Old Bridge Street, Hampton Wick, and that that address is an apartment which is just about four hundred yards away from Kingston Bridge?"

Michael had at first said he would not need the services of a solicitor. This was such an elementary mistake, he said, that he would be able to establish his innocence in just a few minutes. However, the police had insisted, and now he glanced over at the young man who seemed only just a little older than himself and was dressed in a dark gray suit which looked as though it had been borrowed from his father. Earlier he had introduced himself to Michael as Gordon Giles, and now he nodded to Michael to confirm that he should answer.

"Yes, that's my address. Until recently I lived there with my grandmother, but she went to live in a care home a few months ago."

"We'll get on to that in a minute. Let's take a step at a time, shall we?"

Michael felt that his head was swimming, and he looked over at a tiny yellow light on the recording machine which confirmed that the tape was turning. He found himself wondering why the police were not yet using digital recording, but then remembered that he needed to concentrate or more important matters. He wondered whether what he was experiencing was some sort of clinical shock and pushed his fists hard into his eyes to force himself to remain focused.

"Yes, of course. Sorry."

"And can you confirm that your girlfriend's name is Alison Parsons and that she resides at sixteen Arlington Terrace in Brighton and that that address is just about half a mile from Brighton Pier?" Bailey sat back in his chair and raised his bushy eyebrows in inquiry. He used the tip of his index finger to push a pair of steel-rimmed spectacles back from the bridge of his nose.

"I see what you're getting at," said Michael. "But if you just let me explain, I know exactly where I was on all the times and days when these incidents occurred, and you can check my story and we can clear this up within minutes." He looked again at the young lawyer who leaned across to him and whispered.

"Just answer their questions. Don't give them any information they don't actually ask for."

Michael wanted to say that that was probably good advice for a guilty man who was trying to evade suspicion, but that he was not guilty, and so he just wanted to cut to the chase and get out of there. Then he realized that the lawyer was probably giving him advice based on the assumption that his client might indeed be the man the police were looking for. He turned back to face the detective.

"Yes, that's right, and I was with her, in her apartment in Brighton, in bed when the second incident occurred."

"But you confirm that you were in Brighton?" The question came from a younger woman officer.

"Yes, I was in Brighton when the second incident occurred, and as I told you, I was with my girlfriend, Alison. But I was not on Waterloo Bridge when the first one happened, and I have witnesses who can prove it. Also I was not in Kingston when the third one occurred. I was in Brighton, again with Alison, and she can confirm that. Just ask her and we can sort this whole thing out immediately."

"We plan to, Michael," said the senior detective. "She's on her way here right now, and I'm sure she will corroborate your story. But meanwhile, let's make the best use of the available time by allowing us to ask you a few more questions."

The younger detective constable took over the interview and asked him whether he could remember what he was wearing on the relevant days and where those clothes might be now. Michael replied that he could not be certain at this distance in time what clothes he had on, but he was sure that they were not the same as those which the Madman had been described as having worn; if they had been, he would have noted it on the day.

"Do you own a gray sweatshirt, the type with a hood?"

"No, I don't. I never have. I don't like those things."

"And what about blue jeans and white T-shirts?"

"Of course I do. Everyone does. But on the day of the incident in Brighton I think I remember that I was wearing a blue T-shirt and khaki cargo trousers. I recall it because Alison and I both noticed that lots of people seemed to be dressed the same as the news said the Madman was dressed, and obviously I wasn't. But I still don't understand; like I told you, at the time of the incident I was in bed."

"Alone?"

"No, not alone, with Alison. I told you that."

"Yes, I meant alone with Alison. She is your alibi?"

Michael confirmed that she was.

"In fact Alison is your alibi witness on all three occasions, isn't she?" said Bailey.

Once again Michael confirmed that she was. "But there are other people, at the care home where my grandmother is living, who saw me there at the time of the first incident. I was there in the waiting room. When we saw my grandmother on that day she wasn't very well—and the doctor thought she might have been upset by the TV reports of the incident, so she will remember where we were. Dr. Williams, her name is. Bernice Williams, I think."

"What time was that, Michael?" asked the female detective. "What time did visiting at the care home start?"

"About three PM, I think, but we were in the waiting room before that. We sat and watched the news reports about the incident on Waterloo Bridge on the TV."

"But the Waterloo incident happened at one-fifteen, Michael, at which time, by your own account, you were probably on your way to see your grandmother—who is in Battersea, did you say? That's about half an hour from Waterloo on a Saturday afternoon."

Gordon Giles leaned over to him again and whispered that this was the reason he had advised Michael not to say any more than he was being asked.

"In fact," the female detective was continuing, "according to our CCTV, your car was in the area of Waterloo at just about the time the first incident took place. Is there some reason why you didn't take the opportunity to tell us that?"

Michael experienced a sinking feeling in his stomach. It had slipped his mind that they had eaten lunch on that day at the sushi restaurant near the Festival Hall. Still, though, his sense of indignation was stronger than his caution. "So let me get this straight," said Michael, once again ignoring his lawyer. "You think that I went for a walk on Waterloo Bridge, picked up four tiny children and threw them into the River Thames, ran into the crowd, and went to a retirement home in Battersea to visit my grandmother?" Michael's exasperation was beginning to overtake his good sense. "Either you people are mad, or you think I am." He looked across the table and saw the look which passed between the senior and junior officers. Yes, he realized, clearly they think I am the Madman.

After responding as briefly and precisely as he could to a number of other routine questions, Michael was informed that he would be put into a holding cell downstairs at the police station while other aspects of his story were checked. Alison was still on her way under police escort from Brighton, and they would need to question her before anything further happened.

"You'll understand why we need to keep you somewhere secure for the time being, and for your own safety we are going to make sure that you will be in a cell by yourself," said Bailey. "I'm sorry that we're unable to make you more comfortable, but with luck this won't take too long." Bailey and Collins stood up, and he was surprised to find two uniformed constables entering the room and walking around his chair. Each of them took hold of him by a forearm, ready to raise him to his feet.

"Hey, hey, steady," said Michael, and for the first time he felt physically frightened of the situation in which he found himself. He turned to Detective Chief Superintendent Bailey. "Listen, the only person I have in my family is my grandmother, who I was visiting on the day of the first incident. She is very old and very unwell; she has fast-progressing Alzheimer's. If she hears about this on the news, it will kill her in a heart-beat. Is there some way this situation can be handled so that she doesn't find out for a few hours until it's all sorted and I've been released?"

The two detectives gave each other a look which was enough to tell Michael that it was already too late.

"I'm sorry, Michael," said Collins. "We think that someone in your place of work must have tipped off the press. They had already got to Alison by the time we were able to send officers to collect her, and we hear that they've been knocking at the door of the care home where your grandmother is living. I'm afraid that if it isn't already, your name is shortly going to be everywhere."

The escorting officers had not established a grip that was suf-ficiently firm to support his weight, and as Michael's legs gave way beneath him, he slumped sideways, landing heavily on the hard floor. For a few seconds he lay still, but then involuntarily he drew up his legs into a fetal position. Moments later he felt his body begin to shake, a sort of hysteria, as he lost control of his movements. The muscles in his neck were tightening and going into a spasm.

"He's having some sort of fit," said Bailey, who now hurried towards the doorway and pushed an alarm bell. After a few more seconds Michael felt himself being gripped under his arms and again, without any conscious intention of doing so, he began to struggle. The more he moved around, the firmer and tighter their hold on him, and the greater his determination to resist. Then a Klaxon sounded, and two more uniformed police officers entered the room, each of them immediately running to take hold of his flailing legs. Michael felt himself being lifted bodily off the floor, as the four strong men held and pulled on his limbs until he felt that they would be ripped away from his body.

Michael woke up with the sensation of a tight grip on his forearm and felt himself begin to panic all over again until he realized that he was feeling the squeeze of the cuff of a blood-pressure monitor. He looked up and saw that an older man whom he took to be a doctor was examining him, and a few seconds later he could feel a cold spot over his heart as a stethoscope was pressed to his chest. Michael looked at the doctor, who appeared not to have noticed that his patient was awake and simply continued going about his business as though working on a medical dummy. In those few seconds Michael found himself wondering if the doctor was reluctant to look into the face of a monster. A few moments more and the man had collected his instruments and, still without speaking, he stood up and went to the door.

Michael had never been in a police cell before but had seen plenty of them in TV dramas, and this was exactly what he would have imagined. It was a tiny room with one small window made of frosted and reinforced glass, and the only furniture was a bed and a chair. There was a small lavatory with no toilet seat, and the only difference between his imagination and reality was that the walls were clean and apparently freshly painted in pale-green gloss. Michael's head was beginning to clear, and he was regaining some sense of what was going on around him.

"You just make yourself comfortable here, lad." For some reason the broad Yorkshire accent was unexpected and sounded almost surreal in these circumstances. "Try not to worry because it will do no good. What will happen now will happen, and we'll come for you and get you sorted out as soon as we can." Michael raised his head to look at the speaker and found a uniformed sergeant of about fifty-five with a deeply pockmarked face, the kind of marking which might have been scar tissue from an old wound or skin disease. "My name is Sergeant Mallinson, and if you need anything, press the button next to the door." Michael made the shape of *Thank you* with his mouth, but no sound came out, and he felt himself leaning to one side and once again drawing up his legs into his chest. He heard the clang of the door closing and the unmistakable sound of a heavy lock being clicked into place.

A mix of thoughts were swimming around Michael's head like terrified fish in a glass bowl, without any apparent likelihood of organization or process. At one level it seemed impossible to believe that he was in this situation at all. He knew that it seemed a cliché even as he experienced it, but for a moment he really did wonder if he would shortly wake up to find that it had all been an awful dream. Then he struggled to take on board the enormity of it all. Those last words spoken by the detectives in the interview room resonated around his brain. The crimes committed by the Madman were probably the biggest news story of the year in Britain and had undoubtedly been reported internationally. He recalled seeing features on the television about the way that other countries were reporting the crimes, in which tourists planning on visiting the country were advised to take special care of young children. If what the police were now saying was true, his face might already be on every TV news screen in the world. *Police in Britain have arrested a man in connection with the recent spate of deaths of young children in what have become known as the Madman murders.* Michael could imagine the news flashes, and in his mind he saw them presented by newsreaders in different languages, with the only common factor being a picture of himself projected behind their shoulders.

Then Michael began to think about what the police had meant when they said that the press had discovered and contacted Alison before their officers had managed to reach her. He imagined that she might first have been shocked, but then quickly she would have been dismissive and even possibly briefly amused by such a stupid idea, until the real implications of the suggestion fully impacted. He wondered if she had been doorstepped by the press, and now his image of the news bulletins began to include video of her running the gauntlet of a posse of journalists, all screaming questions and accusations at her. But meanwhile, looming in the background of the mental aquarium, the biggest and most menacing presence of all was the question of Grandma Rose. It was probable that whoever had tipped off the press about his arrest in the first place would have known about his grandmother, and it could not take long before the pack descended on Greenacres. The only good thing was that the care home had some security, and in theory it should not be possible for any of them to barge directly into Rose's room. However, if the reports were on the TV, and no one at the home had the presence of mind to intervene, Rose would get the shock of her life to see her grandson's picture on the news—no doubt accompanied by a caption saying "Alleged Madman arrested" or something equally ghastly.

Michael tightened his muscles and screwed up his body into a still-smaller ball, covering his eyes with the palms of his hands to shut out his thoughts and the rest of the world.

Alison looked out from her seat in the middle of a convoy of three fast cars, two in full police livery and one unmarked, as they ignored all the traffic restrictions and swerved dramatically into the rear entrance of Charing Cross police station. Several journalists had attempted to keep up with them on the drive from Brighton, but the police had turned on sirens and ignored red lights, eventually leaving them far behind. The pavement outside the police station was so crowded with journalists and TV news crews that ordinary passersby had to step off the curb, and eventually several officers were sent out to erect barriers to cordon off a safe area. The young officers followed their instructions not to respond in any way to the barrage of questions about the man they had in custody.

There in the backyard of the station, waiting to meet Alison, were Detective Chief Superintendent Norman Bailey, whose face she also knew from the TV news, and Detective Constable Collins. They stepped forward as she got out of the backseat and immediately thanked her for coming and for helping them to clear up a few questions about Michael.

"Did I have a choice? I was bundled into a car and driven here under police guard like I'm a terrorist. Am I under arrest?" Alison was scared, but her fear was overlaid by a pronounced and growing sense of anger about the way she was being treated.

The chief superintendent assured her that she was not under arrest. "But as you're now aware, we have information which has led us to believe that your friend Michael Beaumont might know something about the recent murders of young children, and we think that you may be able to help us to eliminate him from our inquiries."

"Michael doesn't know anything more about it than what we've seen on the telly and read in the papers. He's totally innocent and I can certainly help you to see that."

"That's all we need," said Collins. "If you're able to help us to establish a firm alibi for him on the relevant dates, you'll have done him a great service, and we can all get about our business."

Once inside the police station, she was taken to the same interview room that Michael had occupied less than an hour earlier.

"But just one thing before we start," said Bailey. "As a routine inquiry we asked one of our officers to look into your recent phone records." He paused as if to add gravity to what was to follow. "Can you tell us a bit more about a text you received just a few weeks ago which said, and I quote, 'There's no point in trying to protect him'?"

It was three hours since Michael had been taken to the holding cell, and such had been the turmoil in his head that he started to fear for his sanity. For a few minutes at a time he was able to isolate the individual elements which led to his current situation, and to stay reasonably calm and confident that he would very soon be able to prove his innocence and be out and back to his normal life. But then those thoughts were swept away by the reality of having been arrested and held as a suspect in what was the most notorious series of crimes of his lifetime. He thought he was in danger of losing control and had to work hard to keep a grip on himself.

After what seemed to be turning into a nightmare without end, eventually he heard the key in the lock, and the same two officers who escorted him from the interview room came into his cell. Behind them was the uniformed officer who had introduced himself as Sergeant Mallinson.

"Try not to worry, lad. I'm sure it will all be sorted in a little while." Michael felt he had never been more grateful in his life than at that moment to the scar-faced sergeant who now turned and walked ahead of him back towards the interview room.

"Is Alison here?" he asked. "Can I see her?"

"I'm afraid not right now, Michael," said Sergeant Mallinson. "Maybe later, if the detectives can just get answers to a few more questions."

Something about his tone of voice made Michael wonder for the first time about the "good cop, bad cop" routine he had read about in detective novels, and whether Mallinson's attitude was part of a strategy. He said nothing but was led back into the same room as before, to find that his solicitor Gordon Giles was already sitting with the two detectives, Bailey and

Collins. On the table in front of them was a laptop computer and a brown cardboard file which lay unopened. Bailey reached across and pressed the button which started the recording machine. He reminded Michael that he was still under caution and required him to acknowledge aloud that he understood.

"Well, your girlfriend backs up your story that you were with her on the three dates we are interested in, Michael," said Bailey. Michael closed his eyes and exhaled. He'd known, of course, that she would do so, but having it confirmed went some way to reassuring him that he was not losing his mind altogether. "However, when pushed for details, Alison is unable to say for certain that she was with you every minute on all three occasions, and anyway so far all we've got is her word for it. She is your girlfriend, after all, so is probably inclined to give you the benefit of the doubt." Bailey paused to allow the thought to sink in. "Meanwhile, there are one or two other things that have come to light that we need to sort out with you."

"Now then, Michael." It was the female detective's turn to pick up the questioning. "Can you tell me whether this is yours?" Collins placed a plastic bag on the table in front of him, and inside it he could see the bulky shape of the key fob used to unlock and start his Vauxhall, attached to a USB stick. Of course he recognized it.

"Yes, it's mine," he said, and immediately Giles leaned across and whispered to him. When he had finished, Michael turned back and spoke again to the detectives. "Or what I should have said is that it looks very much like mine, or if it isn't, then certainly I have one like it."

"If I were to tell you that the USB stick attached to these car keys is exactly the same as the one we received through the post from the man claiming to be the Madman, what would be your reaction to that?"

Michael considered for a moment. He remembered thinking when he heard the original news report that he had a USB stick on a key ring, but at the time had no reason to worry about it. There must be tens of thousands of them. He looked at Giles for assistance but was met with a blank stare. "I think I'd say that I got that from a service station which probably must be part of a chain of them up and down the country and that I would imagine that thousands of them had been sold. They were very cheap."

The two detectives showed no apparent reaction to his reply and merely continued to look back at him as though considering whether to continue with the same point or to move to the next.

"Is the phrase 'you are no nearer to catching me than you were when I first started' familiar to you?" asked Bailey.

Michael glanced once more at Giles to see whether he wanted to offer any advice, but again found nothing helpful in his lawyer's expression.

"It rings a bell. Isn't it what the Madman said on the tape you guys played at the news conference?"

"Yes, it is," said Collins. "But it's also very nearly the same phrase as was used by the man who sent recordings to the police hunting the Yorkshire Ripper in 1979. But then again, you knew that, didn't you?"

"Why do you say that?"

"Because you studied the Yorkshire Ripper story, didn't you? Isn't that right?"

"Yes, I think I did, as part of my media course. Yes, as you've no doubt discovered, coverage of the case was a module in my course. But again, I guess it must have been studied by tens if not hundreds of thousands of people. Anyone who has looked at that original case has listened to the tapes and might be familiar with that phrase. Anyway, I don't know what you're getting at or why we need to have these conversations. Haven't my alibis been confirmed? I wasn't there for any of these three incidents."

Superintendent Bailey seemed to ignore the last comment. "So is that where you got the idea from?"

"What idea?"

"To record and send the USB stick."

"I didn't record and send the USB stick."

The senior detective opened a brown folder which had been on the table in front of him. "Look, Michael. We've had further analysis of the comparisons between your voice and the voice on the tape, and the experts have told us that either the person on the tape is you, or there is a million-to-one chance that it could be someone else with a voice exactly like yours. So what I'm wondering is, are you the man who has killed eleven children and has asked his girlfriend to provide him with an alibi for all three incidents, or are you the man who has wasted police time by sending us this recording and thereby diverting us from the real investigation? Because at this moment I'm not considering any third possibility."

"If I could just say something on behalf of my client?" It was the first time Gordon Giles had spoken out loud in the course of the interviews. "If, as you say, the experts tell you that it's a million to one that there could be someone else out there with a voice that's identical to Michael's, that means there are probably at least sixty people in the UK alone, and obviously a huge multiple of that worldwide, who could have recorded it.

So Michael is one of some sixty British people who fit your description."

"Yes," said Collins, hardly missing a beat, "but probably none of the other fifty-nine can be placed about a mile from the first incident, less than half a mile from the second incident, and maybe four hundred yards from the third incident."

"Nor can I," said Michael. "Apart from anything else, I was in Brighton when the murders underneath Kingston Bridge happened."

"So you say," said Bailey.

Once again, Giles intervened. "And so Miss Parsons has no doubt corroborated."

The four sat in silence for a few seconds, and Collins seemed to be about to start on another line of questioning when there was a knock on the door and a young plainclothes detective entered the room and whispered in Bailey's ear.

"For the tape," said Collins, "Detective Constable Squires has just entered the room and is consulting with Superintendent Bailey." As she was speaking, the young detective handed Bailey another USB stick, which he plugged into a port on his laptop.

"May we know what's going on?" asked Giles. "Is this another recording?"

"It's a copy of some material we've just recovered from the Hand-Cutz production house where your client works," said Bailey. Now he was staring at the screen, and Michael could see from the reflection in his spectacles that he was watching a moving image. "It was handed over to us by the team from Matterhorn Productions, which has been making the documentaries about the Madman. It seems that this is from the material they shot on the very first Sunday, just after the incident in Brighton." Bailey was still using the controls on the laptop's keyboard to scroll through the video and was conferring in whispers with Collins as he did so. When he reached the point he was looking for, he half closed his eyes and seemed to smile.

"I repeat," said Giles, now more stridently than before. "May we know what is going on?"

Bailey pressed the pause button and looked again at Michael. "Please, can you remind me again what you said you were wearing on the afternoon of the Brighton incident? When you say you went out with Alison to find something to eat?"

Michael thought for a moment. It was clear that the police had found something they believed to be significant, and he was anxious not to make a mistake. "Yes, it was a blue shirt and khaki cargo trousers. I've told you that already." He looked at Giles, who shook his head. Neither of them had any clue about the significance of the question.

"Then can you tell me who this is?" Bailey's expression was triumphant as he turned the laptop so that the screen faced Michael and his lawyer. The image had been frozen into a still frame and showed a young man, taken from the right-hand profile and just behind him as he walked away. The man was wearing blue jeans and a white T-shirt, and anyone seeing it for the first time would have bet a further million to one that they were looking at a picture of Michael. The time code in the corner of the screen indicated a clock; it was 11:25 in the morning, which was just about forty minutes after the children had been thrown into the sea.

"Michael Beaumont," said Bailey. "I am now charging you with the murder of James Mitchell in Brighton on the tenth of May this year. Once again, you do not have to say anything, but it may harm your defense if you fail to mention when questioned anything that you later rely on in court. Anything you do say may be used in evidence against you."

Immediately Gordon Giles rose to his feet and placed a hand on Michael's shoulder. "My client has nothing further to add at this time."

FIFTEEN

WITH ALL THE furor going on at the front desk and in reception as
a new pack of journalists gathered in the car park at the front of
Greenacres, no one was available to go to sit with Rose to ensure that she was distracted from watching the television. The
stroke must have been very serious and very sudden, according to the doctors who examined her later, because otherwise
there was no way to understand why Rose would not have
reached for the button to summon assistance. By the time they
found her she was in a coma and lying in a position in her bed
which indicated that she may have been writhing in pain for
some while before she lost consciousness. The TV on the wall
was tuned to twenty-four-hour news.

Journalists banging on the outer doors of the care home
would not believe anyone from the staff who told them that
Rose Beaumont had been taken ill and would not be giving
interviews or making a statement about her grandson. Even
when the ambulance arrived with sirens blaring and lights
flashing, the most implacable declined to accept that what they
were being told was true. Several resorted to asking any staff

or visitors going in or out whether they had ever met Michael, his grandmother, his girlfriend, or anyone else remotely connected to the Beaumonts.

Management at Greenacres was in a state of shock after learning that one of their residents could be associated in any way with the murderer who had become known as the Madman, and now they wondered who should be informed about Rose's condition. It was well known that Esme had been especially close to Rose, but she had not been on duty when news of Michael's arrest began to circulate. She changed her plans and agreed to come into Greenacres the moment she received a call from the welfare officer Edwina Morrison.

Rose had been admitted to the intensive care unit at St. Thomas' Hospital, and Mrs. Morrison suggested that in the absence of any available next of kin, Esme should go there and stay close to her bed in case her friend might wake up and wonder where she was. Mrs. Morrison quickly wrote out a letter on headed notepaper authorizing St. Thomas' to allow Esme access. She also had the presence of mind to warn them that their incoming patient needed to be protected from the press.

"Obviously I need to let her grandson know," said Mrs. Morrison, "but I can't imagine that he's been allowed to keep his telephone, and I don't have names or numbers for anyone else."

Esme thought about what Rose had told her a few days earlier about the middle-aged woman who came to visit from time to time—the woman she had identified as Mrs. Rawlinson. She was about to mention her to Mrs. Morrison, but then changed her mind. "I don't think there is any other family—or at least no one I know of."

"It's difficult to believe that he could be capable of something like this, but then I suppose that if the bad people had horns and a tail, we wouldn't need detectives to try to catch them."

Esme shook her head. "I don't know much about anything, but one thing I do know is that unless they've caught that boy red-handed, nothing's going to persuade me that he has done those terrible things. He's a lovely, lovely boy. He's so kind to his grandmother, and that new girlfriend of his is very nice, too. I made them cake!"

"Well, I'm sure the police know what they're doing, Esme," said Mrs. Morrison, her words clipped and clinical. "But anyway, our duty is quite clear. We need to take care of Rose's interests as best we can, and that means being there for her when she wakes up and doing what we can to keep the newspeople away from her."

Esme readily agreed and set off for the hospital.

Gordon Giles had remained at the police station awaiting instructions from his client and spent the time on the telephone trying to raise one of the senior partners from his law firm to seek advice. It was a measure of Mr. Giles's junior status that he had been the on-duty defense solicitor for what should have been a quiet weekday evening in central London. At only twenty-five years old, the most serious thing that the young lawyer had come across in his short career was assault and battery while under the influence of alcohol, and he was terrified of putting a foot wrong. Everyone he tried to call was either out at dinner or the theater, and so when the officers told Giles that his client wanted to see him, it was with some trepidation that he stepped into the holding cell.

"I just cannot believe that this is real," said Michael. He was sitting on the bed, and Gordon Giles had pulled up an upright chair. "It's like a nightmare. Like something out of a horror movie. Stuff keeps happening that I can't take in."

Gordon Giles chose not to reflect on the thought that he was sitting next to a man who might be the most famous mass murderer of the last three decades and decided instead to assume that his client was innocent and would need a good defense. He took a deep breath and plunged in. "I can completely understand that, Michael, but we'd be better off using our time to talk about a few practicalities. What, for example, is going on with that piece of video from the day of the second crime in Brighton? Is there any way that that could have been you?"

"No," said Michael firmly. "I agree that the bloke in the video looks a bit like me, but I've spent the last two hours thinking how they could possibly have taken those pictures. As I told the police, I know that I was wearing my khaki cargo pants and a blue T-shirt on that day because Alison and I noted that so many other people seemed to be wearing the same things the Madman had been described as wearing." Michael paused to recall the possibilities he had considered during his time alone in the cell. "Obviously I do own blue jeans and some white shirts, so either someone has taken some pictures of me at another time and somehow they've been mixed up, or there's someone out there who looks remarkably similar to me."

"When you say 'mixed up,' do you mean accidentally, or do you think it's possible that someone is trying to throw suspicion onto you?" Michael looked up at Giles, his face expressing inquiry. The lawyer continued, "I know that sounds unlikely, but after all, there were a number of people at the production company who told the police that the voice on the tape sounded like yours. Is it possible that a person in there—someone you work with—has doctored the tape, or whatever you do to tapes, to make it look as though you were there at that time and dressed the same as the killer?"

"But honestly, who would do that? Of course it's possible, but who would do that? It's not like a practical joke . . . it's life and death."

"I don't know," said Giles. "Maybe it started as a practical joke that got out of hand? Maybe the real killer? I haven't got a clue, but if you say you weren't wearing those clothes on that day, there are very few other possible explanations."

The pressure which Michael had been feeling inside his head since his arrest was showing no sign of reducing, and he pushed the palms of his hands hard against his temples but obtained no relief. He was about to ask what was going to happen next when the door of the cell opened, and Sergeant Mallinson asked the lawyer to step outside for a moment.

"I won't be a minute, Michael," said Mallinson affably, "I just need a quick word with Mr. Giles."

Alone again, Michael began to pace the cell. He walked its length, and then its breadth, ten feet by six feet, and for a moment he recalled the scene in the classic film *Papillon* when Steve McQueen was kept in the dark in an underground cell for years on end. He had paced out the dimensions and eventually knew he was losing his mind when he lost count and bumped into the wall. The moment of distraction was quickly gone as Michael tried to concentrate on the recent conversation with the lawyer. What possible explanations could there be? Surely it was inconceivable that someone had put footage of him taken at another time in among the footage shot that Sunday afternoon? And yet of course it would be so easy to do, and now he remembered that he had told the director from Matterhorn that he had been in Brighton at that time. Then Michael turned his mind to the matching voiceprints. The spectrograph showing the highs and lows of his voice matched exactly those on the tape from the Madman, and he had been present himself when the two had been played together. As he struggled for another explanation, he realized that an expert sound technician would be able to distort the recording of two voices which were similar to make them seem like a match. He began to rack his brains about who would wish to do such a thing. Surely only the killer himself, or someone else who intended him great harm. His thoughts were interrupted by the sound of the key turning in the lock and the steel door opening. Michael registered that it was Mr. Giles returning, and one look at the expression on his face made clear that something else had happened.

"What is it?" said Michael. "You look as though you've seen a ghost. Whatever it is, it can't be any worse than what has happened already." For a few further seconds Giles said nothing, as if wondering how to express what he needed to say, and then Michael understood that there was indeed something which would be worse than what had already happened. He guessed at what it was the second before Giles spoke again.

"Your grandmother has had a stroke."

"Oh my God." Dreadful though the words were, they were not quite as dreadful as the ones he had feared. Nevertheless Michael felt poleaxed. Unable to move, and yet unable to remain still, Michael literally did not know where to put himself. He stood up straight, then sat down, and then stood up again. "Oh my God. Oh my God. Oh my God. It's a nightmare. They've scared the living hell out of her. That's what they've done. The bastards have damn near killed a harmless old lady." Michael began pacing fast, turning swiftly at each extremity of the cell, ten by six, six by ten, and now he felt a primordial scream welling inside himself and brought his arms up and clasped his hands together behind his head, squeezing his skull between his forearms. "I have to see her," he said, his voice muffled by the sleeves of his jacket.

Gordon Giles had never seen another human being in such distress, and he reached out to touch his new client on the shoulder. "I'm afraid they won't let you, Michael. I've asked already. Basically they say that half the world's press is camped outside the police station here, and the other half is camped outside St. Thomas' Hospital. They just can't make it possible to get you there and back safely. They told me that her condition is serious but stable, which means that nothing is likely to happen overnight. I'll get one of my more senior colleagues here in time for the hearing in the morning, and we'll ask the judge to allow you to visit her."

It was a full ten minutes before Michael was able to speak again, in which time he did his best to absorb and process his situation. His overwhelming emotion was still incredulity — just a few hours ago he was looking forward to the weekend and wondering what he and Alison would do together. Now every important thing in his life was being dismantled before his eyes, and he seemed to be helpless to do anything about it. Suddenly a shudder passed through Michael's body; he realized that he was freezing cold. He looked up and saw that his lawyer was gazing back at him with an expression which might have been sympathy.

"What's going to happen next?" asked Michael.

"You'll stay here overnight, and they'll have to put you before a judge in the morning. You won't need to plead or say anything other than confirming your name and that you understand the charges. I haven't been able to raise anyone else in my law firm, but as soon as I do, I'll get someone down here who will know how best to put the case to the judge that you need to visit your grandmother." Michael's sudden rush of gratitude was out of all proportion to the kindness. He could feel the tears forming in his eyes, but merely nodded to show that he understood.

It had been made very clear to her that she would not be allowed to speak to Michael before she left the police station, but nonetheless Alison begged to be allowed to see him—even if it was through glass or across a room. There was never going to be any possibility, and so after she had given her account of events to Detective Superintendent Bailey and Detective Constable Collins, they said that she could leave the station.

"But Michael will need to appear in court in the morning for the charges to be put to him and for a bail hearing," Bailey explained. He told her that if she wished to, he would arrange for her to be taken discreetly into the back of the public gallery.

"What about fresh clothes?" Alison asked. "Will I be able to bring something for him to wear in court?"

Bailey responded that Michael's apartment was being searched but that he would make arrangements for her to be allowed access. "DC Squires will be there by the time you arrive," he said. "In particular, of course, you won't be allowed to touch or remove any of the clothes Michael was wearing or might have been wearing on the days we're concerned about."

STUART PREBBLE

Arrangements were made for Alison to be driven out of the police station in the back of an unmarked van so that she could avoid the media. She remained out of sight for the entire journey to Kingston, and when they arrived she found that the whole of Old Bridge Street had been closed off with yellow and black police tape, and she was able to duck out of the van and into the entrance leading to Michael's apartment without being spotted by watching cameras. She was met at the door as promised by Detective Constable Squires and immediately became aware that there were three or four other officers, each of them dressed from head to foot in white overalls, spread out in various rooms. They seemed to be opening and closing drawers and cupboards.

"Do you have an idea of the clothes you want to bring for him?" asked Squires. "I guess you know where they are, do you?" Alison said that she did. "We've already collected up all the items we think could be relevant to our inquiries, and so it's OK to take anything you see left there. Just check everything with me before you do, though."

Alison was quick enough to catch sight of a pile of plastic bags containing the clothes and objects which had been collected by the officers. She noted that they seemed to include several pairs of blue jeans and some white clothes which might have been T-shirts.

She pulled herself together as quickly as she could and went to the wardrobe in the bedroom she knew so well. As always, the football posters on the walls seemed entirely incongruous, and Alison reflected that anyone looking for clues about Michael's character would find little that was helpful by searching his room. She knew that it was preposterous for her to be worrying about what Michael would wear for his court appear-

164

ance in the morning, but nonetheless something in her wanted him to look his best and, perhaps more important, to feel as good as he could in the dreadful circumstances. She thought of a blue linen jacket which he had mentioned was a favorite of his grandma's and a pair of black chinos which were probably the smartest trousers he owned. She took a polo shirt from a pile she had ironed for Michael a few days earlier and hung all the items carefully on a hanger.

Alison was about to return to the living room to show them to Squires when she noticed the top of what looked like a piece of card sticking out of the inside pocket of the jacket. She took hold of it and saw that it was not a card but an old photograph. She was about to put it into a drawer when she heard the sound of someone approaching, and instead she put it in the back pocket of her jeans.

"Do you have what you need?" Squires reentered the bedroom and glanced at the clothes she was carrying.

"I just want to get some shoes if I can. I think that at the moment he'll just be wearing sneakers." Once again Alison rooted in the wardrobe, this time on the floor, and chose a pair of black leather shoes which were covered in dust. "It doesn't look as though he's had much use for these recently, but I'll give them a brush and they'll be fine."

"Where will you stay tonight?" asked Squires. "Can I arrange for you to get a lift somewhere? I think we've still got a whole pack of journalists waiting to pounce."

Alison was about to respond when their conversation was interrupted by one of the officers who had been searching and now emerged from Rose's bedroom. "Have a look at this, sir." The policeman was carrying something which he seemed to be trying to show only to Squires, but Alison was just in time to tilt her head sufficiently to glimpse what it was. It appeared to be a heavy cloth top of some kind, and it was gray. Perhaps it was a hoodie.

"Bag it up carefully," said Squires, and turned back to face Alison.

"If that's a gray hoodie," she said, "it isn't Michael's. He doesn't own one."

"You mean not that you know of?" said the detective. "I doubt that you know every item of clothing your boyfriend has ever owned." Clearly the officer had no interest in pursuing the conversation.

"I have no idea where I can stay tonight, so I wondered whether maybe I could find a cheap hotel somewhere near to the court? Can I accept your offer of a lift back into town, and I'll google somewhere when we're on our way?"

Ten minutes later she was back in the police van and retracing the journey around the South Circular and back towards the West End. She felt her head buzzing with a thousand different thoughts and tried to clear her mind so that she could consider her priorities. Then she remembered the photograph which she had found in Michael's jacket and slipped into her jeans. She slid her hand into her back pocket and for a moment could not feel anything and thought that perhaps it had fallen out. She checked her other pocket and found it empty. Then she shifted her weight to enable herself to feel again, and this time Alison traced the tip of the stiff paper against the edge of her fingertips. She was able to pincer a corner of the photograph between her fingers and grip hard enough to slip it out.

The only illumination falling in the area where she sat in the back of the van was coming through the windscreen and side windows, and she looked around and above her head but could see no artificial light. She held the photograph at the corners and turned it this way and that, trying to find the best angle. Through the semigloom she could just make out the shapes of four children. They seemed to be a girl of about eight years old, two boys of around two or three, and a baby in arms. She could not identify either of the boys, but within a few seconds she knew that she recognized the face of the older girl. Alison could almost hear and feel the cogs turning in her brain as a thousand pieces of the jigsaw appeared like birds approaching from over the horizon and began to form into shapes she could remember and recognize. The death by suicide of Michael's grandfather, the dreadful screams from Grandma Rose at their first meeting, and then the various fragments of the pattern seemed to gain speed as they jostled to find their place in the final picture. Alison felt a shudder run through her entire body like someone walking over her grave in the pitch darkness and was unable to suppress an audible whimper of pain.

SIXTEEN

THE EARLY MORNING light was just beginning to penetrate the wire-reinforced windows of his cell when Michael finally fell into a shallow sleep, and it was less than two hours later that he was woken abruptly by the rattling of heavy keys in the lock. For the first few seconds he did not know where he was, and when realization arrived, it felt as though someone had lowered the weight of a boulder onto his chest. He kept his eyes closed tightly for as long as he could, as if it might prevent the reality of his surroundings from invading his inner self.

"Here's some tea. I'll bring you some cereal in a minute." The words were spoken in a strong Yorkshire accent, and it was a voice he recognized.

"I didn't think you'd be here this morning," said Michael. "Weren't you here till very late last night?"

"I should be off today," said Sergeant Mallinson, "but it's not every day we have a celebrity in our cells. You're famous and everybody wants to know all about you."

Michael felt as though someone had shoved a sharp stick into an already very sore place, and he winced at the idea of it.

Immediately his mind went to thoughts of his grandma Rose, and he wondered how she had passed the night. Flooding in hard on the heels of those concerns, he recalled that he would be taken to court this morning and charged with murder. He found it hard to comprehend his situation, but even now his main concern was whether his lawyer would be able to argue successfully for him to be allowed to visit Rose in hospital.

When the sergeant returned a few minutes later, he brought a pile of fresh clothes which he recognized as his own, and it occurred to him that he had hardly given a thought to Alison and how she must have passed the night.

"Your girlfriend brought these from your apartment. It's still being searched, but they let her in long enough to bring you some clothes to wear in court."

"Where did she stay, then, any idea? Is she here now?"

Mallinson said he had no idea where she had stayed and that she had come to the station late last night but left again after being told that she would not be permitted to see Michael. "She's obviously going to be a witness one way or another, and so the detectives will want to compare your stories before you get a chance to make sure they match."

"We don't have to match anything up because I already know that we'll both be saying the same thing. That's because she and I were together when all these three incidents took place."

Mallinson's expression indicated neither belief nor disbelief, but only that he had heard it all and seen it all before. "Hope you enjoy your cornflakes." He closed the door and turned the key.

A follow-up phone call from Edwina Morrison at the care home to the duty manager at St. Thomas' ensured that Esme could avoid the small army of journalists and photographers waiting outside the main doors, and she took directions to the staff entrance at the back where she was expected and ushered through. The male nurse from the intensive care unit who came down to meet and escort her upstairs was obliged to show identification and authorization to three separate sets of police constables en route back to the unit.

The nurse, a tall and very slim black man in his early thirties, introduced himself as Christopher and ushered Esme though a set of double doors leading into ICU, which were then closed and locked behind them. There was something about the atmosphere inside the unit which would have given away its particular purpose even to a person unused to these surroundings. The half-light which was intended to encourage rest and calm instead served only to throw into shadow the shapes and silhouettes of anxious relatives who passed the time as best they could while waiting for news of their loved ones. On one side of the hallway was a series of individual rooms, each of them illuminated from within by the flashing of lights from tiny high-tech monitors. On the other side, strewn around in improvised patterns, were a number of sofas and armchairs, there to provide some comfort for the never-ending procession of husbands or wives, brothers and sisters, parents or children, who spent hour after hour standing by, worried sick, to be on hand just in case.

Now Esme was among those standing by . . . just in case. She was not a parent or sibling or daughter of Rose Beaumont, but she had become closer to her than she had to anyone else she had met at Greenacres these last few years. So close, in fact, that just a week before the incident which caused her stroke, Rose had told her a secret. It was the biggest secret of Rose's life, and before imparting it to Esme, she had made her new friend swear on all she held as holy that she would never breathe a word of it to anyone else. Less than a week ago that had seemed to be a relatively easy promise to make, but now circumstances had changed in a way that no one could have dreamed. What Esme hoped above all else was that Rose would wake up and be clear enough to free her from the unbreakable solemnity of her promise.

Esme closed her eyes several times during the night but at no point would she avail herself of the comforts of the beanbags or sofas. She thought that anyone would be terrified to emerge out of a deep sleep to find themselves surrounded by all this technology, so she dearly wanted to be in Rose's immediate eyeline should she wake up and have no idea where she was. What would it then be like for her friend Rose as her mind gradually reengaged with the circumstances which had undoubtedly brought on her collapse?

Once or twice in the night Rose showed signs of life, and Esme thought that she might be regaining consciousness. She looked at Rose's face, once young and full of hopes, and now showing the battle scars of a life filled with pain and trauma. At one point Rose moved her head and seemed to mumble, and Esme was very keen indeed that she should hear anything that her friend was trying to say. She thought that perhaps it was "Michael" but could not be certain.

When the same early morning light which was illuminating Michael's cell a few miles away began to peep between the blinds in the intensive care unit, all around there was evidence of the unit's regular routine getting under way. Only then did

Esme allow her head to nod and droop, and she had fallen into a shallow sleep when she felt a hand on her arm and looked up to see one of the nurses who had been on duty when she arrived the previous evening. The name on her badge was Roxanne, and she smiled that smile which you only ever see on the faces of people who were born to care for others.

"I'm sorry to disturb you, Esme," she said, "but there is a woman downstairs who is asking if she can visit Mrs. Beaumont."

For a moment Esme did not know how to respond, but then she remembered what Edwina Morrison had said to her the previous day when she left Greenacres. She warned that the press and media would be likely to use any means to get access to Rose, no matter how devious and underhand, and that she should be suspicious of anyone claiming to know her.

"It's probably one of those press people, isn't it? Shouldn't we just send her away?"

"Normally I would," said Roxanne, "but she is saying that you know her—and that her name is Mrs. Rawlinson."

Esme's eyes widened, and it took her a few seconds to take in the significance of what had been said. Collecting her wits sufficiently, she responded: "I think we should ask her to come up."

The short journey to the Central Criminal Court was by far the most terrifying experience of Michael's life. His request for a shower and shave had been refused, and he was only just finishing putting on the fresh clothes which Alison had brought for him when two uniformed officers he had not met before burst through the door, came into his cell, and clamped handcuffs tightly around his wrists. Michael jolted back in pain, but the firm hands gripping his forearms allowed no relief. He was being marched along the corridor towards the outside yard when Sergeant Mallinson caught up with the procession and handed him a piece of a blanket.

"There's no possibility of being photographed between this door and the van because the yard is concealed at the back here, but once you're inside, you might want to put this over your head just before you arrive at the court," said Mallinson. Once again the sergeant's tone of voice was quite distinct from every other aspect of Michael's treatment. "The driver has to slow down to pass through the gates when he gets there, and that's where the photographers will hold their cameras up to the windows and snap away. The windows are high up and have tinted glass, but sometimes they get lucky and can get a shot of you sitting inside. That's the picture they'll put on the front pages, and it makes you look like a criminal. You don't want that. When the van stops, it's a short walk from there into the court, and the officers with you will make sure you can't be seen or photographed."

Again Michael felt a wave of gratitude which was entirely out of proportion to the kindness, and he thanked the sergeant profusely. "Will I see my lawyer at the court?"

Mallinson assured him that he would have an opportunity to consult with Mr. Giles in plenty of time before his appearance. "Chances are you won't be coming back here, I'm afraid. I should imagine they're likely to remand you in custody, so most probably you'll go to the Scrubs Prison. It can feel a bit scary there, but there's nothing to be afraid of. Everyone is just doing their job. I'm sure all this will get sorted out very soon, and you'll be on your way."

Michael remained mystified by the sergeant's attitude, and a few seconds later he felt himself being shunted into the back of a police van and driven off at high speed along the Strand towards the court. Inside the vehicle he was confined to a tiny cell about the dimensions of the cubicle in a public lavatory, illuminated by the overspill from a fluorescent bulb in the ceiling and the dull-blue glow of daylight through a tiny pane of reinforced glass above his head. Immediately Michael felt claustrophobic and frightened, and he wondered whether his legs would move when the time came. The van was escorted by two motorcycle outriders with their sirens blaring, and so it was only a few minutes before he felt the brakes go on and heard the first cries from the crowd outside. He felt the terror rising from deep inside.

"Bastard." "Murderer." "Fucking maniac." "Child killer." The angry shouts were accompanied by the booming noise of fists hammering on the outside of the vehicle, like being inside a huge kettledrum which was being beaten by a frenzied gang. He felt the sides of the van vibrating under the assault and instinctively pulled himself forwards to sit upright and away from the walls. Michael had forgotten what Mallinson had said to him until he saw the flash of light from a camera pressed up against the window and now grabbed the square of blanket and put it over his face. He tightened the material around his neck so that it covered him, pressing his hands to the side of his head to try to keep out the mayhem. Abruptly the banging stopped as the van swung to one side, and he heard the clang of metal gates closing behind him. He was driven a few more yards, and the shouts of the angry mob receded into the distance.

"There is no point in me requesting bail because the judge won't grant it—as much for your own safety as anything else. But I understand from Mr. Giles that you want me to ask the judge for permission for you to visit your grandmother. Is that still the situation?"

Michael had been more or less bundled through a back door at the criminal court and down some stone steps into a stark room with a steel door and no windows. A wooden table and four chairs were the only items of furniture in the room, and sitting on two of them were his solicitor, Gordon Giles, and an older man wearing a long black gown, wing collars, and a barrister's wig. He introduced himself as Richard Ramsey, Queen's Counsel, and got down to business.

"I gather that Mr. Giles has told you that you won't be asked to plead today, but the charge will be put to you, and you will be asked if you understand it. I take it that you do?" The barrister looked up at Michael for the first time, taking off his spectacles and leaning forwards with his arms on the table. "They'll be putting to you a specimen charge of the one murder, but that's just a holding position. Eventually no doubt they intend to charge you with all eleven. We don't think they'll be charging you for the time being in connection with the deaths of the two adults who drowned while trying to rescue the children in the Thames, but we may be inclined to take the view that that's rather academic at this point in time."

Michael nodded. He heard and understood the words, but still did not properly comprehend. "I know I won't be pleading today," he said, "but just so you know it if anyone asks you, or if you want to know it yourself, I am completely innocent. I had nothing whatever to do with these crimes."

Mr. Ramsey continued to stare at Michael for a few seconds

more, as if seeking to ascertain by his appearance whether or not he was telling the truth. Eventually the barrister grunted what might have been affirmation and resumed his examination of his papers.

"Will Alison be at court today?" Michael asked. "She knows where I was on all three occasions. If someone would just listen to her, they would let me out this morning."

"I'm afraid that won't be happening, Michael. Don't get your hopes up. That's not what today is about. It's just a re-mand to give the police time to get their evidence together. No doubt Mr. Giles and your friends can use the time prof-itably to gather proof of your innocence. For the moment, my job is to ensure that you are sent somewhere where you will be safe, and to try to see if I can get you in to see your grand-mother who is, as I understand it, your only living relative and is gravely ill—a condition which was probably brought on by the shock of your arrest?" He spoke the words as though re-hearsing for his performance upstairs. Michael confirmed the details.

"I've been told that we are up first, so we should be asked to go into the court in about five minutes," said Giles. By now he had become a more or less familiar face, and Michael was glad to have him nearby. Nonetheless, his pulse quickened as he cast his mind forward to what awaited him upstairs in the austere courtrooms of the Old Bailey. Even despite the hours he had spent trying to process what was happening to him, Michael felt petrified at the prospect of finding himself actually stand-ing in the dock and having his name attached to these dreadful charges. The judge as he appeared in Michael's imagination was a terrifying figure out of a storybook nightmare, and he felt his insides turn to water when, from the corridor outside, he could hear the sound of approaching footsteps. The two lawyers stood up, anticipating an escort to lead them upstairs. Instead, when the door opened, Michael was surprised to see that the two people who entered the room were Detective Chief Superintendent Norman Bailey and Detective Constable Collins. The two lawyers seemed to be every bit as surprised as Michael was, and when he spoke, Superintendent Bailey had lost some of his recent self-assurance.

"I'm sorry to barge in on you like this. Something unexpected has happened, and I think the formal procedure is that I should speak privately to Mr. Giles, but as you are all here and these seem to be unusual circumstances . . . ?"

The barrister pulled out his own chair and gestured for Bailey to sit on the spare one. The female detective walked the few paces to the side of the room and stood with her arms folded and no readable expression on her face. The four men were sitting.

"Just about an hour ago, a few miles from here in Battersea Park, two small children were standing on the side of the pond and feeding the ducks, when a man ran by, picked up the children one at a time, and threw them into the water." Michael gasped and sat back in his chair, his hands rising up involuntarily to the top of his head as though to prevent it from lifting off his shoulders. The superintendent was still speaking. "The children's mother was a little way away at the time and was more concerned with saving her children than with identifying the assailant. She managed to pull both of the children safely out of the water, and they are recovering, but what description she was able to give us of the person who pushed them in seems to match closely the man we have been looking for as the Madman."

Michael leaned forward and felt his body bend double, his head hovering just above the surface of the table, and he pressed the palms of his hands hard into his face. The surge of emotion came from a deeper place inside of him than he had ever known existed, and he was overwhelmed by the force of it. No physical manifestation could express the sense of relief he felt, and all he could do was to sob for some minutes until the trauma flowed out of him and the waves of fear gradually subsided.

Eventually Michael felt someone's hand on his shoulder and slowly regained awareness of his surroundings. When he sat up straight, he saw that his barrister had packed away his papers into a file and was standing near to the door.

"Congratulations, Mr. Beaumont. I'm sure we are all relieved, if not perhaps quite as relieved as you are. I shall leave it to these good officers to offer you the most profuse apologies in the history of the police force, and to my young friend Mr. Giles to consider the size of the claim for compensation, which I very much hope he will instruct me to pursue. Good day to you gentlemen, and lady." He touched his wig with his index finger and exited.

After the barrister had gone, Bailey left it to Collins to explain what would happen next. There remained the mystery of the matching voiceprint, and the police would still be investigating whether it was Michael who had sent the recording or whether there had been interference with the readings from the monitor. "In the meantime, we will, of course, be dropping the most serious charge of murder, and as soon as we have completed some formalities here, you can be on your way."

"All that's very well and good, but of most immediate concern to my client is that the damage which has undoubtedly been done to him by this unjustified arrest, and the publicity which has arisen from it, should be terminated as quickly as possible and his good name should be restored." Michael thought that his young and inexperienced lawyer was growing in stature with every word. "We will want to approve a statement which we then need you to issue as quickly as is possible." He stood and looked at the detectives, first at Bailey, then at Collins, and then back again. "Are we agreed?" Bailey nodded to indicate that they were agreed.

"But there's just one more thing I'd like to ask you, Michael, before you go," said the detective.

"Yes, what is it?"

Bailey looked intently at Michael as he spoke. "Is there someone out there who hates you?"

"What do you mean? Of course there isn't." Michael paused. "Or not that I know of anyway. Why would you ask that question?"

"Well, if I were you, it's the question I would be asking myself," said Bailey. Again, Michael frowned deeply and urged the detective to continue. "Just think about it. All these incidents have taken place in areas close to where you live, work, or visit. Waterloo, which is close to where you were on that first weekend; Kingston, very close to where you live; and Brighton, just a little way away from where Alison lives and where you and she spend a lot of time together. We still don't know how there came to be video of a person who looks remarkably like you, dressed as the killer was dressed, just a few hours after the Brighton incident. And we still don't know how or why your voiceprint is such a close match to the voice on the recording, but we suspect that it must be possible for someone to doctor the monitor or the readouts. However, we do know that you have access to a sound recording studio, and that we received a recording of someone who says he is the killer, stored on a device like one you carry on your key ring."

"Oh, and just one more thing." Now Collins joined the conversation. "You told us that you don't own a gray hoodie, and yet we found one among the clothes at your home." All that Michael could do was to register further surprise. He remained silent, waiting for the next revelation.

Bailey glanced across the room towards Collins, as if he was trying to weigh up whether to go ahead and share another piece of information. He raised his eyebrows in inquiry, and Michael glanced over in time to see Collins nodding agreement. Bailey sat forward, closer to the table, and continued, now speaking in a lowered voice.

"And there is one other thing which we haven't shared with the public, because when we get our man, we need to have some information which only he and we know if we are to be sure that we've got the right person."

Michael and his solicitor found themselves also leaning forward, both feeling anxious not to do or say anything which might dissuade the detective from sharing his confidence. "A few days before we received the recording which you've heard, we were sent a letter from someone claiming to be the Madman. It was on the same kind of paper and using the same typeface as the note which came later with the recordings, so we are confident it was from the same person." Bailey paused again, as though double-checking with himself that he was doing the right thing by continuing. After a moment he appeared resolved. "The letter said that the writer had been driven to commit the first crime after seeing what he described as 'all the happy couples' on the South Bank on that day. And it didn't occur to me until our CCTV showed that you had been in the area around that time, and the group of people he is referring to, unless I am very much mistaken, could easily have included you and Alison."

Once again there was a pause of a few moments to allow the import of what was being said to sink in. "Maybe it's all just a remarkable coincidence." It was DC Collins who picked up the thread, "but from the outside, it does look very much as though someone somewhere might have been trying to put you under suspicion. And it worked."

"But if for some reason the real killer was trying to do that," said Giles, "why would he then commit another crime at a time when Michael was in custody and therefore couldn't be the Madman?"

The two detectives looked at one other, and Collins shrugged. Suddenly the atmosphere had lightened just a little. "That remains a mystery. Maybe by then whoever it was felt that he had had his fun. Or maybe he's just got a taste for what he's doing and can't stop himself from carrying out more murder and mayhem."

"Or maybe the killer and the person trying to frame Michael are two different people?" The interrogative in Giles's voice indicated that he was in territory he knew nothing about. "Just a random idea."

"We won't know that until we get the bastard. But meanwhile anything you can think of which might help us, I hope you'll let us know."

The speculation had thrown Michael's mind into a further tailspin. Nonetheless he agreed that he would think hard about what the two police officers had said. "But in the end, I'm sure it's just been a dreadful set of coincidences. I'm a straightforward and very ordinary guy—just not the sort of bloke who makes enemies."

Giles turned to Michael. "I'm getting a cab back to the office, but would you like me to drop you off at the hospital? We can telephone your friend Alison on the way."

Just an hour earlier Michael had been absolutely certain that he would be driving out of the precincts of the court on his way to prison at Wormwood Scrubs, where his presumed status as a child killer would guarantee him the most terrible treatment available in the British judicial system, and the likelihood of terrible injury or death if ever he strayed too close to any of the other inmates. In the event Gordon Giles went out before him to hail a taxi, which was allowed through the security gates so that Michael could get in undetected.

"You could, of course, stand on the courtroom steps and say your piece about the police's wrongful arrest. It's probably the fastest way to let the world know that you were falsely accused."

Michael shook his head. "Maybe I could do that, but I'm sure as hell not going to. This has been bloody terrible, but at the end of the day, if you listen to the list of evidence they just talked us through, it's no wonder they arrested me. I'd have done the same. I want to get some answers as soon as I can, but right now all I care about is my grandmother."

The two men agreed that it would be quicker for the taxi to divert a few hundred yards to drop Giles off near his firm's offices in Gray's Inn before taking Michael on. When they arrived there, Michael asked the driver to wait while he got out of the cab to say goodbye. He felt a strong and sudden urge to hug his solicitor, but a second later he knew that would feel awkward, and instead the two young men shook hands warmly.

"It's good that you don't feel rancor towards the police," said Giles, "but what Mr. Ramsey said back there has some truth in it. We should meet in a few days to discuss what you want to do."

Michael agreed to consider the matter. "Right now I just want to make sure that the news that I'm no longer a suspect is spread as widely as the news of my arrest. I don't know whether they're going to catch this lunatic, but whatever happens I don't want to go through the rest of my life being thought of as the man who might be the Madman."

Michael got back into the taxi and asked the driver to take him to St. Thomas' Hospital. All this time he had been wondering what had happened to Alison, and now he switched on his mobile phone, hoping to find some contact from her. When it came to life, the screen showed that he had thirty-seven missed calls. He dialed his mailbox and began listening to a series of messages from journalists who seemed keen to be his friend. He lost patience after five or six, rang off, and then pressed the speed dial for Alison's cell phone. By now the taxi was crossing Blackfriars Bridge, and Michael looked over the water towards Waterloo, where this still-unbelievable nightmare had all begun just a matter of a few weeks earlier. The steel girders flashed past like a motorized camera shutter taking photos of the dark gray water swirling down below, and he thought of the children whose lives had been cut short when they were thrown to their deaths. Once again he felt the welling up of emotion as the sound of Alison's phone ringing clicked through to her recorded voice. Simply hearing her brought on yet another barely controllable wave, and when the tone ended he found that he could not speak the words he wanted to say. "Please call me. It's Michael," he said.

When the taxi pulled up outside St. Thomas' Hospital, Michael stepped out onto the pavement and fished in his pocket to pay the fare. He found he had only ten pounds left, which he handed to the driver through the open passenger window.

"That's all right, mate," said the taxi driver. "I've been listening to the radio while we've been driving. You're that bloke, ain't you? You've had a terrible time. Have this one on me."

"That's very good of you," said Michael, "really kind. Thanks very much."

"That's no problem. Think of the great 'you'll never guess who I had in the back of my cab' story I've got now. This one'll last me a lifetime." The cab drove away, leaving Michael standing alone on the pavement to contemplate his own notoriety.

He was about to enter the hospital when he realized that once inside the intensive care unit, he would have difficulty making or receiving any further phone calls. His anxiety about Alison was now rising quickly, and he could think of no explanation for why she had not picked up his call or responded to his message. He had hoped and expected that she would be as anxious to speak to him as he was to speak to her, and would be standing by for any news. It occurred to Michael that if anyone knew where she was, it was likely to be the police, and so, still standing on the pavement outside the hospital, he called directory inquiries and asked to be put through to Charing Cross police station. Eventually, after several delays and diversions, he was connected with the officer he was looking for.

"Hello, Sergeant Mallinson. It's Michael Beaumont. No doubt you've heard what's happened?"

Mallinson said that of course he had heard and was very pleased with the turn of events. "I'm sure you think we are all the same, but I reckon I've been in this game long enough to spot a mass murderer when I see one. Or if I can't, I certainly can spot someone who definitely isn't one." Immediately Michael felt ashamed about his "good cop, bad cop" suspicions and was about to say so, but Mallinson was still speaking. "I'm sorry about what you had to go through, but we were all just doing our jobs. So what can I do for you?"

"I was wondering whether you have any idea what has happened to my girlfriend, Alison? I know you were questioning her, and that she went to my home and brought in these clothes for me, but do you know where she went next? She's not answering her phone, and that's not like her."

There was a brief pause while Mallinson considered the question. "Maybe she's getting some sleep somewhere, Michael. She certainly looked all-in when I saw her late last night. Or maybe she's turned off her phone because every call she was getting was from some lowlife journalist." Michael was relieved to hear the suggestions, and he reckoned that both explanations were entirely plausible. He assumed that the conversation was coming to an end, when Mallinson spoke again. "There is just one thing, though, that you might like to know." The policeman waited for Michael to confirm that he would. "I shouldn't be telling you this, and it's something we would have followed up on if the case against you had continued, but with the turn of events we had no reason to pursue it." Michael was increasingly anxious to get inside the hospital to see his grandmother, but now his curiosity was soaring once again, and he felt impatient for the policeman to complete his story. "I'm not quite sure how best to put this, Michael, but Alison Parsons as such does not exist."

"What do you mean she doesn't exist?" For a moment

Michael wondered if Mallinson was cracking some ill-judged joke. "I know she exists. We've all met her. Do you mean she's an android?"

Mallinson laughed halfheartedly at what he in turn took to be a weak attempt at humor and continued, "No, Michael, I don't mean that she's an android. What I mean is that the person you know as Alison Parsons is real enough, it's just that whoever she is, she isn't Alison Parsons. Obviously there are plenty of people called Alison Parsons, but she isn't one of them. We were in the process of finding out her real name and who she actually is when the news came through that you are no longer a suspect, so we've been told not to waste any time on it."

Michael stopped the sergeant in midflow. "I don't get it. Why aren't the police trying to get to the bottom of who Alison really is?"

"Well, Michael, it's not really our business if someone wants to call herself something she's not, so long as she's not doing it for criminal purposes, and in this case there is no reason for us to believe that she is."

"So what you're saying is that Alison Parsons is not Alison Parsons, and you don't know who she is?" The policeman confirmed that that was what he was saying. "And you don't care either?"

"What I'm saying is that we have no reason to care unless she is doing something illegal, which we don't think she is. In fact I shouldn't be telling you this at all because it isn't really our business, but I just thought that in the light of what you've been through . . ."

Michael was on the point of telling Mallinson that only a few minutes ago he had been asked to think about who might want to cast suspicion on him for the Madman murders, and here they were having discovered that the person other than his grandmother who was closest to him was not who she said she was. In those few seconds, his mind raced over the way she had deceived him about her acquaintance with Joanna Potts, and the unexplained calls and text she had received when they were walking in Brighton. THERE'S NO POINT IN TRYING TO PROTECT HIM? Was that from Joanna? From someone else? And protect who from what? Michael had also been shocked to hear, less than an hour ago, of the discovery of a gray hoodie among the clothes at his apartment, when he knew for certain that he did not own one. Once again, his thoughts and feelings were equally divided between suspicion and trust, and he hated to feel that way. He breathed deeply and made a further effort to get ahold of himself. He knew that he needed to choose, because going on like this was no longer an option.

"Thank you for telling me that," he said to Mallinson, "I don't quite know what to make of the information, but I promise you that your confidence will be respected. I won't tell anyone else what you've told me."

"Well, we probably won't meet again, Michael," said Mallinson, "but perhaps you'll just remember that we all wear the same uniform, but not all of us are exactly the same."

Michael thanked him once again and turned towards the hospital, his thoughts speeding around his head at a hundred miles an hour.

SEVENTEEN

THE STEEL CROWD-CONTROL barriers were still in place on the pavement outside St. Thomas' as part of the police attempt to corral journalists and sightseers, but where just a few hours ago there had been a vast melee of the curious, now only a handful of hapless-looking photographers had stayed the course, waiting for whatever happened next. Their patience was rewarded when one of them spotted Michael as he finished his phone call to the police and turned to enter the hospital. With his thoughts now deep in other matters, Michael had not noticed the flurry of activity and he looked up to find five photographers walking backwards as he advanced, and now the motorized camera shutters were for real. He tried to walk around them, and then through them, but they kept retreating in front and alongside him like iron filings backing away from a magnet. Michael found himself wondering whether any of these were the same photographers who had stuck their cameras against the tinted windows of the police van on the way to the court as the crowds bayed for his blood. He shuddered at the memory, so vivid and recent. The photographers knew better than to try to follow him into the hospital, and they stopped at the main entrance when he went in.

Michael felt a sense of relief to be rid of the crowd, which was further deepened when the receptionist did not seem to recognize him as she pointed out the way towards the intensive care unit. He got into the lift and pressed the button to the second floor, and he thought again about his grandma and what she had been through in the last twenty-four hours. All he knew were the barest facts about what had happened, but he could imagine the horror she would have felt when she saw the news that her grandson had been arrested as the Madman. She had always been his one firm anchor, and now she was lying prostrate in an intensive care ward because of the shame and shock he had unwillingly brought upon her.

He arrived at the ICU and paused for a moment to collect himself before pushing open the heavy double doors. Michael breathed deeply. He wondered what he would find and felt a sense that a page was turning and that another chapter of his life was beginning. He tried to resist the thought. The male nurse who was on duty seemed to be expecting him.

"Hi," he said, "I think you're here to see Rose Beaumont, aren't you?" The young man extended his hand. "I'm Christopher, and I'm in charge of her care today." Michael shook the nurse's hand and was surprised to see a dense pattern of tattoos all up his forearm. The design seemed to involve a gathering of cherubs and angels, but the ink was indistinct. "The good news is that her condition is unchanged since she came in here yesterday; no better, but no worse either. She has been unconscious for most of the time, but her vital signs seem to be stable. I think she has come around a couple of times, but none of the staff was by her bedside at those moments."

Michael nodded. "How do you know she regained consciousness if no one was with her?"

"I think she said a few words to one of her visitors. I'm not sure now which one it was." Christopher looked down at his desk and moved some papers as he looked for the ones relating to Rose. "The woman from the care home"—he paused as he consulted his notes—"Esme, is it?"

"Oh, yes, of course I know Esme," said Michael, "but did you say 'one of her visitors'? I'm not sure who the other person could be. Rose and I don't have any other relatives."

Christopher frowned. "Oh, well, that's a mystery then. I was here when Esme first arrived but not when the other woman got here. Esme seems to have vouched for her. I hope there's no harm done. Actually I think they might not be far away. They may have just gone down to the canteen for some tea. Would you like to see your grandmother now?"

Michael said that he would and Christopher offered to lead the way. The two men walked slowly through the semidarkness towards a corner room, and Michael could make out the shape of a single bed surrounded by medical monitors, all of them bleeping and flashing. He felt a renewed wave of emotion welling up inside him as he realized once more how dependent he was on this frail and fragile old lady. She was entirely motionless and her skin looked pale and smooth. Instinctively he took her hand and immediately felt that it was cool to the touch. He looked at her face and was glad that she seemed to be in no pain or apparent distress. That at least was something. He could hear her shallow breathing, and now he saw the slight movement of the bedclothes. Her eyes flickered beneath her eyelids as though she was experiencing a vivid dream, and Michael wondered what thoughts might be filling his grandmother's subconscious mind. He felt a sense of dread. If only she could be made aware that he was here alongside her and that what must have been the worst nightmare of her life was over.

"Hello, Grandma." He put his lips close to the side of Rose's head and whispered, "It's me, Michael. I'm here beside you. We've all had a terrible time, but it's over and I am back with you. It's all been an awful mistake, but now it's all cleared up and I am here." Michael's voice thickened, and he had to swallow hard. He closed his eyes and gave her hand a further small squeeze. She showed no sign of response or understanding, and he sat in silence for a few more moments.

"I'll leave the two of you together." Michael had forgotten that Christopher was behind him and now turned to acknowledge his presence. The nurse's words were spoken softly and in a tone which offered instant comfort. "I'll be at the reception desk if you need me. Don't hesitate to ask for anything, and you can take as long as you like."

Fifteen minutes went by, during which Michael spoke several more times to his grandmother, sometimes repeating his whispered reassurance and at other times relating more mundane news. "Don't worry about anything, Grandma, I'll let them know at Greenacres that you're doing fine and hanging in there." Eventually he wondered about Esme and the other woman, and whether they might return from the canteen. He guessed that the second visitor must be the person he had seen in Rose's room and in the corridor at Greenacres and remembered once again that he had intended to make inquiries about her, but had been overtaken by events. Was it Rawlinson? Eileen Rawlinson, he thought Esme had said. Now, perhaps, he would find the answer to the mystery. He walked back to the reception desk and asked Christopher for directions.

The canteen was situated in the basement and was shared by staff and visitors. Michael took the lift down, and as soon as the doors opened the unmistakable smell of hospital food filled the air. He could hear the clanking sound of plates and trays as he approached. He stood at the double doors and looked around; it was a large area and there were perhaps a hundred people at tables spread around the room. The strong fluorescent lighting caused Michael to squint as his eyes adjusted, and after a few seconds he saw that Esme was sitting in a booth next to a far wall. On the other side of the booth, with her back to the door, Michael could see the outline of another woman. The two were engaged in conversation, and neither looked up as he walked towards them. Only when he was a few steps away did the movement catch Esme's eye. Her expression when she saw that it was Michael quickly went from joy to anxiety, but then a moment later was back to joy and relief. She got to her feet and threw her arms around him.

"Oh Michael, Michael, I am so glad to see you," she said, and he felt a surge of happiness to see her smiling face. He hugged her in return. "We've all been so worried, but thank the Lord you are safe now."

All the time Michael was aware of the other woman, who had remained seated. She had not moved nor spoken, and now he turned again towards Esme, as though expecting an introduction, and saw from her expression that she did not know quite how to proceed. After a few seconds Esme suggested that they should all sit down. She slid back into her side of the booth and gestured to the seat beside her. Michael sat, too, and was facing the other person, and in those few seconds he registered a face which was handsome but care-worn and more lined than merely her years would explain. She seemed to be about fifty, but wore no makeup, and dark shadows beneath her brown eyes hinted at a life lived hard. Only now was he able to be sure that he had seen her before — at Greenacres.

"I think it's time that I should introduce myself," said the woman, her voice carrying a tremor. She stretched out her right hand across the table and waited until Michael responded and held it in greeting. "My name," she said slowly, "is Margaret. Margaret Beaumont." There was a momentary pause before she spoke again, enough time for Michael's expression to flinch, as if in anticipation of a blow. "I am your mother."

Alison could not explain what had persuaded her to take her walk in Battersea Park. News that this was the location of the most recent incident involving the Madman meant that a large area next to the lake had been cordoned off, and in the distance she could see a line of about fifty uniformed officers standing side by side and walking forward slowly, examining the ground beneath their shuffling feet. No one had said anything on the news about the search for a weapon or for anything which might have been dropped during the incident, but Alison guessed that the police investigation was at a stage where they quite literally left no stone unturned. Neither of the children who had been attacked most recently had been seriously injured, and the news said they were expected to be released from hospital later that same day.

The radio and TV had also been playing and replaying the statement read out by Detective Superintendent Bailey from the steps of the police station indicating that Michael Beaumont was no longer a suspect and had been released from police custody. The TV people kept showing a picture of Michael which looked like a mug shot but which she recognized as his photo ID from the Hand-Cutz production house. Alison had never liked that picture of Michael when she had seen it on his identity card, and she liked it even less now that it was on the television. The only consolation, she thought, was that it looked so unlike him that he might soon be able to show his real face in public without fear of being recognized.

There had been a few recent days with unseasonably cold winds. Today was one of them, and Alison pulled up the collar of her jacket and continued to walk as close to the perimeter of the park as access permitted. Usually she loved the sunshine, but today she liked the fact that she could turn up her lapels and tuck her chin down into a turtleneck shirt. She was keen to be as inconspicuous as possible.

After completing a full circuit of the park, Alison eventually sat on a bench which had a vantage point over the water and dug her hands deep into her side pockets. She had been crying for most of the previous twenty hours, and now her eyes felt so dry that she wondered if she would ever be able to cry again. In the distance, walking along a path bordered with pink and yellow flowers and shrubs, she could see a mother and three small children toddling along around her. The woman also had a Labrador on a lead, and one of the children seemed to be issuing detailed instructions to the dog, which in turn was plodding on exactly as though nothing was being said or done to him. Alison felt a moment of envy and then even of anger, until she remembered that these people's lives were entirely average and normal, and it was hers which had been so far from average and so very far from normal.

Now she took out the photograph which she had been carrying with her since she had found it in the pocket of Michael's jacket the previous day. She looked again at the four silhouettes in the shot, and tried to remember the time it had been taken. She could not, but guessed it must have been around 1997 when she was eight and the two boys were aged just three and two. The baby must have been just a few months old, and only weeks away from the tragedy which would affect all of their lives forever.

———————

Michael was running. He ran and he ran at the limit of his speed and ability, and he ran until the pain in his chest made him feel that it would explode. He stopped and bent double at the side of the pavement, and now he was gasping for breath and retching, in imminent danger of throwing up in the gutter.

The scale of the revelation on its own was so immense that even against the background of a normal day it would have been difficult to take in. Coming as it had, hard on the heels of his arrest and then sudden and unexpected release, the turn of events propelled an already extreme situation into a level of trauma which was difficult to absorb. He would never be able to explain how he managed to retain his sanity.

It had not been his intention to leap to his feet and dash out of the hospital canteen. Nor did he have a moment to think about the need to get out of the hospital building, into the air, and to fill his lungs. He made no conscious decision to turn on his heels and sprint along the pavement, and he was scarcely aware of the screech of brakes and the shouting from a cab-driver who had to swerve hard to avoid him as he raced across the south side of Westminster Bridge.

His involuntary reaction had hardly given Michael time to take in the expressions on the faces of the two women left sitting at the table in the hospital canteen, nor did either have time to react to his sudden movement. Nothing he did in those few minutes was the product of logic or process; he simply knew that he had to get out of there or lose whatever mental stability he was still clinging to.

After standing for a full minute on the edge of the pavement, Michael became aware of the looks of concern on the faces of passersby, and now he thought that two younger men who had been walking along the other side of the road had worked out who he was. Out of the corner of his eye Michael could see that one of them was punching numbers into his phone, and it occurred to him that in a moment he would be surrounded by journalists. The thought was quickly reinforced as he saw that the other man was using his phone to take pictures of him. Michael forced himself to stand straight, and he turned his back on the two men and walked away as briskly as his legs would oblige, back in the direction of the hospital.

There was no sign of Esme when he reentered the hospital canteen, but Margaret Beaumont was still there. For a minute Michael stood silently and looked at the woman who had walked out of his life eighteen years earlier and never, to his knowledge, tried to see him since. She still had her back to the main door and remained unaware that he had returned. Michael wondered what she must be thinking, and immediately he realized that he could have absolutely no idea about anything she was thinking: she was his mother, but he knew almost nothing about her. Among his surprises was that she had introduced herself by the name which was unfamiliar to him. If he knew this woman in any way at all, it was as Eileen Rawlinson, the mystery woman who had visited his grandmother in Greenacres.

Michael felt angry, but his anger was mixed with a deep sadness. Right at this moment, though, all of his other emotions felt secondary to an irresistible curiosity. Within a few minutes he was back inside the hospital canteen, and the woman who had walked out of his life eighteen years ago was turning to greet him.

———————

"I've spent hundreds of hours wondering how I'd start this conversation if ever the time came when I could have it." Michael and his mother had moved to a booth in a far corner of the canteen. They had paused long enough to buy fresh tea and to try to steady their nerves, and now they were once again sitting, each trying to find a way to cope with the overwhelming intensity of their feelings. "I don't think I ever found an answer, so all I can do is to start at the beginning. But before I do, I just need to say that you will find what I have to tell you very painful and difficult to deal with. My only wish is that when you are eventually able to think about it, you might come to understand why your grandmother and I did what we did — which was to make it our number one priority in life to shield you from the memory of it all."

———————

*There had been nothing unusual about the courtship and early re-
lationship between Henry Bannerman and Margaret Williams which
might give an indication of the tragedies which would eventually befall
them. The couple met when he was twenty-three and she was nine-
teen and had fallen in love. Henry had gotten along well enough with
Margaret's parents. He was a mechanic in a local light-engineering
works which made parts for the motor industry, and Margaret's father,
George, was a school inspector but loved to tinker with classic cars in
the garage at the side of their house in Hove. Margaret's mother, Rose,
also liked Henry from quite early on.*

*Henry and Margaret were married in 1990, and both were keen to
start a family, but for several years nothing happened and they began
to think that perhaps parenthood would not be for them. Eventually,
though, they had three children: two boys just a year apart and then a
daughter.*

*For a while everything in their lives seemed happy. There were
occasional incidents where the two small boys seemed jealous of the attention paid to their new baby sister, but nothing about them seemed
untoward or out of the ordinary.*

*Then, out of the blue, Henry fell in love with a secretary at the en-
gineering firm and went away with her, leaving Margaret with three
young children to bring up on her own. Deserted and impoverished, she
had no choice but to move in with her parents, and for a few months
the grandparents, their daughter, and the children lived together in
the cramped town house in Hove. Her new situation threw Margaret
into a depression. Her parents rallied round to give what support they
could, and Margaret also welcomed the occasional break provided by
the daughter of next-door neighbors. Elizabeth was only eight years
old but, like many girls of her age, she was very fond of playing "house,"
so she was glad to stage make-believe tea parties which entertained the
two toddlers, giving some brief respite to their mother.*

One weekend, Rose suggested that Margaret should take a break from her responsibilities and the children and go away for a few days. She and George were perfectly happy to take care of their grandchildren, and Elizabeth from next door could always lend a hand in helping to distract them. Elizabeth's mum and dad were only too pleased to allow her to help out.

Rose had a few errands to run on the Saturday morning, but Grandpa George adored the kids and was perfectly able to cope with all of them for a few hours until she returned. He was restoring an old Morris Countryman, and an engine part he had been on the lookout for had just been delivered, and he was keen to get on with installing it. Three times that morning he had interrupted his work in the garage to go into the house to stand at the foot of the stairs to make sure the children were still playing nicely. On the last occasion he could hear Elizabeth asking the two brothers whether they wanted cake with their tea, and he smiled at the thought that one day the eight-year-old would make a wonderful mother.

Rose was cross when she returned from the shops and found George occupied in the garage when she thought he should have been keeping a closer eye on the children. He assured her that they had been playing together quite happily, and so she put on the kettle before going upstairs to check whether they wanted anything to eat or drink. Elizabeth had helped Rose to make butterfly cakes the evening before, and they were looking forward to tasting them this morning.

At first Rose could hear no sound as she started up the stairs, and she wondered whether the children had sneaked into the bedroom she shared with her husband. She used to allow Elizabeth to dress up in the old clothes that she kept in a trunk at the end of her bed, but the child had been told not to play in Rose's bedroom when Grandma wasn't present. Now Rose suspected that the silence was a sign that some mis-

chief was afoot, and there was a smile in her voice as she called out Elizabeth's name.

There was no sign of any of the children in the bedroom they had been sleeping in, but still Rose felt only slight anxiety. She was never completely happy when she saw Elizabeth lifting the boys and the baby around, but she seemed to be capable and gentle enough for it not to be a problem. When she walked into her bedroom and found Elizabeth and Michael sitting next to the dressing-up box, her concern suddenly increased.

"Where are Martin and the baby?"

"I don't know, Mrs. Williams," said Elizabeth. "They were playing with the water, and Martin was going to give Amy a bath."

Less than a minute later, Rose started to scream.

It was only at the inquest that the evidence of the family, the police, and the pathologist, all taken together, enabled the coroner to piece together the likely sequence of events. Elizabeth, it was stated, must have lifted the baby into the bath but had then gone to play with Michael, leaving Martin to take care of his little sister. The pathologist's evidence was that someone had held Amy under the water until she drowned, and that since Elizabeth and Michael had been playing together in the bedroom at the time, the person responsible could only have been Martin.

The inquest was adjourned for several weeks to allow a child psychologist to prepare reports on all of the three surviving children. She concluded that Michael was simply too young to have been left alone anywhere near the baby, but that whatever role he might have played, he could not be responsible for anything that had taken place. Though Elizabeth was older and perhaps might have been expected to know better, she, too, was declared to have had no malicious intentions towards Amy, and her involvement was accidental. The psychologist's report on Martin, however, concluded that he was a child with no sense of right and wrong, who had become jealous of the attention being given to his newborn baby sister. She believed that Martin had been aware of the likely outcome of what he was doing.

The court case provided newspapers with their lead stories for days on end. Though none of the children could be identified by name, they were widely labeled in mile-high headlines as "unnatural," "evil," and "baby killers." Every columnist in every publication opined on every aspect of the story from the responsibility of the parents to the age of criminal culpability.

No similar restriction of anonymity applied to the children's grandfather, and when asked by journalists outside of the inquest whether he felt responsible for the death of his granddaughter, George replied with an unequivocal yes. If he had felt any doubt about his own guilt, the tabloid newspapers left little room for debate; his picture was splashed over every front page.

For Elizabeth's parents, the stress proved too much to bear. After three weeks of lurid headlines, they abandoned the girl dubbed by one newspaper as their "devil-daughter" into the care of the local authority, where she grew up and never saw her mother and father again. Martin was sent to a secure unit for children for an indefinite period until he was determined not to be a danger to others.

Two days after the verdict, Rose, Margaret, and George went for a walk to try to clear their heads. George said he felt unwell and went back to the house, closed the doors of the garage, turned on the newly restored engine of the Morris 1000, and asphyxiated himself.

Once, when he was a small child, Michael had been playing a game with friends in the school playground. Alongside the playground was a football pitch where a group of older boys were playing a match. One of the bigger boys had kicked the leather ball high in the air and, without any warning, it had hit Michael hard on the side of his head. The explosion caused a bright light to flash and an immediate screaming sound in his eardrums, and when he had come to in the headmaster's study, he felt as though his brain had been loosened and was rattling around within his skull. That, as nearly as he could have described it, was how Michael felt now. These astonishing revelations all but knocked him sideways. When, after a few moments, his head cleared just a little, he looked up to see that his mother was still speaking.

"One minute I had been a wife, daughter, and mother; the next minute my husband had left me, my father had committed suicide, my baby had drowned, and my elder son had been held responsible." Margaret had been telling the story for twenty minutes, almost as if on autopilot, having turned over these events in an almost constant stream for much of the past eighteen years. "The only people I had left in the world were you and Rose, and so she and I decided that the best thing we could do was to try to find a way for you to start a new life, and to do whatever we could to erase every aspect of those terrible events from anywhere in your memory."

And that, Michael's mother now continued, was what she and Rose had determined to do. They had gone through all the formalities of changing their names, they moved from the south coast to Kingston in west London, and began a new life in a place where no one knew them. All their family documents were replaced with new ones bearing their adopted names, and the idea was to try to start afresh. That had been the plan, except that what she had not reckoned on was that she found herself unable to cope with the enormity of everything that had happened, and gradually she had resorted to drugs and alcohol. Eventually incapacitated and in a state of constant torment, she left the family home, wandering for many years all over Britain and Europe. She had lived in squats and communes and become involved with a number of unsuitable men.

"But then finally, just about a year ago, I managed to clean up my act and eventually had sufficiently come to my senses to reestablish contact with Rose. I came to see her, and she was happy to know that I was safe, but by that time her only concern was for you and your well-being. She said that you had apparently no memory whatsoever of the things I have described and insisted that the worst thing that could happen was for me to come back in your life and raise a lot of questions in your mind. I took her at her word and got myself a rented place not far away in Wimbledon, and from that day to this I have kept in touch with her from a distance, just close enough to ensure that you were all right, but I would never go anyplace where there was a chance that I might bump in to you. Except that I did exactly that, by accident, a few weeks ago at Greenacres."

Michael sat quietly on the cushioned bench seat with his back against the wall and watched the staff and patients perambulating backwards and forwards with their trays of tea and coffee. The mix of cooking smells filling the air was dominated by the odor of frying bacon, and the familiar clatter of plates and cutlery seemed strangely reassuring. At one moment, it seemed as though the extraordinary story he had just been told offered a resolution to all the unanswered questions which had provided the background of his life so far. At another, the sheer horror of this personal history felt so violent and wretched that he could scarcely find a way to begin to address it. And all the time, fleeting fragments of single images stole out of the depths of his recall and vied for ascendancy in the forefront of his consciousness. Suddenly he had a vision of a tiny baby cooing and gurgling on a plastic mat. The image was instantly replaced by the sound and smell of an old man leaning into the engine compartment of a dilapidated car. Then both were whisked away as he recalled a vivid memory of throwing his tiny arms as tightly as he knew how around the body of another human of about the same size and shape as himself, and clinging for dear life as four strong men pulled at each of his limbs and dragged his brother away. The screams of terror and pain echoed down the corridor and through time and space until they filled Michael's brain up to and beyond its capacity and right to this moment.

Slowly his head began to clear, and Michael focused once again on Margaret. She was gazing back at him and contemplating for the ten-thousandth time all the important moments between mother and child which had never been. The bruised knees and the hurt pride, the days out and the first day at school, the first girlfriend and the graduation ball. She had missed all the milestones of his life, and now she sat opposite her son, confronting her loss. Michael stretched out across the table and closed his hands around hers.

"So what happened that led to us so close to meeting at the care home?" Michael felt that he had a hundred questions to ask, but before he did so, he wanted to come up-to-date with recent events.

"Rose told me a while ago about the plan you and she had made for her to move to Greenacres. I had been to visit her a few times when I knew you would not be there. I used to sign in using the name Rawlinson, Eileen Rawlinson. It was the name of my first teacher at primary school, but heaven knows why I chose it. Luckily nobody bothered to check. Sometimes Rose was like her old self, and sometimes she seemed to be in terrible distress and was unrecognizable. But she and I were beginning to get used to each other, and I think she was starting to forgive me. Then one day I got a message from her to say that she needed to see me urgently. Something had happened that had upset her very badly, which she said she needed to talk to me about, but I had no idea what it was. I assumed it can only have been something to do with you. When I got to the hospital, I got the shock of my life when I nearly bumped into you in Rose's bedroom, and then events took over and I never did find out what it was that she needed to tell me."

Michael remembered that day at Greenacres and thought how extraordinary it is that a person could literally bump into his own mother but have no clue of any relationship. So strange that two people who had once been part of the same being could later meet up but experience no feeling of recognition.

At this moment, however, the only thing he could be sure of was that he was incapable of any considered or even coherent response, and that above all else he needed some space to take in what he had heard. At the same time he had an inkling of the appalling emotional trauma which his mother must have gone through in relating her story and felt a need to try to give her whatever reassurance he could. He did not know what he was going to say next until he found the words forming in his mouth.

"I'm sure I will never begin to understand what you've been through. I'm also sure you'll understand that this is an extraordinary story for me to try to get my head around. I've got so many things to think about." As he spoke, Michael gently shook his head, a mix of incredulity and denial. "But meanwhile, you obviously know what's been happening to me in the last few days with the police and this false arrest, and what you've told me has triggered a train of thought in my mind which I have to work through before I decide what I need to do next. So I need some time to myself. I guess you can see that?"

Tears were streaming down his mother's face. "Of course I understand," she said, "and I wonder if you can understand how terrified I have been of this meeting. You're entitled to be angry with me for having walked out on you, and I wouldn't blame you if you don't want to see me again. But what you've said confirms what Rose has told me about you—that you are a young man with a big heart, and I can see for myself that you are a credit to what she has done for you."

Once again Michael found himself in danger of being completely overwhelmed and felt the need to get away before the breakdown which was threatening overtook him. He squeezed his mother's hands and walked out of the hospital and into the street, where he stood on the pavement for a moment, wondering in which direction to walk. The swarm of extraneous thoughts and ideas crowding into his head seemed likely to swamp his ability to process them, and he needed space to try to find some access point into his new reality. He was just about to turn away when he heard someone calling his name and looked up to see that Esme was heading quickly towards him.

"Is it Rose? Has something happened?" Michael's first assumption when he saw her was that his grandmother had taken a turn for the worse and there was some kind of emergency. Unable immediately to regain sufficient breath to speak, Esme simply shook her head by way of reassurance.

"No, it's nothing like that," she said eventually, still trying to catch her breath. "Can we sit? I know that your head must be spinning, but there is something more that I need to talk to you about." Still in turmoil from the story he had just heard from his mother, Michael wondered how on earth he would be able to deal with anything more right now. In the half hour or so since he had heard her account of things, his mind had been racing, but if there was more to know, then he felt glad that it was from Esme that he was going to hear it.

After she had regained herself sufficiently, they walked for a few hundred yards until they reached a bench on the riverside between Lambeth Bridge and the hospital. Both of them stood for a moment and looked out upon the water, which today seemed to sparkle in the sunlight.

"I guess you've now heard from Margaret the story of what happened when you were a baby?"

Michael nodded. "How long have you known yourself?"

"Only just a very few days," said Esme. "One day, when she was doing well and in a good frame of mind, I asked Rose what was troubling her, and she ended up telling me the whole thing. But she swore me to secrecy and insisted that I should never tell a soul unless she gave me permission."

Esme looked as though she was getting ready to tell the rest of what she knew but perhaps had been rehearsing it all and felt the need to follow the narrative she had been forming in her mind. They sat together on the bench, and she reached across and took Michael's hand. "You already know your grandmother is an extraordinary woman. When you think of what she went through on her own account—losing her grandchild in those circumstances, and then her husband. And then to decide to spend the rest of her days taking care of you, and having to change her own name and every aspect of her life—just so that you could be protected as much as possible."

Michael turned to face Esme full on and smiled. "Thank you, Esme, but I promise you that whatever else I am in doubt about, I don't need to be persuaded of any of that."

Esme was happy to hear it. If she had any concerns that Michael would be angry at everyone for having kept all these secrets, she now felt comforted. After a few moments she went on.

"But, Michael, in view of what you've had to deal with in the last few days, I don't even know how to start what I have to say. I've agonized over it, because when she told me the full story, Rose swore me to secrecy; but in view of what's now happening, I've decided that you need to know." She paused, waiting for this new thought to sink in. "It's the reason why Rose called Margaret into the hospital urgently. She wanted to tell her something that she had realized for herself only in the previous few days; something she didn't know how to handle. But by the time Margaret got to her, Rose was beyond being able to communicate, and so she was never able to tell her daughter that one of their worst fears had come to pass."

Michael tried to brace himself for whatever new horror Esme was about to impart to him. "And what was that?"

"That the girl who was in part to blame for Amy's drowning, and who everyone thought had gone away for good, has turned up."

"She has?" asked Michael. "I realize that I didn't ask what happened to her after she left wherever it was she went to. That must have been years ago."

"Rose had heard that she had changed her name and probably left the country to start a new life where nobody knew her history. Everyone assumed that we would never hear from her again, but then a few weeks ago she just arrived unexpectedly at Greenacres."

"She did?" Michael had thought he was past the stage where he could be amazed. "How come? How did she track Rose down?"

"She didn't. When she came to Greenacres she didn't know who Rose was. She came to visit her. With you. Her original name as a child was Elizabeth, but she changed it when she left child custody. The girl who lived next door to you as a child, and was there on the day your baby sister died, is your girlfriend, Alison."

EIGHTEEN

LESS THAN HALF a mile away, on a bench close to Horse Guards Parade, Alison sat and contemplated the faded and blurred photograph she had picked out of Michael's jacket pocket on the previous afternoon. She had been unable to sleep even a moment since her discovery, and every minute of every hour since then had been spent in a state of the most excruciating torment. Now she felt completely exhausted by the stress of it all.

She reflected upon all of the effort she had gone to after leaving the children's home at age eighteen to put her old life behind her and to begin completely afresh. She had been determined for many years to explore the possibility of leaving Britain altogether, to try to begin a new life in another country. She shared her hopes with the authorities, and it was agreed that her best chance of retaining anonymity was for her to emigrate. She was so excited and relieved when an agreement was reached with the Australian authorities that she could go there, and as part of the process she had changed her name from Elizabeth to Alison and taken a new surname.

Over the years there were a regular stream of inquiries from the press and media about the likely timing of Elizabeth's return back into society, and so the Home Office agreed that no announcement should be made and that she should be assisted to go more or less directly from the institution to the airport.

During her years working as a tour guide in Sydney, she began to feel for the first time that there was a possibility that she might put some distance, in time and space, from all the dreadful memories which had been the background to her life so far. No one there had heard of the appalling tragedy which happened a decade earlier, and she was able to invent a whole new past; a past which, from constant repetition and elaboration, she could easily come to believe in herself. When she told people she met for the first time about the terrible car accident which had killed her parents when she was a small child, the looks of sympathy seemed so much easier to deal with than the dark suspicions which had always accompanied her before she left England. So real did her newly invented history become, and so solid did her made-up identity feel, that eventually it seemed to her to be entirely possible that she could move back to England in the persona of the woman she had created.

When the authorities informed her that what was left of the original Bannerman family had changed their names and moved to another part of the country, and that the elder brother Martin was still being kept in a secure unit with no imminent prospect of release, she felt it was worth the risk of returning to the town she had known as a child. She moved back to Brighton, managed to get an apartment and a job in the travel agency, and effectively reinvented herself once again. Alison Parsons had made a few good friends among the young women at work but had not found any boyfriends until she caught the eye of a good-looking young man across a noisy and crowded bar. The attraction had been powerful and instant, and nothing could have given her even the smallest indication of the extraordinary events which were shortly to unfold.

The empathy she had immediately felt with another person who had also lost his parents at a young age had reinforced the bond between them, but now she marveled that the coincidence had not disturbed her until she discovered the photograph, and the pieces all tumbled into place. Only then did she put together the reason that his grandmother had reacted as she had on her first visit to Greenacres, and everything else up to the point where Michael had been mistaken for the Madman. The realization of her shared history with the man she had fallen in love with hit her with the force of a juggernaut, and now she was sitting on a public bench in the center of London, with absolutely no idea what on earth she should do next.

The only moment of even small relief she had experienced in the last day and a half was when she heard the news that Michael had been released from police custody. Hours later she saw his call coming in on her cell phone but had not yet been able to find it within herself to reply, simply because she did not have the first idea of what she could possibly say.

Alison put away the photograph and set off for the short walk towards the meeting which she had arranged by telephone on the previous evening. A few minutes later she could see through the window of the Starbucks on Trafalgar Square that Joanna had arrived ahead of her and was sitting on a stool and slowly turning a spoon through the foam on the top of her coffee. There were only a handful of other people in the place, and so after she had ordered her drink, Alison gestured to a table in the corner where there was a better chance of keeping their conversation private. The two women sat opposite each other for a moment, as though sizing up the enemy before battle. Recent years seemed to have been more kind to Joanna than those she experienced at the children's home, but still Alison thought that she had the look of someone whose life was a battle against adversity. Her bleached hair was showing half an inch of dark roots, and her makeup seemed designed to terrify. Eventually it was Joanna who spoke first.

"So have you told the police yet?"

"Have I told them what?"

Joanna looked at Alison with an expression which suggested that she knew the answer to her own question. "Have you told them that you know the name and identity of someone who answers the description of the Madman and who has a proven liking for drowning tiny children?"

Alison knew that she had made many mistakes in her life, but now she understood that one of the greatest of them had been to confide in a person she had once considered a friend her belief that Martin Bannerman had deliberately murdered his baby sister. When Alison had first been placed into care, aged only eight years, the circumstances which had sent her there were nationally notorious. Everyone was curious to meet the girl whom the press had dubbed an evil monster. She had not been named in court, but of course it was impossible to keep these things a secret. She had resolved from the beginning not to discuss her memories or experience with anyone, and it was only to Joanna that she confided her suspicion that Martin had known exactly what he was doing; that all along he had intended to murder the baby.

"No, I haven't. First, because I have not seen or heard from him since he was three years old, and so I would have no way to know whether or not he resembles the descriptions of the Madman. Second, we don't know for certain that he killed his baby sister because it might well have been an accident. Third, I have absolutely no idea where he is—for all I know he may still be in custody. And last, I don't believe for one moment that Martin is the person who has been taking every possible opportunity to throw tiny children to their deaths."

Alison had no clue about where the look of malevolence on Joanna's face came from or why it should be there. While the two girls had not gone their separate ways as friends, they had not been enemies either. Nonetheless, when Joanna spoke again her words were full of poison.

"Look, Lizzie," she said, "I asked you nicely to warn the police, and then I asked you a bit less nicely, and when I sent you those texts, it was just because I worked out, like you must have done, that you know who the Madman really is. What I didn't know then, but can work out just like you can, is the reason why the Madman is the spitting image of your new boyfriend. He must be his brother, which is partly why dear Michael was arrested. So the fact that Martin looks like Michael, and has a nasty habit of drowning babies, sort of gives you the complete answer."

Alison felt a repeat of the same shudder she had experienced when she had first looked at the photograph from Michael's pocket, but this time it transitioned into a wave of anger which was reflected in the tone and volume of her reply. "What the hell are you talking about, you dozy bitch?"

The environment they had shared as children guaranteed that neither of them was easily intimidated, and now Joanna leaned across the table, her face almost touching Alison's, and spat out her reply.

"Because, you stupid fucking cow, I can work it out. Just as you must have worked it out. If it was Martin who has been doing these killings, and your Michael has been arrested, chances are that Michael must be the spitting image of Martin. Or to put it even more simply for you"—and now Joanna's voice rose another few decibels and was attracting the attention of their neighbors at other tables—"either Martin is the killer, and for some reason you aren't grassing him up. Or it really is your boyfriend, Michael, and you and Martin are covering up for him." Her short speech ended with a snarl. "Geddit?"

Everyone in the coffee shop turned as the collection of cups and saucers and plates and condiments hit the floor with a clatter, and the noise of the crash bounced around the sharp corners of the walls and ceiling. At first no one seemed inclined to intervene as the two young women grabbed at each other's hair and fell, struggling and scratching, onto the hard tiles. Three or four young helpers who had come to London from various parts of Eastern Europe ran back and forth in panic, and a full thirty seconds passed before the most senior of them reached down and grabbed Joanna by the collar of her jacket and dragged her backwards. By now both girls' faces were a mass of cuts and scrapes, but Alison was still screaming to be allowed access to her enemy.

"She knows who the Madman is," Joanna was shouting. "She knows and hasn't told the police."

"I don't know anything of the kind, you stupid bitch." But now every survival instinct that Alison had learned through her years in the children's home kicked in, and all she wanted to do was to retreat. She scrambled to her feet and steadied herself on the edge of the table, turning towards the man who had been restraining her and shaking herself free. "Sorry about the mess."

NINETEEN

MICHAEL GRADUALLY BECAME aware of the sound of a bell ringing. At first he thought it was coming from inside his head, but then it seemed to have been going on forever, and he realized that he was in his apartment and it was the telephone next to his grandmother's bed. The sound was joined up to such an extent that there was no way to detect whether the same person was calling repeatedly, or there was a queue of people trying to contact him, one after another, in a way which had the effect of an unbroken series. From time to time he reached across from where he lay and lifted the handset an inch from the cradle and replaced it. The ringing would stop for perhaps ten seconds, only to begin afresh. Eventually he reached over and pulled the connecting wire from the socket in the wall.

The only people who had the landline number, to his knowledge, were the management at Hand-Cutz, and Michael presumed that whoever had sold his identity and details to the press had also revealed the phone number at the apartment. He had little doubt that the calls would be from journalists, and he was equally certain that he had nothing to say.

Michael did not know how long he had been lying in his grandmother's room. The sky had turned from blue to urban yellow, and the shadows cast upon the walls were tinted from the light of streetlamps. He could hear in the background the continuous hum of distant traffic, and the only other discernible sound was the ticking of a pendulum clock, which he had wound up every week for as long as he could remember.

Just as his mind floated over any one aspect of what he had learned in recent hours, some other aspect appeared to be more urgent and fought for precedence. At first he thought that the vital priority was to consider what now seemed to be the unavoidable answer to the mystery of the identical voiceprint and mistaken identity. But then, nothing was more demanding than the fact that the woman he had fallen in love with had in some way been partly responsible for the death of his baby sister. The information was too shocking and fresh for him to begin to come to terms with everything it meant, but at the very least, it felt impossible that Alison could ever again be his lover. He had left several messages on her phone but was almost relieved when she did not pick up.

Eventually it was clear to Michael that the most important thing he needed to focus on was the revelation that he had a brother who was just a year older than he was. The experts had said that only one in a million other people might have a voiceprint which matched his so exactly, but they had not commented on the likelihood of a match between siblings. Add to that the mystery of how Michael had managed to appear in the video taken in Brighton that Sunday afternoon, but wearing clothes he knew he had not been wearing, and circumstances seemed to be pulling inexorably towards only one conclusion. If he added the further revelation that his brother had originally been taken away from their family because of his involvement in drowning a small child, there appeared to be little further room for doubt. He had been asked by the police to consider whether there might be anyone out there who hated him enough to wish to implicate him in the most appalling crimes of his lifetime, and now his brain was splitting itself in two as part of it was pulled towards an unavoidable conclusion, and an equal and opposite part of it was attempting to resist.

What, though, was he to do with this information? The first and most obvious thing must be to take it to the police: to tell them everything he had learned in the last few hours and leave it to them to find and arrest his older brother. However, there did seem to be an alternative, which might be to do nothing with the authorities for the moment, but to locate and track down his brother to satisfy himself as to whether or not he was the person the police were looking for. A third possibility was, of course, that he could pull a blanket over his head, sleep for a thousand years, and hope that if and when he woke up the nightmare might be over. At that moment the third alternative seemed by far the most attractive.

Michael must have fallen asleep because the next thing he knew he was still lying, fully clothed, on top of the covers on his grandmother's bed but was feeling cold and shivery. The streetlamps outside had been switched off, and the room was too dark for him to be able to make out the time by the clock; only the sound of its apparently perpetual ticking reminded him of where he was. He pulled up the duvet and slid under it, still fully clothed.

His thoughts turned back to Alison and that most important of life's lessons he had learned from his grandmother: always to do his best to put himself in the shoes of the other person. Try as he might, however, he could not find a way into what must have been going on inside the head of his lover all this time. There were so many unanswered questions. Still he did not know what her true role had been in the death of his baby sister. He knew little or nothing of her real experience when she had been taken into care. Nor did he know for sure whether or not she had any idea of his own identity when they had first met. He thought once again about the overheard telephone conversation in the apartment in Brighton, the mysterious text she had received when they were walking on the cliff top. Who could the text have been from? THERE'S NO POINT IN TRYING TO PROTECT HIM. Who had she been trying to protect? Himself? Someone else? The killer? Now he again considered the gray hoodie which had appeared in his apartment at the time she had gone there to collect clothes for his court appearance. Surely she couldn't have been involved in framing him. Michael cast his mind back once again to that first time he had taken Alison to Greenacres and Rose's dreadful reaction upon seeing her.

Then he remembered what Alison had said in the car after they drove away from Greenacres on the day of the first Madman killings. About how the witnesses had simply been unlucky to be in a certain place at a certain time and had unwillingly become a party to an event which would haunt the rest of their lives. From that perspective, Alison was as much a victim of circumstance as he was, and it was only by sheer chance of the calendar and their relative ages that he had not found himself in exactly the situation in which she found herself. "There but for the grace of God," he whispered, but there was no one there to hear him.

There were so many questions and so few answers, but whatever they would turn out to be, Michael desperately wanted to believe that Alison had loved him, and from the bottom of his heart he hoped against hope that the generous interpretation he so badly wanted to put on all of her actions would turn out to be justified.

Now, though, the woman who had sacrificed her life for him was lying in a hospital ward ten miles away, stricken by yet another tragedy which had befallen their family. Of course she was eighty-five and already seriously ill, but Michael had no doubt that the shock of hearing that her grandson had been arrested for murder had pushed her over the edge. Even with all the anxieties and concerns which had arisen from the many revelations he had been given in the last hours, it remained his greatest wish that his grandmother would regain consciousness for long enough to hear and understand that he, Michael, was not guilty of anything; that he remained the devoted and loving grandson she had brought him up to be. If he could be granted that and only that, he thought, he would ask for nothing else.

Michael's telephone call to the police incident room was answered by a junior officer who sounded as though she had been working for longer hours than might have been wise. When Michael gave his name, however, he immediately got her full attention. He had been the only suspect seriously under consideration for the Madman murders, and so was well known to the hundreds of officers of all ranks who were allocated to the inquiry. When he asked to speak to Detective Chief Superintendent Norman Bailey, he was asked to hold, but he waited for less than a minute before the voice he recognized came on the line.

"Yes, Michael?" he said. "How can I help you?"

"Actually, I'm calling because I may be able to help you. I think it's possible that the man you are looking for is my older brother. His name is Martin."

Ninety minutes later the senior detective and his assistant, Detective Constable Georgia Collins, were sitting across from Michael at the kitchen table in Rose's apartment. He and Collins had set off straightaway after Michael's phone call, but had asked DC Squires to use the time while they were on their way to find out everything they could about his older brother, Martin. Now Bailey was speaking on the phone to Squires and told the junior officer that he was about to put the call onto the speaker so that all of them could hear it. He placed his cell phone on the table between the three of them.

"The name of the person we are interested in is Martin Bannerman. That was the family name before it was changed by Michael's grandmother to Beaumont. Martin, of course, kept his original surname while in detention, and we think that that's what he is probably known as now."

"And where do we think he is?" asked Bailey.

"He was transferred from Feltham into the normal system three years ago when he reached the age of eighteen," said Squires. "His conduct while inside doesn't show anything out of the ordinary. They do vocational training there, and in fact the only thing it does show of any note is that he had an aptitude as a sound engineer. Interesting coincidence that he has the same talent as his brother. He seems to have become something of an expert. Feltham thinks they still have some tapes somewhere of him speaking, so they're sending them over."

"Did no one there think to check any voice recordings when we put out our appeal?" asked Collins.

"Apparently they have quite a few voice recordings in the files and were planning to start going through them on Monday," said Squires. The two detectives sitting at the kitchen table both looked at the ceiling and shook their heads as Squires continued.

"It seems that Martin was released on life license four months ago."

"What does 'life license' mean?" asked Michael.

"It means that technically he is still serving his sentence," said Collins, "but he's doing so in the community and could be recalled back into custody at any time."

"Yes," said Squires, "and theoretically he's supposed to report to a probation officer. It seems that he did so regularly for the first few weeks but has disappeared off the radar these last two months."

"And nobody in the system thought to draw this to our attention?" Bailey banged the flat of his hand down on the table. "A bloke of the right age, who was originally put away for drowning his baby sister, and who likes to record his own voice. What were we waiting for, a signed confession?" No one had any answers that they wanted to share. "OK," said Bailey. "That's it. Let's get an up-to-date picture from the records and circulate his photo and description to the papers and media."

"Just wait a minute," said Michael. "You are about to put out a mug shot of me! Martin is just a year older than me, but we already know that he may as well be my twin. I've just been through hell on earth by having my name and photo splashed all over the world's press and media." He was close to losing control, and his voice cracked with emotion. "My grandmother has quite literally had a stroke as a result of it and is clinging to life in the intensive care unit of St. Thomas' Hospital. And now you're about to publish a photo which looks exactly like—guess who?"

"I'm sorry, Michael. Obviously I see the point you're making, and I sympathize, but what choice do we have? This precious brother of yours is killing little children. At random. Whenever and wherever he likes. Knowing who he is and what he looks like but not doing whatever we can to apprehend him as soon as possible is not an option."

"So once again the world will think it's me you're looking for? Wherever I go, I am well and truly fucked."

For several moments no one in the kitchen spoke, and after a silence lasting a full twenty seconds, the next words came from the disembodied voice of DC Squires.

"Can I suggest something?"

Two hours later Michael was again sitting between Bailey and Collins, but this time they were all facing outwards into a phalanx of perhaps a hundred journalists and photographers at a hastily called press conference at New Scotland Yard. Word had spread that the young man who had been arrested earlier as a suspect would be appearing with the police who arrested him, and what would anyway have been a scramble for the best positions turned into a frenzy. The flash of cameras and whir of motorized lenses threatened to make Michael dizzy, and after five minutes of mayhem Chief Superintendent Bailey called the meeting to order.

"Michael Beaumont has kindly agreed to join us here today because we have reached what we believe is a crucial breakthrough in our investigation as a result of his assistance. I want to make as clear as I possibly can that Mr. Beaumont is not a suspect in our inquiries. We have been dealing with a case of mistaken identity and some other confusion, which we have now cleared up, and I am happy to confirm once again that Michael Beaumont is completely innocent of the crimes we have been investigating and has nothing directly to do with them. However"—Bailey paused, and for a moment it almost seemed as though he might be enjoying the anticipation of what was to follow—"we do now have what we regard as a reliable lead, and I am in a position to show you a photograph of the person we are looking for in our murder inquiry."

There was a renewed buzz of anticipation in the room, and Bailey turned to look offstage and signaled to a technician who was operating a large screen which had been set up behind the desk. A moment later the white space was filled with a full-face photograph of a young man of twenty-one years of age—who looked almost exactly like Michael Beaumont.

"This man is called Martin Bannerman. As you can probably see, he bears a striking resemblance to Michael Beaumont here, and that's because he is Michael's older brother. I have asked Michael to join us today, first of all to make totally clear to everyone that the person we are looking for is not him. And second because, in case Martin Bannerman is watching, Michael would like the opportunity to speak to him directly." He turned. "Michael?"

Michael was not sure exactly what he was going to say. A range of thoughts and feelings had been churning within him, but had reached a new climax of emotion with the full realization that he had no choice but to betray to the police what he had worked out about his brother. Now, as the cameramen turned towards him like snipers at target practice, he tried to focus his thoughts by reflecting on what his mother had gone through, what his grandmother had gone through, what his grandfather had gone through, and what he himself had gone through. Alongside those thoughts, though, he retained the gnawing suspicion that his brother had played some part in incriminating him in the killings. The thought disturbed him deeply, not least because he could think of no reason whatsoever that anyone should do such a terrible thing to his own sibling; but then immediately he reflected that set against the far more appalling crimes which Martin was suspected of, framing a younger brother fell into pale insignificance. Right now, though, Michael was determined to marshal all his resources, and once again to try to do the thing that Rose had always urged upon him. His task was to try to see the world from the point of view of his brother and, in doing so, to determine what he would need to say to persuade him to stop his campaign of terror and hand himself in to the police.

Michael looked around and eventually decided to select one camera and to look directly into the lens.

"Martin. We have never met. Or at least, obviously, we have met, but not for the past eighteen years to my certain knowledge. Stuff happened when we were tiny kids which you have had to deal with ever since then. I don't know what's going on with you, but I do know that we have to bring all these killings to an end, so you need to come forward and tell the police whatever you know. It's what our mother wants, and it's what our grandmother would want. Of course the long separation means that I don't feel I know you as I would like to know you, but I feel I do know something about you because we are brothers, and that must count for a lot." Michael paused, unsure about whether to continue with the thought he had in his mind, but then swallowed hard and once again looked straight into the camera. "I don't remember much about all those times, but I do have a memory of us clinging together for dear life when they tried to separate us, and I felt that half of me was being ripped away when they took you. So please, if you feel and remember any of that as I do, then for me and what's left of the family, come forward and give yourself up before anyone else gets hurt. Give us a time and place, and I will be there to meet you and make sure that you are safe. I promise you that."

The room was full, with perhaps two hundred people, but when Michael finished speaking there was complete silence. It was as though the world held its breath as the realization of what had just happened sank in. The moment was about to be broken by a barrage of shouted questions when DCS Bailey picked up the threads of what Michael had said.

"So, to make that clear to Martin Bannerman if he is watching. Your brother and the rest of us are asking you to contact us on a number which we will give in a moment, and we will meet you wherever and whenever you say. Michael will be with us to guarantee your safety. Please give yourself up, before anyone else gets hurt."

DCS Bailey now turned to Michael and told him that he could leave the stage while he and Collins dealt with any more inquiries from the press. There was a further chorus of shouted questions as he stood up to go, but Michael was emotionally drained and was glad to leave the rest of the news conference to the police. When he opened the door and went into the corridor outside, he was happy to see the kind face of Sergeant Mallinson.

"Hello, Michael," he said, and Michael was surprised to see the sergeant extending his right hand. He took it in his and shook it warmly. "That must have been incredibly difficult, but you managed it brilliantly well. You hit exactly the right note. It was a brave thing to do. Very, very brave." Michael thanked the sergeant and accompanied him along the corridor to an outer hallway. "What happens now, do you think?" he asked. "I guess we wait to see if Martin contacts us?"

Before Mallinson could answer, Michael looked up and saw that the door on the other side of the hallway was opening, and a uniformed officer was showing two women into the room. The officer looked across and caught Michael's eye, and then pointed him out. Because of the unexpected context, it took a few seconds for Michael to realize that the two women were Esme and his mother, Margaret. He felt a hard knot forming in his stomach in anticipation of terrible news, but when he was able to see the expressions on their faces their anxiety was of a different kind.

"She's awake, Michael, and she's asking for you," said his mother. Michael scarcely dared to believe the words, and his face showed instant relief and joy, but straightaway he felt Esme's hand on his arm, and her face was close to his.

"She is very weak, Michael, and you know that in any event she has not got long, but it's important that you see her if you can."

"I'm there," he said, and turned back to Sergeant Mallinson. "Can you spare me the use of a fast car?"

Fifteen minutes later Michael burst through the doors leading to the intensive care unit at St. Thomas' and headed directly towards the room in which he had last seen Rose. Esme and his mother had suggested that they should make their own way from the hospital's main entrance while he went on ahead. Michael walked quickly, and a renewed wave of fear gripped him as he looked through the glass and saw that a doctor and nurse were standing at the bedside, but there were three other people whom he did not recognize. He was about to push open the door when he felt a hand on his shoulder and looked around to see that it was Christopher, who had been looking after his grandmother when he last visited.

"Don't worry, Michael," he said, "your grandmother has been moved to another room. The one she was in has specialized equipment which she doesn't need anymore, so we have put her in a more comfortable place just down the corridor." His voice was soft in the way that people speak to the newly bereaved. "Let me show you."

Christopher led the way along the corridor towards a far corner, which seemed to be tucked away from the hustle and bustle of the rest of the unit. Rose's room was in semidarkness, and when he entered Michael was immediately aware that there were none of the flashing lights and bleeping machines which he associated with intensive care. He looked over and saw his grandmother's head resting on the pillows and that there were no tubes or drips by her bed. Her eyes were closed, and she was breathing deeply.

Michael stood at her bedside and looked at her face. He felt relieved to see that there was no trace of pain or discomfort in her expression, and nothing about her suggested that she was fighting demons; she was at peace.

"She was conscious a little while ago, Michael," said Christopher. "We told her you were on your way, and she was trying to stay awake. She agreed to go to sleep if we promised to wake her when you got here. I'm afraid I did make that promise, and if it's OK with you, I'm going to keep it."

Michael's instinct was to refuse. "But she's sleeping so peacefully. Surely if she's going to get better..." Merely speaking the words made him realize that they were inappropriate, and he stopped and nodded his head. "OK, well, that would be good then. I'd be so happy if I could feel that she could see and maybe understand me just one more time."

"She was quite cogent," said Christopher. "She is in no pain."

Christopher walked to the other side of the bed, and very gently he put his hand on Rose's shoulder. Once again, Michael saw the shapes of cherubs in the tattoos on Christopher's forearm and noted the contrast between his healthy flesh against the yellowing and dying skin stretched over Rose's collarbone. The nurse brought his lips quite close to her ear and whispered very softly, "Rose. Rose. It's Michael. Your grandson Michael. He has come to see you, Rose. He's here with me now. Can you open your eyes? He'd love to talk to you."

At first Michael thought there would be no response, but then within a few seconds he heard a murmur of what might have been acknowledgment and saw a tiny flicker under her eyelids. It was as if she was in the deepest of sleeps and was struggling to climb up and out again for a last visit to the conscious world.

"Michael," she said, and he saw that she was moving her bony hand towards him, and he took it as gently as he knew how. Her flesh seemed cold and clammy to the touch, and nonetheless he lowered his head to kiss the back of her hand.

"Grandma. Yes, it's me. It's Michael. I'm here. I'm here with you. I'm safe and you are safe and we are here together, and everything is going to be all right."

"Michael?" Her voice expressed disbelief and a need for further reassurance. "Is it you? Are you safe and OK?" He could see that she was struggling to open her eyes just a fraction, and perhaps she could see enough to make out the shape of him against the light.

"Yes, Rose. It's Michael. And I'm fine. I promise. Everything is going to be all right. I promise you." He saw her face relax, and she exhaled deeply. It was a second before she began to breathe in again, and Michael felt a moment of anxiety. He looked at Christopher, who closed his eyes and mouthed the words *Not long.* He turned and walked to the edge of the room, on hand if needed but allowing a few private moments.

"Grandma." Michael leaned in so that his face was inches from hers on the pillow and spoke as softly as he could. "I don't want you to worry about anything. Not ever. You are a truly wonderful person, and you have been a truly wonderful grandmother to me. I will never be able to thank you, and for the rest of my life I'll be grateful for what you have done for me. I shall try to live my life as you would have wanted me to." He was still holding her hand and thought he could feel a slight squeeze on his. "You can let go now, Grandma. You've done everything you could do, and you've done it all very well. I hope I will see you again one day, but meanwhile, go and be at peace."

Michael detected a small sound at the door and turned to see that Esme and his mother were standing silently. He stood straight and beckoned them forward. The two women and Michael stood at Rose Beaumont's bedside and watched her fade away.

TWENTY

THERE WAS NEVER any answer from the scores of calls which Michael made in the following days to Alison's landline and her cell phone. Both eventually clicked onto her voice mail and both eventually declared that the available capacity had been exceeded and no more messages could be recorded. At one point Michael considered trying to involve the police in the search for her, but he had no reason to believe she had any idea where his brother was, and it would be inexcusable to persuade them to use resources to locate her.

The need to make arrangements for the funeral meant that Michael and his mother spoke regularly in those few days, and the necessity to make practical decisions and plans was a useful diversion from the intensely emotional circumstances in which both found themselves. Discussions about the location of the ceremony and the type of coffin were of sufficient importance and gravity, ironically, to divert their thoughts from other immediate concerns. They sat together through the evenings discussing who needed to be invited, and at one time they even found themselves laughing when they considered what could possibly be said by the minister at the service about the loss to the family. In the context of the carnage which seemed to surround every aspect of the Beaumonts like a Greek tragedy, Rose's death from natural causes at the age of eighty-five might be considered light relief. Their laughter did not last for long, and mother and son retreated into their own thoughts; but for the first time in eighteen years, they slept under the same roof, and Michael thought that Rose would have been happy to know that her daughter was sleeping in her bed.

There seemed to be an unspoken pact between them in those few days that they would not venture back into the distant past or the series of horrors which had led them to where they now were. Many times Michael wondered what it must be like for his mother to know that she had given birth to someone who may be responsible for the murder of all those tiny children, but instantly he tried hard to expel such thoughts from his mind. That way lay madness for all of them, it seemed, and for the moment it was as though the normality brought by the ordinary business of everyday life was the best way to survive and get through the coming ordeal. They preferred to try to get used to each other gradually, building a new bridge towards dry land, rather than churning up the quagmire which had made the connection necessary in the first place.

The police had scheduled a twice-daily telephone call with Michael to touch base about any developments in the hunt for Martin. Once again every newspaper, magazine, and news bulletin in the land headlined the story, and once again pictures of a face which could be Michael's were everywhere. This meant that Michael could leave the apartment in only the most controlled circumstances, always having given prior notice to the police so that they knew to ignore tip-offs from the public in the relevant areas. The police had warned people not to approach Martin Bannerman if they saw him, but nonetheless it was impossible to rule out vigilante action by some public-spirited individual, with potentially appalling consequences for Michael in the case of mistaken identity.

Michael spent many hours studying the face in the police photo. It was indeed very like his own face in shape and structure; but then again it was not his face in all the ways that environment and nurture can overlay. He thought that his brother's complexion had a pallor which was no doubt consequent on having spent less time outdoors or in the sun. Possibly the frown lines on his forehead were the result of having spent more of his life in unhappy or challenging circumstances. The trace of a scowl around the mouth need not be permanent, but the physical record of recent years had left what was probably an indelible shadow. Michael wondered how this person, this parallel human being, could be so like him in so many ways, and yet unlike him in so many others.

The police had agreed to keep the press and media as far away as they could from Rose's funeral, and Michael and Margaret reckoned that there would be only twenty or so people attending. There was Elsie from next door, whose son Raymond was going to bring her. There was Mrs. Morrison and some of the other staff from Greenacres, including, of course, Esme. Three or four of the other residents from the care home were also able to attend, and Detectives Bailey and Collins had asked if they could come to pay their respects. Michael was pleased and surprised to receive a message that the nurse from the intensive care unit, Christopher, would also be present.

Mrs. Morrison had kindly offered the use of a private room back at Greenacres for tea and some refreshments after the service.

Michael went on calling and calling the numbers he had for Alison right up to the morning of the service. The travel agency said it had not heard from her, and her voice mail remained over capacity and unable to record anything further.

It was a dry but windy day in June when the group of mourners gathered together to say goodbye to Rose Beaumont, formerly Rose Bannerman, formerly Rose Williams. It had been arranged that Michael would drive to Wandsworth Crematorium with Margaret, and Rose would be brought directly there by the undertakers. Two uniformed officers stood on each side of the iron gates at the perimeter, and there was a barrage of clicking and bright lights as Michael maneuvered the aging Vauxhall among and through the melee. The chapel was out of sight of the main road, and Michael saw that a number of people had arrived before them and were parking nearby. As he got out of his car, Michael was happy to see Esme just emerging from the passenger side of a blue VW, and a moment later was surprised and puzzled to see that her car was being driven by Sergeant Mallinson, who was dressed in civilian clothes and who now got out and walked around to stand next to his passenger. Michael went over and gave Esme a hug, and she smiled the smile he remembered so well from happier days at Greenacres.

"I think you know Peter, don't you?" She gestured towards the sergeant, who looked slightly uncomfortable out of his police uniform. "Peter lives three doors down from me. He's been a good friend over the years." Suddenly a number of questions which Michael had been asking himself for weeks were answered, and he also smiled broadly and extended his hand. Mallinson's face eloquently reflected their mutual understanding.

"Obviously I wasn't able to say anything," said the sergeant. "But I always knew that you couldn't be the Madman. Not after what Esme had told me about you. I hope you understand that I had to go by the book?"

Michael said that he understood completely. "Whatever was the reason, I'm grateful. Your few kind words gave me something to hang on to at the worst time of my life." Once again he chose not to share the suspicions he had harbored at the time that Mallinson might be playing "good cop" to Bailey's "bad cop." They turned and went inside the chapel.

Rose had been a regular churchgoer and had attended the same Methodist ministry in Hampton Wick ever since she moved into the area with Michael eighteen years earlier. The vicar who had known her originally retired some years before and was in the congregation, but the man who conducted the formalities had also known her for several years. As Reverend Tibbets began to recite the familiar words of the funeral service, Michael looked around, discreetly acknowledging the presence of anyone who caught his eye. He was keen to know who had come to his grandmother's funeral, and most keen of all to see if there was any sign of Alison. There was not, and so Michael tried to concentrate on the words being spoken by the minister.

"Rose Beaumont was someone we would simply call a good woman. Someone for whom nothing was ever too much trouble, and who was always looking for an opportunity to do a good turn for other people. There is no doubt that she was the epitome of that old cliché 'a pillar of the community,' but much more than that, she dedicated her life to bringing up her grandson Michael, who is here with us today. And Michael"— the minister turned and addressed him directly—"I know that she was very proud of you." Michael attempted a smile of acknowledgment, but above all at that moment he felt relief that Rose had known in her last moments that he was no longer suspected of any crime and that he had been able to say goodbye to her properly. He was also grateful that she had died without ever knowing that her other grandson, Martin, was now the prime suspect in the hunt for the Madman.

Eventually the recorded organ music was playing, and the coffin began to move away on the rollers which would take it behind the velvet curtains and on its final journey. Michael noticed that his mother remained seated for a few moments after everyone else was edging out of the chapel, and he stood beside her patiently, waiting for her to complete her thoughts. Outside, people were shaking hands and speaking of "a lovely service," and Michael invited everyone to head back to Greenacres for tea.

Michael opened the car door for his mother and was walking around to the driver's seat when he looked up and saw a figure in the distance he immediately recognized. It was Alison. She appeared to be staring into space and only looked directly at him when he called her name. At first he thought she was about to turn and head in the other direction, but then Michael called again, and she remained still as he ran up behind her. She was facing away when he reached her, and he put his hands on her shoulders. He was about to turn her around to embrace her, when he felt a sudden jolt from the reality that the woman he thought of as his lover was in some way involved with the death of his baby sister, and he did not know how to be with her. When she turned to him, her face was wet from a fast-flowing stream of tears, and he was shocked to see cuts around her eyes and lips. Now they embraced, clinging together like two lost souls, and both with their hearts entirely ready to break.

TWENTY-ONE

ALISON HAD ARRIVED at the service in a taxi and said she would prefer to go in it back to Greenacres rather than to meet Michael's mother for the first time, after so many years, in the crematorium car park. Once there, Michael made sure that those who had returned to the care home were directed to the private room which had been set aside. Esme told him that he need not worry about them — she would ensure that everyone was offered tea and sandwiches — and that they would all be content to talk among themselves. She had also spoken to Mrs. Morrison, who agreed to allow her office to be used for a small and very strange reunion.

The two women greeted each other with courtesy and coolness, neither yet able to shake off the inhibitions caused by the circumstances and the history, and most of all by so many unanswered questions. Now the three of them sat on individual chairs, each in a separate corner of the room, and Michael felt like the referee between two combatants who were trying to get the measure of each other. Margaret was gently nodding her head, still trying to take on board the sequence of events from the time she had received the emergency message to go in to visit Rose at the care home.

"I think that Rose must have worked out that Alison was Elizabeth," said Michael to his mother. "And that's why she had called you so urgently that day. She wanted to know what to do."

"I see that. None of us had seen Elizabeth for eighteen years, since she was eight years old, and we'd been told by the police that she had gone abroad. They didn't say where it was, but we got the impression that it was far away. I'm sure we were all certain that we would never see or hear from her again." She sipped her tea and thought for a few moments longer. "In her heart, I think that Rose always blamed Elizabeth for what happened to your baby sister, and then for the fact that her husband took his own life."

Michael caught sight of the renewed twinge of pain which flickered across Alison's face, as though she had been physically slapped. "Which is, of course, entirely unfair," he said quickly.

"It may have been unfair, of course it probably was unfair, but nonetheless, that's how she would have seen it. You two brothers were always the apple of her eye, and you can understand why it would have been tempting to blame an older child from outside the family who should have known better." Nothing in Margaret's tone indicated to what extent she herself believed what she was saying. "And then she dedicated her entire life to making sure that you had no knowledge, Michael, of all those events. You were so young at the time that you could easily not remember anything about them. So she must have had the shock of her life when Elizabeth turned up and she worked out who she was." She put down her cup, again speaking her thoughts as they were coming to her and she was sorting them out in her own head. "But I still wonder what could have been so urgent. It had taken her a while to work things out, but once she had, I wonder why she regarded it as such an emergency."

Michael was at first confused that the reason for Rose's alarm was not obvious to Margaret, but then he realized that she might not yet know the circumstances of Rose's first meeting with Alison and himself.

"Well, because it was me who brought Elizabeth to see Rose in the first place. I introduced her to Grandma as my girl-friend," he said. "If it wasn't bad enough that someone she thought she would never see again had turned up out of the blue, she must have understood that I was involved with a girl she held responsible for the death of my sister. She will have been horrified, and wanted to speak to you to discuss what to do. If she told me what the problem was, she'd also be telling me about the past, and that's what she had spent her whole life trying to avoid."

Michael felt uncomfortable about having left the other mourners to their own devices, and the three of them agreed that they would return to the wake and then come back together a little later. They went to the common room, where Michael noted with some amusement that Esme had produced a bottle of sherry and that one or two of Rose's former card-playing partners were in danger of getting tipsy. As he tried to focus on the niceties of friendly conversation about memories of Grandma Rose, Michael could not prevent his attention from returning over and over again to Alison. He watched her chatting to Rose's former neighbor Elsie and the Methodist minister, apparently without stress or anxiety, and found himself amazed that she had been able to remain apparently so sane and stable in spite of her appalling ordeal.

After the last of the guests had drifted away or returned to the dayroom, Michael asked Mrs. Morrison if it would be okay to use her office for a little longer to catch up on some lost time.

"I don't want you to think that the children's home was some sort of Dickensian nightmare," said Alison when everyone had resettled. "It wasn't. Probably they did their best in difficult circumstances. Every kid in there had come from a tough situation of some sort, and they all had their own histories. Mine was worse than most because of the terrible stories which everyone had read in the papers before I got there — stuff about child monsters and evil incarnate — and for most of the time, no one was really certain whether or not I was guilty of anything. Either I was some dreadful child killer who had drowned a baby out of pure evil, or I was the victim of a horrible injustice which had taken me away from my family and led to me being blamed for something I had nothing to do with."

She stopped speaking and there was a long pause. Both Margaret and Michael were desperate to hear Alison's own answer to the question which had been left hanging in the air, but neither wished to be the one to ask it. Alison was every bit as aware of the suspense as they were; she had faced comparable situations hundreds of times.

"And do you want an honest answer?" Michael and his mother exchanged a look before nodding their heads. "The honest answer is that I don't know. It was all a long time ago. I was eight, for heaven's sake. I was playing in the house.

Martin was somewhere else. I think he wanted to play with Amy in the bath, but I have no memory of running any water into it. I also have no memory of even lifting the baby into the bath, but I know that I must have done so, because Martin wouldn't have been able to lift her without help. I remember being completely involved in a game I was playing with you, Michael, and the next thing I knew, I could hear your grandma starting to scream. Then all hell was let loose, and I was crying and crying, and people were yelling at me. I remember someone shaking me and calling me an evil witch, and being roughly handled as I was taken away. The rest is a complete blur. I get flashbacks of newspaper headlines and my parents in hysterics. In the end both had something like a breakdown and told the authorities they couldn't cope. No one else wanted me, for obvious reasons, and I was more or less locked up. I never saw them, or any of the rest of you, ever again."

There was another extended pause, and finally Michael spoke. "Not until the bar in Brighton?"

"No, not until then."

"But what about Joanna? Tell me what happened with her." Michael turned to his mother and related the story of when they met Joanna in the French restaurant in Brighton. Then he returned to Alison. "Where does she figure?"

"I was determined that when I left the children's home I would start a new life. I changed my name and made a plan to go to Australia. I was there for eight years and eventually thought it would be safe to come home. I'd spent most of my time in the Midlands and the north, and so I thought that after eighteen years and a complete change of appearance, it would be safe to go back to Brighton. I got a job in the travel agency, and it was all going well, and then you and I met in that bar." Now Alison turned to Margaret. "He and I hit it off straightaway, but I had absolutely no idea who he was. I thought that finally I'd met someone who could really mean something to me, and the last thing I wanted was for him to know about my past. So when a girl I'd known in the children's home approached me when Michael and I were in a restaurant, I pretended that she had mistaken me for someone else." Alison went on to tell how she had stupidly confided to Joanna when they were in the children's home that she believed Martin had deliberately killed his baby sister by drowning. "Martin was taken to a secure place, and I hadn't seen him since. Anyway, when she heard about the Madman murders, Joanna took it into her head that Martin might be the person responsible. She started pressing me to inform the police of the possibility, calling and texting me every hour of the day and night, telling me that I was trying to protect the killer and that I shouldn't be doing it. Then things eventually got a bit out of hand." Alison related the story of the meeting in Starbucks and how ashamed she was of what had taken place.

For the entire time since Esme had told Michael about who Alison really was, his mind had wandered over every possible explanation for how she had come back into his life. He had agonized over his feelings for her, his emotions alternating between doubt and hope, and between suspicion and faith. Now her clarification of the history made him feel reassured, and her description of their first meeting in Brighton was a reminder of their happy times together. He reached across and took Alison's hand in his. She looked back towards him, a half smile on her face, and he thought his heart might overflow.

After a further few moments Michael turned again to his

mother. Since they were in the full flow of revelation, it was important to understand everything he could about how they had come to the situation they were now facing. "Was there ever any sign when we were growing up that he was different? Anything at all which would give a clue as to what might have been going on in his head when he did what he did to Amy?" He had to summon a renewed effort of will to move on to what must follow. "Or what we suspect that he may have been doing these last few weeks?"

"You can probably imagine that I've spent a lot of time agonizing about that. In the end there's no escaping the fact that all of us grown-ups were guilty in some way of what happened to Amy. I shouldn't have been away, Grandma shouldn't have left you kids with Granddad, and he should have kept a closer eye on things. Elizabeth was far too young to be in charge of any of you. We've had to live with that and, as you know, your grandfather just couldn't. I also paid a price, but there is no getting away from what Martin did. Was he jealous of the attention paid to Amy when she was a newborn baby? I guess so, but not more so than happens in lots of families. Could I put hand on heart and say there was anything about him which might have given any hint that he was capable of what he did then, and what everyone thinks he has done now? Despite what the psychologist said at the inquest, I believe I'd have to answer no."

She had only just stopped speaking when there was a knock, and Mrs. Morrison put her head around the door.

"Sorry to disturb you, but the two detectives who were at the funeral are here and are asking if they can have a word with Michael. I didn't know if you minded being interrupted?"

Michael said he would come out to speak to them.

"Hello, Michael," said Superintendent Bailey. "Sorry to bother you. We went back to the office after the funeral, and there's nothing new to report. It's just that we agreed that we would speak twice a day, and I've been calling your number. I think that maybe you forgot to turn your phone back on after the ceremony. I've left a few messages."

Michael apologized and felt his pockets to find his phone. He took it out and switched it on, and saw that he had five missed calls. "Let me just listen to these and make sure there's nothing relevant." He pressed the speed-dial for his messages. The two detectives stood facing Michael as he placed the phone at his ear, and the service clicked on. "First one's from you," said Michael, continuing to press the phone against his ear. "So's the second"——he smiled at the DCS, waiting for the next playback——"and so's the third! Sorry about this." A few seconds more passed and Michael nodded his head. "This one's from my work asking me when I think I'm going to be able to get back." Still Michael was pressing the phone to his ear and was about to end the call when he heard a voice he instantly recognized. The words were spoken slowly and calmly.

"Michael. You know who this is. If you are with the police now, just act normally and pretend this is a routine call from a friend." There was a pause. "Tell them it's just an old mate, and then listen to the rest of this when you are on your own." Michael was aware that the two detectives were looking at him with curiosity. He had a moment of indecision and was about to reveal the truth when something stopped him. He clicked off the call. "It's just a bloke from work sending sympathy about Rose. I'll call him back later."

Perhaps there was something in Michael's tone which made Superintendent Bailey wonder, and he continued to look at

Michael for a few moments, as though trying to work out whether he was telling the truth.

"Are you sure, Michael? Nothing we need to know about?"

"No, nothing." Michael tried to sound as casual and convincing as he knew how. "Just a friend from work."

"What's his name?"

"What?"

"I just wondered what your friend's name is? The one who's a liability."

"Oh, it's Stephen. He's my boss at work. It's just Stephen. I'll phone him back later."

The two detectives seemed satisfied with the answer. They apologized once more for disturbing the family and said they would be back in touch tomorrow. Michael watched from the window as they drove out of the car park, then returned to his phone and called voice mail again. He played through to where he had interrupted the recording and listened intently.

"OK, so I'm assuming you're now on your own. Well, Michael, it's been a long time, hasn't it? A lot of water under the bridge, as you might say." There seemed to be an underlying sneer in the voice, and Michael found that he was shaking his head in disbelief at what he was hearing. "So I guess you must have been wondering what really happened all those years ago — what I did, what Elizabeth did, and most of all what you did yourself. And also why everything that has happened to you in the last week has happened. Well, I'll be happy to tell you, Michael, but if you want to know the truth, the whole truth, and nothing but the truth, we will need to meet up. Yeah, that's right, but no police. If you bring them, I will clam up tight and you will never ever learn what really happened. So I'll call you at six o'clock tonight. Make sure you're on your own, and I'll tell you a time and place where we can meet. Cheers," said the voice, "and by the way, Michael, I know exactly what you were talking about in your appeal on the telly about being torn apart. Always tight, always one. Isn't that right, little bro?"

TWENTY-TWO

THE TELEPHONE MESSAGE from his brother sent Michael into a renewed state of shock, and he knew he would need to dig deep into his reserves of self-control if he was to stand any chance of acting normally as he returned to Mrs. Morrison's office. He stood outside the door for a few moments, taking time to breathe deeply, but all the while feeling that the air was constricted in his lungs. He stuck out his chest and spun both of his arms like windmills, willing his heart to start pumping the oxygen through to the extremities of his body. Finally he inhaled as deeply as he could, mouthed a silent prayer to his grandma to give him strength, and reentered the room.

"What did the police want?" Margaret did not look up.

"Just the routine stuff," said Michael, but he still felt breathless as the words came out. He coughed and swallowed hard. "Had I heard anything? Seems like I forgot to turn my phone back on after the ceremony and they couldn't contact me."

Neither woman appeared to notice his disarray, but still Michael turned aside, afraid that his facial expression would give away his state. He suggested that it was time to bring what had already been a very long day for all of them to an end, and no one disagreed.

Michael and Alison gave Margaret a ride to her rented home in Wimbledon. There was an unspoken understanding that events were likely to bring them together again soon, and so they made no arrangement. Alison remained in the car as Michael walked his mother to her door, and there was a moment of awkwardness before, for the first time since their reunion, he put both of his arms around her and held her closely to him.

"Your grandma was very proud of you Michael." Margaret pushed her face into the lapels of Michael's jacket and held her son tightly around his waist. "And she was right to be." Then she loosened her arms and turned and headed indoors. "Let's talk again in the next day or two."

Michael and Alison continued the drive back to the apartment in Kingston, and he wondered whether or not to share the latest extraordinary twist in the unfolding series of events. Part of him wanted to spare her the further turmoil which would inevitably arise from knowing that his brother had contacted him. On the other hand, he had no firm idea what he should do about the call he had received and felt an overwhelming need to seek her opinion.

"Something happened today." He kept looking at the road ahead as he spoke, but Alison turned towards to him in amazement.

"Are you kidding? Your grandmother's funeral, an agonizing confession from your mother, and you and I talking again. Yes, I think something happened."

Michael half turned back towards her with a smile and placed his hand on hers. "But even with all that going on, I'm afraid you need to get ready for another shock. It happened when I went out this afternoon to talk to Bailey and Collins." Alison said nothing, but the expression on her face encouraged him to finish what he had to say. "I had a phone message from Martin."

Less than an hour later they were sitting at the kitchen table in Rose's apartment. Alison had been unable to react beyond the briefest expression of surprise and alarm, but now there were only twenty minutes to go before the promised phone call from Martin, and they knew that they had an urgent decision to make. For her, at least, their choice seemed clear.

"For one thing, there's the small matter of the law. If we know the whereabouts of a dangerous criminal and don't tell the authorities, we could end up going to jail. And that's not to mention the moral point of view. If we don't tell the police and he kills again before they catch him, we'll be indirectly responsible. Surely we don't want that on our consciences?"

"All that's true, and I get it," said Michael, "but I can't just ignore the fact that he is my brother, and we don't have a single shred of firm evidence that he's the Madman. I know that everything points to him, but remember that just a few days ago everything seemed to point to me. Don't you think that the very least I owe him as his brother is to give him the benefit of the doubt? He didn't say anything directly in the phone message about being responsible for the Madman killings, and if we hear him out, we'll know in a moment if he's guilty or not. If he is, we will obviously have to tell the police straightaway."

Alison found his logic difficult to resist, and now Rose's antique clock showed that the time was approaching 6:00 PM. Michael's heart seemed to be pounding at about five beats to every one sweep of the pendulum.

They waited as the minutes went up to and then past the top of the hour, and Michael had begun to wonder if the call would come when his phone started to ring. He and Alison shared a last moment of doubt before Michael nodded and put the phone to his ear.

"Hello."

There was silence on the line, but then Michael thought he could hear someone breathing. Alison's expression turned from anticipation to inquiry, and so he put the phone on the table and pushed the speaker button. The static hum which filled the room seemed to have the sound of the sea in the background.

"Well, well, well, if it isn't my little brother. We get to talk after all these years. Are you alone?" The voice was unmistakably the same as they had heard at the police press conference—undoubtedly that of the person claiming to be the Madman.

"I'm here with Elizabeth," said Michael. "She and I are both very keen to know what you have to say."

"Hello, Elizabeth," said the voice from the speaker. "It's nice to talk to you, too, after so much time. Thanks for coming to see me in the detention center." There was another pause while Michael and Alison wondered how to respond. It was broken by a single word from Martin. *"Not."*

"It's very strange to be speaking to you, Martin," said Michael. "A few days ago I had no idea that I even had a brother or had ever had a baby sister, let alone anything about what happened when we were all children. And now here you are, and there's all this Madman stuff going on. I don't know where to start asking you questions."

"Exactly," said Martin abruptly, "but I don't want to talk for long on the phone. We should get together, just you and me, and I'll tell you everything you need to know. You can ask me anything you like. Do you want to do that?"

"Of course I do, but it's not possible. How can it be? The whole world knows our faces and everyone is looking for you. How could we possibly meet without you being arrested?"

"I've got pretty used to going out in disguise, Michael. I'm out and about right now, and people are walking past me. I think you're resourceful enough to do the same. Meet me at midday tomorrow—tell you what—at the end of Brighton Pier. That should bring back some memories from when we were little kids together."

"I just don't see how we can do that, Martin." Michael suddenly felt a desperate need to keep his brother on the line. "But just tell me one thing before you go."

"What's that? Be quick."

"It's bloody obvious that someone set me up as a suspect in the murders of all those children. I've been working hard to come up with an alternative answer, but it seems to me that the only person who could have done that is you. Did you all along want me to be arrested for the Madman murders?"

Martin laughed. "I wanted you to get just the smallest taste of what I've had to go through all these years. So, yes, I set you up just a little bit. After that first time, I watched you for weeks before I chose the places where I would do what I did. It was simple enough to break into the apartment to check out your wardrobe so I could make sure you had a set of clothes to match mine. Nice place, by the way, and what a cute picture of you on your first day at school."

"So that was you . . . ?" but Michael's words were cut off sharply.

"I dropped back later on, too, just to make sure you had a gray hoodie, but I couldn't find one, so I made you a little present of mine. And it was easy enough to get into your work and make a few minor adjustments to the sound monitors. After that, I sat and watched it all take its course."

"But why, Martin? What did I do to deserve that? And what on earth did any of those kids do to deserve what you did to them? What the hell were you thinking?"

"I'll explain it all," said Martin. "But that's enough for now. I'll tell you everything you need to know tomorrow. Twelve o'clock, midday. Brighton Pier. No police." The line went dead.

A further ten minutes passed before either Michael or Alison could express anything sensible about their thoughts. "So that's that then," she said finally. "There can be no more doubt that Martin is the Madman. He admitted it. Surely we have to tell the police straightaway, don't we?"

"I guess we do," said Michael, "but just think, if we do that right now, the chances are that neither of us will ever know what happened on that day. He's told us already that he'll clam up and we may never know the truth. As it is, whatever he thinks happened has caused him to believe that I deserve this nightmare I've been put through. I have to find out what that's all about. And it's only one day. I don't believe that even a fucking Madman is going to kill anyone else before tomorrow."

Later the couple set off in the car towards Brighton, and while neither of them felt certain that they were doing the right thing, events seemed to have taken on their own momentum. It was beginning to grow dark outside, and the driving rain caused the oncoming headlights to blur and dazzle. The defrosters were not working, and Michael asked Alison to reach across to wipe the inside of the windscreen so that he could see the road ahead. They drove for most of the journey in silence, each of them scouring the deepest corners of their memories but discovering nothing further.

It was late and dark by the time they arrived and unpacked the car, but still Alison suggested that they should take a walk to stretch their legs and clear their thoughts. They set off to retrace once again the route they'd taken together on the morning after their first meeting. The rain had stopped, and after a few hundred yards they lengthened their stride and began to suck in the fresh sea air.

"God, it's so good to feel some oxygen in your lungs," said Alison. "It seems like days since I've been able to breathe freely."

"Yes, it feels good," said Michael, "and even more so when I think how it's only just over a week since I was looking at the possibility of an indefinite stretch in jail."

"Just like Martin," said Alison.

"I guess so," said Michael, and wondered whether she was thinking about what his brother had faced before, or what he was facing now. "But maybe he should have thought of that before he started throwing tiny kids into the river?"

The time was approaching 11:00 PM and neither of them had discussed how they would spend the night ahead. Since the moment that Esme had told him about Alison's true identity, Michael had been trying to reconcile himself to the notion that he and she would never be intimate again. All the while her role in the death of his baby sister remained unclear, he could not imagine how it would be possible to be so close to her. It was not until earlier today, as he listened to her own account of events, that the weight of all that began to be lifted from him, and he allowed himself to wonder whether they might be able to pick up their lives where they left off.

Still, though, Michael knew that there was one more hurdle he had to get over before all barriers between them could be swept away. He feared the consequences of yet another difficult revelation, but even more than that, he feared embarking on the next stage of his life with Alison without complete honesty. If they were ever to have a chance of moving forward together, this was his opportunity to start with a totally clean sheet.

"Now that Martin has admitted what he's done, there's something else I need to tell you." Alison looked at him with renewed apprehension, but then once again the expression on her face encouraged him to continue. "I'm sure you understand that one of the most difficult aspects of all this for me was the discovery that someone has been trying to put me under suspicion for the killings. Framing me for these terrible crimes." He hesitated momentarily as though to check on his own resolve, but quickly decided to continue. "It's been a terrible blow to me to learn that my own brother was responsible for doing so.

I still can't imagine why he did, but in a way it was also a relief to hear it from him."

"How so?" said Alison. Michael paused again and took a deep breath.

"Because right in the middle of all that, before I even knew of the existence of Martin, the thought occurred to me that the person trying to incriminate me could possibly be you."

Alison's footsteps slowed, and within a few more seconds she had come to a halt. He stood alongside her, waiting for her to react, his anxiety increasing moment by moment. He was getting ready to try to row back from his statement when she spoke.

"Oh my God." Her words were punctuated by short pauses as each of her next thoughts tumbled into her mind. "All my secrecy about Joanna. What I told you about my mum and dad. The unexplained calls and texts. Your grandmother's reaction when she first met me. You must have wondered . . . it's not surprising"—but then she paused again, interrupting her own flow—"but surely not planting the hoodie in the apartment? Surely you didn't think that I was capable of doing something like that?" She raised both hands to clutch the sides of her head. "After what we've been to each other?"

"I'm sorry," said Michael. "I'm so, so sorry. Of course it now seems madness, but you have to understand that my head was all over the place. So much was happening, and for a while back there I lost my mind. Lost it entirely. All I can do is to ask you to forgive me."

Alison made no further response, but after another minute she slowly resumed walking, and Michael fell in alongside her. Out of the corner of his eye he could see that she was gently shaking her head, still grappling with her own reactions. After a few hundred yards more he thought that perhaps the tension in her shoulders was dissolving, and finally she edged alongside him once again and took his hand.

"Look," she said, "all of us have got a lot to deal with, but even with everything that's happened in the last few days, that's a lot for me to take in. It's going to take a while to get my head around what you've just told me." She paused again, still working out her feelings as they came to her. "Right now, though, all I can say is that you've been through some kind of living hell in the last few days, and no one could blame you for whatever you felt. That's stuff we have to work through in the future. Right now we've got more urgent things to worry about."

A surge of relief flowed through Michael, and he released his grip from Alison's hand and put his arm around her shoulders. For the first time since they had become lovers, the doubts and secrecy which had formed a constant but invisible barrier between them were put aside, and he had a chance to be with her in a way which had never previously been possible. They exchanged a further look which was far more eloquent than any words, and again they lengthened their stride, anxious to return as quickly as possible to her apartment. Once inside, neither of them spoke as they left a trail of clothes between the front door and the bedroom.

Even so, they were tentative at first, as they had been on their first time together. Their kisses were gentle and hesitant, but gradually the need to lose themselves began to take over. They moved together slowly and tenderly, with more and more urgency, until their inhibitions fell away entirely. Michael and Alison made love that night with the passion of two people with a deep and profound commitment but who had come to believe that they would never make love again. Their embrace was without consciousness, each of them subsumed in the other as they put aside all their dreadful cares and concerns, on a journey which led them away from the traumas of their shared history and into oblivion.

Afterwards they lay beside each other on the bed, still entwined, and looked at the shadows dancing on the ceiling. By now it was completely dark outside, and the streetlamps threw cold light against the curtains.

TWENTY-THREE

AND YOU ARE the only person called Stephen working at Hand-Cutz, are you?" asked Detective Constable Collins. "Michael Beaumont couldn't have another friend here with the same name?"

"No, I don't think so," said Stephen.

"And you definitely didn't telephone Michael yesterday afternoon, after his grandmother's funeral?"

"No, I didn't. Should I have done? Maybe I should have phoned to express our sympathy, but to be honest it didn't really occur to me . . ."

"No, it doesn't matter. You've been very helpful. Please don't tell Michael that we've had this conversation. We don't suspect him of anything, but it would just be better if he didn't know."

Stephen nodded agreement, and Collins walked out into the street and phoned Superintendent Bailey.

As night turned into day, Michael and Alison held each other tightly and spoke little about what the hours ahead would bring. Both had their own apprehensions about what might unfold, but both also felt for the first time in their lives that their deepest and most secret emotions could safely be shared with another person. It was no longer necessary to disguise what they were feeling or to erect a barrier against intimacy. Each had emerged from a stark isolation which they had not identified because it had been their normality, and they were glad.

They made breakfast and sat up in bed, waiting for the morning to pass, both immersed in their own thoughts.

"Penny for them," she said at one point, "as if I couldn't guess." He gently shook his head and said his thoughts had not been exactly as she might have expected.

By now it was getting close to the appointed time for the meeting, and they renewed their focus on what lay ahead of them. Michael dressed in his usual clothes but put on a baseball cap and a pair of dark glasses to disguise his appearance.

"Let's not go to the pier until just before twelve," he said. "We don't want to take any more risk than we have to of being recognized."

"What do you want me to do?" asked Alison. "He said he wanted to see you on your own. If I'm with you, it's likely to freak him out."

"I want you to be right next to me as we hear whatever he's got to say," said Michael. He could see that she was hesitant, and he knew that it was hardly surprising that she should be reluctant to come face-to-face with a mass murderer. However, he doubted if he could get through the next few hours if she was not with him. "We're going to have to decide together what we do next, and so it's important that you hear his story at the same time as me. Neither of us has much chance of being objective, but you're more likely than I am to get a sensible take on it all."

"I'm not sure that I can see the logic of that," said Alison, but Michael was continuing.

"I also think you're right that he'll be freaked out, so you should hang back while I go and talk to him first. I will tell him that you are close by and that I'm only going to speak to him if you are part of the conversation. After that I'll give you a wave, and you can come and join us."

They agreed that this would be the plan and then took a circuitous route towards the pier. Even now they could not be sure that they were not under surveillance by the police or the press, and they wanted to take as few chances as possible.

Eventually the clock on the esplanade said 11:55, and Michael and Alison went through the turnstiles onto the pier and began to progress along the wooden boardwalk. They agreed that she would approach the far end of the pier from the left-hand side, and Michael would walk along the right. They would keep watching each other, and whichever of them saw Martin first would signal.

The cacophony of music and voices, the bright lights from the amusement arcades, the thrill rides and the evocative smells of fried food and cotton candy all combined to produce the unique experience that was Brighton. The sound and sight of the sea below, visible through the gaps between the wooden slats, added a hint of danger, which made the place all the more magical for generations of tourists and their children.

Michael and Alison both scanned faces among the crowds. Most were mums and dads with their kids, and Michael noted once again that—in this location in particular—small hands were being gripped with more vigilance than would be usual. They progressed slowly along opposite sides of the boardwalk, taking the opportunities of the spaces between buildings to keep sight of each other. Michael tried to make sense of the mix of emotions he was feeling. Most intense was his apprehension about meeting a man who stood accused of committing the murder of tiny children, thrown to their deaths in front of their horrified parents who would relive that dreadful moment for the remainder of their lives. How could such a person even be countenanced? Suddenly he felt a wave of revulsion and contemplated retracing his steps and immediately dialing 999. But then Michael thought about the photograph which Elsie had found in the envelope. The two small boys, their younger sister, and the babysitter from next door: ordinary people going about their everyday business, who would soon be caught up in a single dreadful incident which would infect the rest of their own lives. Who could ever know at such distance where the real responsibility lay, but all three of the survivors were destined to exist in the shadow of what happened on that single afternoon. If there was any kind of explanation to be heard, Michael needed to hear it.

He saw the top of a red baseball cap and a glimpse of the side of the face below it, moving quickly through the crowds, and something about it seemed familiar. He looked across to where he expected to find Alison, but instead he saw that suddenly the other side of the walkway was crowded by a party of schoolchildren who had become mixed up with a large group of Chinese tourists heading in the other direction. He scanned the sea of black hair, trying to locate her, and suddenly felt a sharp bump which momentarily winded him. His cap was knocked from his head and fell to the ground behind him, making Michael feel exposed and even more vulnerable than before. He turned his head and saw that he had collided with an overweight man whose bare upper torso and arms were covered with multicolored tattoos.

"Watch where you're bloody going!" said the man, and Michael muttered apologies, turning quickly to pick up his cap. He replaced it on his head and looked again for Alison, who had by now put herself in his eyeline and was anxious to reconnect. Michael nodded towards the man he had spotted and lengthened his step to follow in the direction of the walking figure. Once or twice the crowd thinned out, and he could see the back of a pair of blue jeans and a darker-blue T-shirt, but still he was unable to be sure. The man seemed to be of the right height and build and was now striding towards the far end of the pier. A vendor selling helium-filled balloons on a string obscured his view for a moment, and Michael quickened his pace still more as his target reached the farthest edge of the platform. He turned suddenly to face his pursuer, and Michael and Martin found themselves looking directly into what might have been an only very slightly distorted mirror.

Even despite the buildup and the anticipation, Michael felt unprepared for the experience. In just those few seconds he was able to take in a face which was so much like his own, and yet in small and subtle ways was not. Were Martin's features slightly larger than his? Were his eyes just slightly more turned up at the corners? Perhaps it was Michael's imagination playing tricks, or a function of the extreme circumstances, but was there some trace of cruelty around his brother's mouth?

Thirty yards farther back, Alison had been able to watch the two men converging in the distance and slowed down in good time to conceal herself behind the corner of the ticket office for the helter-skelter ride. She looked on as the two men stood squarely facing each other, seemingly a perfect match in size and shape and in the way they carried themselves. For a few seconds neither appeared to be speaking, but then she saw that Martin was extending his arm for a handshake. Michael hesitated before taking it, but then they shook hands only briefly before the younger of the two brothers took a step back and an animated conversation began.

Alison did not take her eyes from the pair of them, and after a few seconds she saw Michael turn towards her, beckoning for her to approach. She began to move forwards, but then instantly it was clear from his movements that Martin had not agreed, and she saw him take a step back. Now, however, she was within earshot of the brothers, and Martin was speaking.

"Obviously I know you can't remember anything about it. You were too young to know what was going on, and anyway you've had a normal life growing up and every chance to forget. But I was too young as well. I had no idea what I was doing either. Yet it was me who was labeled the monster, and it was me who had to spend my whole life locked up, being watched and checked up on every minute, like I was a freak of some kind. Probably they just wanted to see if I would drown the fucking cat if I got the chance."

"But whatever the rights and wrongs of what happened back then," Michael's tone carried an urgency to hear the answers he so badly needed, "why the hell would you wait all this time for freedom, and then start killing more children and trying to frame me?" The volume of his words was rising, and he was beginning to attract the attention of people walking close by. "You've murdered a whole load of totally innocent kids, wrecked dozens of lives, and caused bloody mayhem all around you. I've been through hell on earth, and you've killed our grandmother in the process!"

"You want to know why?" said Martin, his volume was also rising, but he spoke in a hoarse whisper. "I'll tell you why, because for all those years locked away, the only thing I could think about was you and Elizabeth. The two of you. Every bit as responsible for Amy's death as I was, but it was only me who got the blame."

"What are you talking about?" said Michael. "Apart from anything else, Elizabeth lost her family and was locked away in an institution for years and years."

"Yes, and I took some comfort from that. Some consolation that at least she had suffered a small part of what I had suffered. And when I first got out of the nick I was prepared to forgive and forget. That was the reason why they let me out, and it was a condition of my release that I didn't try to find you or her. But you are my brother, and so I couldn't stop myself. I had to know what you were up to." Martin paused and seemed to intensify his gaze at his younger sibling. "You'd had your name changed and took a lot of finding, but eventually I did track you down. I thought I'd watch you for a bit while I decided what to do. Probably I wouldn't even have spoken to you or let you know who I was, but then when I finally located you, you'll never guess what I saw."

"What did you see? When was that?" asked Michael.

"Surely you remember the day? It was *that* day. I saw you and Elizabeth. Together. Walking on the South Bank. Laughing together. Laughing at me. The two of you were walking arm in arm. Hand in hand. Not a care in the world."

"And that was . . . ?" Michael had a sudden moment of clarity.

"Oh, for God's sake, no," he said, "and that was the first day? The day of the first murders?"

"At that moment it was obvious to me that while I'd been labeled a monster and locked away, you two were just like every other happy couple. I was surrounded by all of you, taunting me about your good fortune. And then suddenly it all became clear to me. If I couldn't have a normal happy family life, why should anyone else? If I could have my family taken away from me for no good reason, why shouldn't that happen to other people? And why should you two, every bit as guilty as I was, have found each other and live in blissful ignorance of what I've had to go through?"

Michael could not speak and turned towards Alison, to find her expression reflecting the same horror as was his own. There was a moment of paralysis, as the full implications of Martin's words swept over both of them like a giant wave, rooting them to the spot, neither of them able in their minds or in their bodies to move forwards or back.

"So that was it," Martin was continuing. "Something exploded in my head and I went straight up onto Waterloo Bridge and set about doing to young families what had been done to mine. Wrecking them in an instant. And I haven't stopped since. It's been so easy. I even enjoyed it. Just a flick of the arms, and they're gone. Those kids weren't being properly looked after, just as little Amy wasn't being looked after properly all those years ago."

Only now was Alison able to clear her head sufficiently to speak for the first time. "And you then set about framing your own brother for the crimes? And making sure he was with me whenever you did them?"

"Exactly," said Martin, and finally it seemed that he had said what he came to say, and his face formed into an expression of complete satisfaction. "Finally you understand."

For a few moments no one spoke any further, then suddenly Alison saw that Martin was pointing with one arm towards the area behind her, and he began to shout.

"You fucking bastard, Michael. You've brought the police! You've sold me out and brought the fucking police." His last few words were drowned out by a voice from behind her, amplified through a bullhorn.

"Martin Bannerman. Armed police. Remain where you are. You are surrounded and cannot escape. I say again. Armed police. Do not move."

Alison turned and saw that a row of six uniformed policemen, all wearing peaked caps and bulletproof vests, was walking forward slowly, each of them carrying a large pistol in outstretched hands. The guns were pointed in the direction of Martin and Michael. All around them parents and young children began to scream and were turning to run towards the shore. A movement above her head caught her attention, and Alison looked skywards to see a bundle of twenty or more multicolored balloons rocketing towards the heavens. She screamed and ran forward to put herself in the line of fire between the marksmen and the two brothers, and the force of her momentum made her crash into the pair of them. In a single movement Martin stepped forward and wrapped his arm around her neck, dragging her backwards against the railing. Now he was shouting again.

"If you come any closer, we're both going into the water."

Michael took a step backwards, holding up his hands to try to calm the situation. "Martin. I didn't bring them. They must have followed us. I wouldn't. We wouldn't have."

"Well, they're here now, and so that's an end to it. I'm not sorry for anything I did, and if I'm going down, it's only right that Elizabeth should be going down with me, because I would never have been in all this in the first place if she and you hadn't been a part of it."

"Let her go now, Martin, there's a good lad." Michael turned and saw that the voice was that of Detective Chief Superintendent Norman Bailey, who was edging forward slowly, flanked on all sides by the marksmen.

Michael held up his arm to stop the police from approaching. "What do you mean?" he said. "You said it was me who should have shared the blame. That's why you did what you did to have me arrested. To give me a taste of what happened to you. She couldn't have helped you. She was playing with me when Amy was drowned."

"Yes, she was, but it wasn't me alone who wanted to play with the water, to play with our little sister. It was you and her, too. We were all playing with her, all of us together. But she was the one who lifted the baby into the bath, and she was the one who turned on the taps and left us. Read what they said at the inquest. If wrong was done, it's as much the fault of the two of you as it was mine, but I'm the one who has had to carry the can, and now it's time for some proper justice."

Michael looked into Alison's face and saw her staring back at him with the expression of someone about to pass through the gates of hell. Every dark shadow of her entire life was concentrated into that moment, and all the realities of the guilt she had felt, the doubt about the part she had played, her share of the responsibility for the death of Martin and Michael's baby sister and their grandfather, had all been focused into that single instant. She was suffering her own special torture of deep water.

"It's not true, Alison," shouted Michael. "I don't believe that's what happened, and you don't believe it either."

"Yes, it is true. What he says is right. Of course it is. I am every bit as much to blame as he is." Alison was screaming at the top of her lungs. "It was me who put Amy in the bath. It was me who turned on the taps. It was me who did it all. It was me, it was me, it was me..." and the shape of her mouth continued to form the words as they guttered into a wail and were overwhelmed in the gusting wind.

"That's rubbish," Michael shouted. "The coroner said that someone held her down, pushed her down under the water. That can only have been him." He pointed directly at his older brother. "And he has proved that in the last weeks. Murdering tiny defenseless children like they're nothing. He is the Madman. It's him. Not you. Not me. It was never either of us."

"No." Alison screamed with renewed vigor. "I killed Amy every bit as much as he did, and it's me who deserves to be punished every bit as much as he does. Either way..." She lunged herself backwards, tilting the top half of her body against Martin, and at the same time reaching down to grab his legs to lift him off his feet. Michael propelled his body forward, trying to take hold of anything, and managed to gain a grip on flaying limbs, which may have been Alison or may have been Martin. He tried to hold tighter and to press himself backwards and away from the railing, when he felt the pressure of strong hands from behind, and now he was being wrestled backwards. The police were pulling all three of them away from the water's edge, but at that moment Martin jolted with what seemed to be unnatural strength and shook loose from Michael's grip. Two other police officers rushed forward a few steps to grab at whatever they could but were too late to prevent Martin and Alison from toppling over the railing and then plunging down towards the water. Michael rushed to the edge and looked over, just in time to see both bodies bounce off the metal parapet and twist into unnatural shapes before they hit the surf below.

EPILOGUE

FOR THE SECOND time in just two weeks, uniformed police officers were stationed at the gates of Wandsworth Crematorium
with instructions to prevent journalists or the ghoulish from
gaining access to what was intended to be a private family funeral. Nonetheless, Michael and Margaret felt their hearts sink
as their car reached the brow of the hill leading down towards
the cemetery, and they could see the size of the crowd awaiting
them. News of the dramatic cornering of the notorious Madman who had been terrorizing families in the south of England
for months had dominated world headlines ever since the incident, and it seemed as though every news organization on the
planet had sent a representative.

On this occasion, unlike the last, Michael and his mother
had heeded advice to accept the services of a driver, prefer-
ring to sit in the back of the funeral car rather than handle
things themselves. In the event, unknown to them, the man
in the dark suit driving the vehicle was a plainclothes police
officer rather than an undertaker. The public mood remained
volatile, and Superintendent Bailey wanted to do everything

possible to avoid any demonstrations from getting out of control.

As their car covered the last few hundred yards before the iron gates, Michael reached for his mother's hand. Lines of police officers were struggling to hold back the crowds, and when they slowed to turn the corner, he was able to take in a variety of facial expressions—ranging from the natural solemnity which might be appropriate at a family funeral, to what seemed to be the totally uncontrolled rage of others. Perhaps some of these were friends or relatives of the murdered children, though Michael thought it unlikely. He noted that most of the dozens of news cameras were tilting towards the noisiest and most vociferous of the demonstrators, and these would no doubt be the images flashed around the world.

Michael tried to decipher any of the constituent words making up the barrage of abuse which was being directed towards himself and his mother. Not for the first time, he wondered what might be the purpose of all that aggression and anger. Some of those present were there because their job required them to be, but others were merely rubberneckers, that strange crowd of people who no doubt in times past would have turned up to see public floggings or executions.

Michael and Margaret renewed their grip on each other's hands as their car swept through the gates. Suddenly the camera flashbulbs were exploding strobelike through the windows, and Michael had time to recall the advice he had received earlier about avoiding the appearance of a fugitive being driven into a jail. Nonetheless, both mother and son found it necessary to raise their forearms to shield their eyes from the glare, which gave the photographers the shot they wanted.

Their vehicle eventually drew to a halt behind a clump of

trees which took them just out of sight but not out of earshot of the crowds, and Michael saw that a number of what he took to be unmarked police cars had arrived before them. There were two further vehicles—one a shiny black upright van which was used for transporting corpses as discreetly as possible from hospitals or crime scenes to mortuaries. Parked behind it was another midsize van, this one also unmarked and painted black.

Michael and his mother got out of their car and stood silently. He turned to his right and saw that a small group over to one side included Esme and Sergeant Mallinson. Behind Esme he could see the outline of another figure, and he had to take a step back in order to see that it was Christopher—the St. Thomas' nurse who had been their guardian angel at the recent death of Grandma Rose. Michael was very glad to see him, and the two men exchanged a smile. There also were the detectives Bailey and Collins. Bailey removed his trilby hat and seemed to contemplate the ground in front of him.

The rear double doors of both vehicles were opened, and Michael and his mother watched as six men wearing dark suits gently eased the plain wooden coffin backwards so that it slid smoothly onto a trolley. All at once from over on his right he heard someone shout something which sounded like "They're moving the bastard now," which provided the cue for several hundred other voices to join a chorus of yelling. "Murdering bastard!" "A funeral is too good for him." "Just throw him in the water," and this last comment was followed by a burst of raucous laughter.

Michael turned to look at the activity at the back of the other vehicle and was aware of the workings of an electronic lift gradually being lowered. Unable to remain still any longer, he took a few steps forward towards the wheelchair so that his movement caught her attention. She turned her head slightly towards his approach, and he had to brace himself to suppress his instinctive reaction to her appearance. The vivid bruising on the side of Alison's face was already turning a variety of shades of blue and black, and her hair had been shaved to the scalp to allow access for the twenty-six stitches which were holding the top of her head together. Her right arm was in plaster, and her left leg stuck out straight in front of her, providing an effective battering ram against anyone who came too close. Carefully avoiding any chance of contact which might produce further agony, Michael leaned down and kissed her on the cheek. He moved round to the rear of the wheelchair, gripped the handles, and started pushing her towards the chapel.

"Imagine if it had been you who drowned and he that had survived," said Michael. "He'd be in a maximum-security hospital for the criminally insane." They watched as Martin's coffin was lifted off the trolley and hoisted awkwardly onto shoulders, as though the corpse inside had somehow corrupted its container, turning it into something unclean or untouchable.

Such had been the injuries to her head and neck in the fall from the pier that after emergency treatment in Brighton, Alison had been airlifted to the intensive care unit at St. Thomas' in London. For several days and nights, she had hovered between life and death, drifting in and out of consciousness. In her brief moments of lucidity, Michael whispered reassurance that she would survive and be well. The doctors advised that she should not attend the funeral, but she insisted, and now the couple hung back as the mourners slowly filed into the crematorium.

"I don't know if there will ever be a good time to ask you,"

Michael leaned close to her and spoke hardly above a whisper, "but sooner or later I need to be able to understand what was going through your mind on the pier." He watched Alison's face carefully as she registered his words. Her eyes were turned towards the sky, and she blinked slowly but did not speak, so he continued, "I can work out why you took it into your head that Martin's life had to come to an end, but surely not at the cost of your own?" Suddenly all the weight of pain and grief which he had worked so hard to suppress during recent days threatened to overwhelm him, and he brought up his forearms across his chest as if to defend himself against further hurt. His voice cracked as he spoke again. "Didn't you think I have lost enough already without also losing you?"

Still Alison did not turn to look at him, but she reached out with her hand and took hold of his, gripping it tightly. For several moments she could not find the right words, but then began to speak.

"I don't know if I will ever be able to make you understand, any more than I do, but let me try." She closed her eyelids, and behind them the pupils were darting around, as though she was involuntarily reliving the story. "Those few words that Martin spoke on the pier suddenly brought back to me a clearer memory than I've ever had of that day. In those few seconds, I could see you playing, I could see Martin playing, I could see myself playing, and there was little Amy giggling happily. None of us apparently had a care in the world." A trace of a smile flickered across Alison's face, but was instantly replaced as though she had been stabbed by a sharp knife. "Then suddenly all those images were lost, and instead I was confronted by the sight of Amy's tiny body lying quite still but facedown in the water."

The vision she described was familiar to Michael. It was the same as he had imagined many times since hearing the story from his mother only two weeks earlier. "I can see why that would be absolutely bloody awful," he said, "but I still don't get it. Why did that thought make you want to throw away your life as well as his?"

"Don't you see?" asked Alison. "That image of Amy lying facedown is not from my imagination, it's from my memory. If it's something I saw rather than imagined, it means I must have been with Martin in the bathroom when Amy died. Exactly as he said I was. It wasn't until I heard him say it that I realized that it must be true." She paused to allow Michael to absorb the import of her words. "Even now I don't think I will ever know exactly who did what, but what I can't deny is that I was more involved in the death of your sister than I have ever admitted. Surviving the fall from the pier has made sure I have to face up to the fact."

Michael was about to protest again but stopped short, and finally he understood something more about what Alison had said on the journey home from Greenacres on that day of the first murders. About how any of us can find ourselves caught up in events which change our lives forever, but there is no such thing as a pure truth of anything which follows. In this case there had been his grandfather's truth, there had been Martin's truth, and now, after all these years, Alison had arrived at her own version of the truth. Michael knew that it would be a long and difficult journey for both of them but that he would be there to help her to find a way to live with it.

By now the pallbearers had carried the coffin containing the last earthly remains of Martin Bannerman into the chapel. The handful of witnesses had also gone inside, and Michael stood alongside Alison, his hand resting on her shoulder. He was about to speak, but then something moved in the corner of his vision, and he turned from her to see that Christopher had been sent to find them and was indicating that the funeral service was about to begin. Michael remained still for another moment, and then he turned to take a firm grip on the handles of her wheelchair and began to push it forwards.

ACKNOWLEDGMENTS

I would like to thank the teams at Curtis Brown, Gelfman Schneider, and Mulholland Books who have helped to bring this novel to publication, and especially Gordon Wise, Deborah Schneider, Wes Miller, Emily Giglierano, Betsy Uhrig, and Sue Betz.

ABOUT THE AUTHOR

Stuart Prebble is the author of four novels, five comedy books, and a history book and is also a producer of documentary and current-affairs programs for television. He was formerly CEO of the UK television network ITV and is currently chairman of the TV production company Storyvault Films. He lives in London.

MULHOLLAND BOOKS

You won't be able to put down these Mulholland books.

RED RIGHT HAND *by Chris Holm*

TELL THE TRUTH, SHAME THE DEVIL *by Melina Marchetta*

IQ *by Joe Ide*

RULER OF THE NIGHT *by David Morrell*

KILL THE NEXT ONE *by Federico Axat*

THE PROMETHEUS MAN *by Scott Reardon*

WALK AWAY *by Sam Hawken*

THE DIME *by Kathleen Kent*

RUSTY PUPPY *by Joe R. Lansdale*

DEAD MAN SWITCH *by Matthew Quirk*

THE BRIDGE *by Stuart Prebble*

THE HIGHWAY KIND *stories edited by Patrick Millikin*

THE NIGHT CHARTER *by Sam Hawken*

COLD BARREL ZERO *by Matthew Quirk*

HONKY TONK SAMURAI *by Joe R. Lansdale*

THE INSECT FARM *by Stuart Prebble*

CLOSE YOUR EYES *by Michael Robotham*

THE *STRAND MAGAZINE* SHORTS

Visit mulhollandbooks.com for
your daily suspense fix.